The Man
Who Married a Mermaid

FROM THE SAME AUTHORS

Alexandre Dumas:
The Return of Lord Ruthven (stage play)
ISBN 978-1-932983-11-1

Paul Lacroix:
Danse Macabre
ISBN 978-1-61227-205-4

The Man
Who Married a Mermaid

by
Alexandre Dumas
and
Paul Lacroix

Translated, annotated and introduced by
Brian Stableford

A Black Coat Press Book

ISBN 978-1-61227-612-0. First Printing. April 2017. Published by Black Coat Press, an imprint of Hollywood Comics.com, LLC, P.O. Box 17270, Encino, CA 91416. All rights reserved. Except for review purposes, no part of this book may be reproduced or transmitted in any form or by any means, electronic or mechanical, including photocopying, recording, or by any information storage and retrieval system, without permission in writing from the publisher. The stories and characters depicted in this novel are entirely fictional. Printed in the United States of America.

Introduction

Les Mariages du Père Olifus, signed by Alexandre Dumas, here translated as *The Man who Married a Mermaid*, was originally envisaged as an episode in a vast compendium of supernatural stories titled *Les Mille et un fantômes*, which was planned as a kind of supernatural *Decameron*, intended to run initially as a potentially-infinite series of *feuilleton* serials in the daily newspaper *Le Constitutionnel*, but the project apparently ran into trouble during the economic difficulties that caused and became much worse after the Parisian Revolutions of 1848. The publisher of the book version, A. Cadot, issued the beginning of the frame narrative and the first few stories in two volumes, under the original title, in 1849, and subsequently gathered the other completed materials, extracted from the frame, in a five volume set published in the same year, titled for the present story, although there is also an edition of the five-volume set published in Brussels entitled *Les Mille et un fantômes*. The story of Père Olifus had by then been considerably elaborated, becoming by far the longest individual story in the group.

It is not obvious how and why that transformation occurred. *Les Mariages du Père Olifus* started to run as a serial in the 10 July issue of *Le Constitutionnel*, but the first three episodes—the first three chapters of the story—have little to do with Père Olifus, and look suspiciously like deliberate procrastination. The "intercalation" inserted into the middle of the text was definitely written as the serialization was continuing, because it reacts to an event occurring on the 26 July; Père Olifus' story was suspended for five days after the 27 July, the three episodes of the insertion appearing on 2-4 August; Père Olifus' story did not resume, however, until the 21 August issue of the newspaper, and was interrupted briefly again before finally concluding on 30 August. As to the reason for that long pause, we can only speculate.

An illustrated edition of *Les Mariages du Père Olifus* was published in 1856 by Maresq in a volume that also contains *Les Medicis*; it is presumably a reprint of that version, issued by Calmann-Lévy, that is reproduced by the Bibliothèque Nationale's website *gallica*. The Calmann-Lévy version is, however, abridged, omitting the first three chapters of the version published in *Le Constitutionnel* and included in the Cadot set. The full version was subsequently reprinted as a single volume in a uniform set of Dumas' works issued by Michael Lévy frères, initially in 1861, and reprinted in 1873 and 1882. A version of the story translated into English as "The Nuptials of Father Polypus," began serialization in New York in *The Gazette of the Union, Golden Rule and Oddfellows' Family Companion* in September 1849, but that version, which is available for inspection on Google Books, does not seem to have been continued after its first episode, consisting of the third chapter and the fourth. The full version was translated into English by Alfred Allinson in 1907, in a volume entitled *Tales of Strange Adventure*, but that text was very scarce until it was reproduced in an e-book omnibus of Dumas' works issued in 2013. That version is a trifle difficult to follow for modern readers; hopefully the present translation will be much easier, especially with the aid of the explanatory footnotes.

Although the autobiographical chapters of the novel are obviously written by Dumas, the story told by Père Olifus was farmed out to another writer, Dumas having planned to function more as an editor than an author in compiling the initially-envisaged compendium. That work is credited by various secondary sources to Paul Lacroix (who signed most of his work "P. L. Jacob le Bibliophile") and "Paul Bocage" (Paul Auguste Touchez).

It is difficult to be certain, but important evidence regarding the composition and authorship of the narrative can be derived from the account of the collaboration given by Lacroix to his biographer "Eugène de Mirecourt" (Charles Jacquot), as reported in *Le Bibliophile Jacob (Paul Lacroix)* (1867). Lacroix told Mirecourt that he agreed to furnish Dumas with the "elements" of the "great collection" entitled *Les Mille et un fantômes*, that he sent Dumas his written notes every morning and went to his house in the evening to hear his oral comments. He claimed that all went well until the series reached the Père Olifus episode, when, according to Lacroix, Dumas "wearied." Lacroix told Mirecourt that he had supplied a scenario of fifty pages, with books on the various countries of the Indies to assist Dumas to revise it for the serial version, but that Dumas then came back to him and asked that the work be "more completely done." Lacroix apparently did the work—he asserted, according to Mirecourt, that not only almost the whole of the present story but the whole of "La Femme au colliers de velours" (tr. as "The Woman in the Velvet Collar"), the last and second-longest story in the series, was his work, and that the inscription in the copy of the printed proofs that Dumas sent him, which read *cui pars magna fuit* [a large part of which was] was an understatement—but whether it was delays in his delivery, delays in Dumas' reprocessing of what he delivered, or some other reason that caused the interruption of the serial is anyone's guess.

Everything Lacroix told him, according to Mirecourt is, of the "utmost exactitude," but it is worth noting that Mirecourt was not an unbiased observer. In 1845, he had published an "exposé" of Dumas's extensive use of collaborators, entitled *Fabrique de romans: Maison Alexandre Dumas et cie* [The Novel Factory: Alexandre Dumas & Co.] which had annoyed Dumas and instituted a hostility between the two men that lasted for decades. There might, therefore, be reason to doubt the "utmost exactitude," of Mirecourt's reportage. At any rate, there can surely be no doubt that the first three chapters of the novel, the two chapters of the intercalation and the final pages, are all Dumas' work. What also seems certain is that Dumas initially commissioned Lacroix to provide a novelette of much the same length as the items collected in the first two volumes of *Le Mille et un fantômes*, but that he changed his mind and decided to stretch the story far beyond the original plan, at which point he asked Lacroix to provide a much fuller text.

Perhaps Dumas made that request, as Lacroix suggested, simply because he "wearied"—and he was certainly very busy with other matters in late July 1849, as the intercalation makes clear—but it is also possible that the editor of *Le Constitutionnel* requested the inflation for some reason, or that the difficulties Cadot was experiencing caused Dumas to rethink the strategy of the series. The decision to issue the story in the five-volume set titled for it, along with other materials intended for the aborted *Mille et un fantômes* could well have been

Cadot's idea rather than Dumas', and there might have been an interval when Dumas thought that the story needed to be inflated to novel lengthy in order that it would be able to stand alone, if necessary.

It is difficult to know, too, what to make of Paul Bocage's claim to have made a contribution to the work, since Lacroix did not mention his involvement at all, but it seems probable that Bocage's claim referred to other stories in the five-volume set—only one of which Lacroix claimed to have had a hand in—rather than specifically to the story of Père Olifus. That, at least, is the assumption I have made in crediting the present volume simply to Dumas and Lacroix.

Assuming that the above account of the novel's troubled genesis is approximately true, it helps enormously to explain the peculiar patchwork quality of the final text, which must initially have been planned and executed as a supernatural short story, before being twice padded out. The expansion of the short story converted the greater part of into a curious adventure story of the "travelogue" variety, which was beginning to enjoy some popularity at the end of the 1840s before it reached a heyday during the latter days of the Second Empire, especially in the work of Dumas' protégé Jules Verne, and then degenerated after 1870 into tedious repetition in the work of Verne's many imitators. That fantasy-cum-adventure story was further supplemented, before the serialization even began and again during its interruption, by the addition of the autobiographical frame and the intercalation, and eventually by the conclusion of the frame narrative. That ultimate closure is of a kind that subsequently became clichéd, but it had not yet been done to death in 1849, and is excusable in that context.

An argument could certainly be made out for the contention that the story would work better as the relatively compact weird tale that Dumas and Lacroix had initially planned to incorporate into the continuing *Mille et un fantômes*, and that the decision to inflate it into a novel, in a stumbling fashion, merely succeeded in spoiling it, and rendering it, in narrative terms, somewhat monstrous. Indeed, the project of "restoring" that lost original might be an intriguing one. It cannot be doubted, however, that for all its eccentric untidiness, the inflated version is certainly not without interest, especially as a significant early contribution to the subgenre of "travelogue fiction."

As might be expected, we can see with the hindsight of modern geography and history that the details of Olifus' journey to the East are almost all preposterous, but their ludicrous aspects do include several themes that were later to become staples of feuilleton fiction—including the admittedly crude use of the myth of orangutans stealing and raping human women, which became the basis of a whole subgenre of French fiction in which lurid sensationalism sometimes overlaps and mingles with serious philosophical speculations about the nature of the evolutionary relationship between orangutans and humans.[1]

Although the ending attached to the novel version of the story is a distinctly modern one, frequently invoked as an apology for fantastic stories told in an era where belief in the supernatural supposedly is no longer licensed, it is worth noting that even the original story must have carried an implicit ambiguity of the same

---

[1] See *The Missing Link and Other Tales of Ape-Men*, Georges T. Dodds., ed. Black Coat Press, ISBN 978-1-935558-14-9.

kind, as almost all tales of mermaids and sirens are inevitably afflicted the particular uncertainty attached to the whole series of mermaid and siren sightings reported by seamen.

As Dumas notes in the early chapters, that mythology is particularly tenacious in the Low Countries, not merely because of their rich seafaring traditions but also because they were once a center for the manufacture of fake mermaids that often ended up in Cabinets of curiosities, and sometimes in museums, and were popularly known as "Jenny Hanivers," the city of Antwerp being thought to be particularly prolific in their manufacture. Literary mermaids have always had a particular character of dubiousness, which must have been reflected in the oral anecdote of which even the short version of Père Olifus' story might well have been an adaptation (as several, but not all, of the other stories in the series certainly were, including "La Femme au collier de velours").

The addition of the autobiographical chapters to the original text might seem to some readers to be a bizarre artifice, and such readers might well criticize the abridged version of the novel on the ground that it did not remove the intercalation as well as the introductory chapters. Perhaps the abridged version is preferable, and would be even more so without the intercalation, although the omission of the author's visit to the mermaid in the museum in The Hague is detrimental to some extent. The chapters in question do have a definite value, however, in providing a powerful reminder and illustration of the circumstances in which the contained work was produced: the confused interval between the collapse of Louis-Philippe's monarchy and the advent of Louis Napoléon's Empire, when the Second Republic battled unavailingly with adverse circumstance and many of the authors in Paris suffered difficulties, often including real privation, as their opportunities shrank alarmingly and many projects collapsed.

At first glance there might appear to be little or no connection between the social environment in which it was produced and the content of the story, especially the part of the story that is a wry misogynistic fable of supernaturally-punished infidelity. It was, however, in that unremittingly hostile domestic climate that tales of the Far East and the economic possibilities of colonial enterprise gained a firm foothold in French popular culture, and the account of Père Olifus' various profiteering endeavors, especially the sarcastic quasi-picaresque spirit in which it is rendered, can be easily linked to the escapist temptations of the day.

Those chapters also help to highlight the curiously ambiguous situation of Dumas himself during the Second Republic, when he seemed a sufficiently dangerous Republican to be subsequently exiled by Napoléon III and then to have his work carefully monitored by the censors when an amnesty allowed him to return to Paris, but when he was simultaneously a hate figure for those revolutionaries who considered him "a friend of princes"—as, of course, he was, being a fervent snob as well as an enthusiastic Republican.

Although the result of the inflation of *Les Mariages de Père Olifus* into a quasi-novel can hardly be reckoned esthetically satisfactory, therefore, it is not without interest, and if the ultimate product is a chimera, might that not be reckoned an apt fate for a story which is itself a celebration and reexamination of a species of chimera? If the novel was raised uncertainly from the ruins of what *Les Mille et un fantômes* was originally supposed to become, the manner of its peculiar genesis is not entirely out of keeping with the deliberately confused and inherently ambivalent spirit of the original.

Modern lovers of fantastic fiction are certainly obliged to regret that the compendium as originally envisaged was aborted, and that its chances of market success were wrecked by the dire economic circumstance in which it had to be issued. Had it made its debut in a kinder epoch and extended successfully through ten, twenty or fifty volumes, it would have provided a highly significant benchmark and exemplar for the development of fantastic fiction in France, and in Europe as a whole—but it was not to be, and the endeavor became a casualty of hard times, parts of which survived only in scarred and injured form..

What remains of the project faded into insignificance for a long period, although the early fragments at least—especially the vampire story not separately titled in the original but known in English translation as "The Pale Lady"—have now acquired a kind of classic status among the aficionados of the relevant genre. *Les Mariages du Père Olifus* has mostly been excluded from that belated celebrity, partly because the 1907 translation was so very hard to locate and partly because it is a trifle unwieldy, but it is certainly one of the most fascinating items to survive the wreck of the projects, and even though it has to be read with certain advantages of hindsight in order to get the best out of it, it nevertheless has rewards to offer the contemporary reader that make it entertaining as well as intriguing, and it deserves to be reckoned one of the flawed classics of its subgenre.

This translation was made from the London Library's copy of the 1861 Lévy edition of the novel.

Comparative reference was also made to the abridged version of the novel reproduced on the Bibliothèque Nationale's *gallica* website, which is the illustrated reprint published by Calmann-Lévy, in a volume that also contains *Les Médicis*.

Brian Stableford

THE MAN WHO MARRIED A MERMAID

I. The Crow-Catcher

One morning in the month of March 1848, on going from my bedroom to my study, I found a pile of newspapers on my desk, as usual, and on that pile of newspapers a pile of letters.

Among those letters there was one whose large red seal immediately attracted my gaze. It did not bear any postage stamp, and was addressed quire simply to Monsieur Alexandre Dumas, Paris, which indicated that it had been delivered by a third person. The handwriting had a strange character, suspended between English and German styles. The person who had traced it evidently had the habit of command, a certain firmness of mental resolution, mitigated by emotional impulses and capricious thoughts, which sometimes made him a person quite different from the apparent individual.

When I receive a letter in an unknowing handwriting, and when that letter appears to come from an important person, I rather like to anticipate and to obtain from the insignificant lines traced by that person in the address an idea of his rank, habits and character.

Having made my reflections I opened the letter and read the following:

The Hague, 22 February 1848

Monsieur,

I do not know whether Eugène Vivier, the great art-ist who came to visit us during the winter, and whose acquaintance I was fortunate enough to make, has told you that I am one of your most assiduous readers, and whether I say can so, numerous as they are, for to say that one has read Mademoiselle de Belle-Isle, Amaury, Les Trois Mousquetaires, Vingt ans après, Bragelonne *and* Monte-Christo *would be to accord you a compli-ment that is too banal.*

I have therefore thought for some time of offering you a memory and, at the same time, making known to you one of our greatest national artists, Monsieur Backuisen.

Permit me then, Monsieur, to send you herewith four drawings by that artist, which represent the most striking scenes of your novel, Les Trois Mousquetaires.

Now, I shall bid you adieu, and be you to believe, Monsieur, that I am your affectionate,

> *William, Prince of Orange*[2]

I confess that that letter, dated 22 February 1848—which is to say, the day on which the Parisian Revolu-

---

[2] The William, Prince of Orange, in question (1817-1890) ruled the Netherlands as William III from 1849 to his death. He had married his cousin Sophie of Württemburg in 1839. The first reference in his letter is to the prolific writer, com-poser and librettist Eugène Vivier (1817-1900) but the refer-ence to Backuisen is puzzling, as the 17th-century master of that name cannot have produced illustrations to *Les Trois Mousquetaires*.

tion burst forth, received a day or two after an attempt had been made to kill me on the pretext that I was "a friend of princes," gave me a sensible pleasure.

In fact, for a poet, the foreigner is posterity, being placed outside our petty literary hatreds and artistic jealousies. The foreigner, like the future, judges a man on his works, and the crown that crosses a frontier is woven from the same flowers as those that are thrown on a tomb.

Curiosity, however, prevailed over gratitude. I began by opening the folder that had been deposited on a corner of my desk and I did indeed find within it four charming drawings. One represented d'Artagnan's arrival at Meung with his yellow horse; the second the ball at which Milady cut the diamond tags from Buckingham's doublet; the third the bastion of Saint-Gervais and the fourth Milady's death.

Then I wrote to the Prince to thank him.

I had known for some time that the Prince was an artist. I knew that he was a distinguished composer, and two other artists who are rarely mistaken about men or the arts, the Duc d'Orléans and Prince Jérôme Napoléon,[3] had often mentioned him to me.

It is well-known that the Duc d'Orléans engraves in a charming fashion; I have prints emerged from his hands that are models of etching and aquatinting. As for Prince Napoléon, I have read—something that he has probably forgotten—Republican verses that earned him

---

[3] The Duc d'Orléans in question is Ferdinand-Philippe (1810-1842), the eldest son of Louis Philippe. Jérôme-Napoléon Bonaparte (1784-1860), Napoléon I's youngest brother, was King of Westphalia from 1807-1813, and later used the title of Prince de Montfort.

a good pension from the College of Stuttgart, and which were given to me in Florence in 1839 or 1840 by the beautiful Princesse Mathilde.

I had, above all, heard mention of the Princesse d'Orange as one of those superior women who, when they are not called Elizabeth or Christine, are called Madame de Sévigné or Madame de Staël.

In consequence, when the Prince of Orange was called upon to succeed his father on the throne of Holland, it naturally came to my mind to undertake a voyage to Amsterdam to witness the new king's coronation and to present my compliments to the ex-Prince of Orange.

I therefore departed on 9 May 1849.

On the tenth, the newspapers reported that I had gone to Amsterdam in order to write an account of the coronation celebrations. The same thing had been announced when I had left for Madrid on 3 October 1846. I beg the pardon of the newspapers who are kind enough to take an interest in me, but when I go to the weddings of princes, I go as a guest, not as a historian. Having said that, I shall return to my departure.

In addition to the pleasure of locomotion, and the need to breathe from time to time air other than that what normally breathes, an excellent surprise was reserved for me. As I was about to leave the waiting room at the railway station, I felt someone tug the flap of my frock-coat.

"Where are you going like this?" asked the person who had just attracted my attention by means of that gesture.

I uttered an exclamation of surprise. "And you?"

"To Holland."

"Me too."

"To see the coronation?"

"Yes,"

"Me too. Have you been invited directly?"

"No, but I know the King as an artist prince and as, since the death of the Duc d'Orléans, there are not many artist princes left, I'm going to see this one crowned.

My traveling companion was Biard.[4]

You know Biard by name if you do not know him personally; his is the intelligent brush that has depicted *La Revue de la garde nationale dans un village, Le Baptême du Bonhomme Tropique* and *Les Honneurs partagés*. His is the poetic brush that has shown you, at the foot of a cracking and splitting mountain of ice, two Laplanders passing one another in pirogues and embracing in passing. Finally, he is the author of all those ravishing portraits of women full of coquetry and light, which you might have seen at the last Exposition and again at the present one. Above all, however, and more than all that—for I have the bad habit of putting the man before the artist—he is the charming intelligence, the indefatigable storyteller, the voyager of the south and the north, the benevolent friend, the colleague devoid of jealousy, who forgets himself when he speaks about others. In sum, he is the traveling companion with whom I wish my reader could go around the world, and whom I was delighted to have found in order to go to Holland.

It was a year or two since we had last seen one another. Ours is a strange life; we like it when we meet one another, we are glad to see one another, we spend hours,

---

[4] The painter François-Auguste Biard (1799-1882) was a great traveler whose most famous paintings included scenes of Africa, including graphic representations of the slave trade, and several depicting such Arctic scenes as hunting walrus and fending off attacks by polar bears.

days or a week joyfully in the coupling that chance has determined; we come back in the same railway carriage, and continue in the same cab, we shake hands and say, in the most serious fashion in the world: "But it's stupid not to see one another, let's keep in touch!"—and we do not see one another again, for each of us goes back to his own life, throws himself into his work, builds his ant-like or giant edifice, to which posterity alone will assign its veritable height, and time its veritable duration.

It was a good night that my son and I spent with Biard on the road to Brussels. There were five or six other people with us in the same diligence; did they understand anything we said? I doubt it. After fifty leagues of road and five or six hours of traveling, did we seem to them to be intelligent men or imbeciles? I have no idea. Our mentality is so strange; it leaps so rapidly from the heights of philosophy to the depths of the pun; it has such a peculiar, individual and eccentric character. It belongs so particularly to a caste that it requires a long intellectual initiation of sorts to comprehend it.

But as one wearies of everything, even laughter, by two o'clock in the morning, the conversation dried up, and by three o'clock we were asleep. At five o'clock we woke up again to visit our trunks, and finally, at eight o'clock, we arrived in Brussels.

In Brussels, everything was perfectly tranquil, and if we had not heard so many bad things said about France, in French, we might have been able to forget that France existed.

We had reentered the heart of monarchy.

Belgium is a singular country, which keeps its King because its King is always ready to leave. It is true that Leopold I is a highly intelligent man. At every Revolution that occurs in France or every mob that complains in

Brussels, he runs to his balcony, his hat in his hand, and signals that he wants to speak, and people listen.

"My children," he says, "you know that I have been made King reluctantly; I had no desire to be one before being one, and since I am one, I desire no longer to be one. If, therefore, you are like me, and have had enough of royalty, give me an hour, and in an hour's time I will be out of the kingdom; that is the only reason that I have encouraged railways. Be good, though; don't break anything; you can see that there's no need."

To which the people respond: "We don't want you to go. We felt the need to make a little noise, that's all. We've done that; we're content. Long live the King!"

After which, the King and the people part, more satisfied with one another than ever.

All along the route, Biard had told me not to worry, that when we arrived in Brussels he would show me something that I had never seen before. And in my pride, every time that he made me that promise, I shrugged my shoulders. I had been to Brussels ten times over; in those ten voyages I had seen the Park, the Botanical Gardens, the Prince of Orange's palace, the Church of Saint Gudule, the Boulevard de Waterloo, the shops of Méline and Cans and the palace of the Prince de Ligne. What, then could be left for me to see?

So, scarcely had we arrived than I said to Biard: "Let's go see what I haven't seen before."

"Come on," he said, laconically. And Alexandre, Biard and I set forth.

Our guide took us straight to a rather fine house situated in the vicinity of the cathedral, stopped at a coaching entrance, and rang the bell without hesitation.

A domestic came to open up. His appearance was immediately striking. He had blood on his fingertips; his waistcoat and trousers were literally covered with feathers, or rather down, belonging to all kinds of birds. Furthermore, he moved his head in a singular fashion, a semicircular movement similar to that of a wryneck.

"My friend," Biard said to him, "would you be kind enough to tell your master that foreigners passing through Brussels would like to visit his collection?"

"My master isn't here, Monsieur," said the domestic, "but in his absence, I'm charged with doing the honors of his showcases."

"Damn!" said Biard. Then, turning to me, he said: "It won't be as curious, but it doesn't matter; let's go anyway."

The domestic was waiting; we nodded our heads, and he went ahead of us.

"Watch him walking," said Biard. "That's already a curiosity."

In fact, the worthy man who was guiding us did not have a human gait, but that of a bird, and the bird from which he seemed to have borrowed his particular gait was the magpie.

To begin with we traversed a rectangular courtyard populated by a cat and two or three storks. The cat seemed suspicious; the storks by contrast, immobile on their long red feet, seemed full of confidence.

While we were traversing the courtyard, I did not observe anything extraordinary in the stride of our guide, except for the rotation of the head I have mentioned and a grave impression given to him by his fashion of putting one leg in front of the other. In fact, as I have said, he walked like a magpie, when magpies walk gravely.

We arrived in the garden.

The garden was a kind of small botanical garden, rectangular like the courtyard but larger, with a multitude of labeled flowers divided into a number of plots separated by pathways, in such a fashion that the flower-beds could easily be tended.

As soon as we were in the garden, our guide's gait changed, from the grave tread to a hopping motion. At a distance of three or four paces, he perceived an insect, a caterpillar or a beetle; immediately, with an indescribable thrust of the hips, he made three or four little forward jumps with his feet together, then a sideways hop landing on one foot, leaning over at the same time, captured the animal, without ever missing, between his thumb and index finger, threw it down on the pathway and brought the foot that was still in the air down upon it, with the full weight of his body. In that fashion, there was not a second lost between the discovery, the capture and the execution of the animal.

The execution terminated, he returned, with a little sideways leap, to the same path as us. Then, at the first glimpse of another animal, he recommenced the operation—but so rapidly, I repeat, that we could continue our route without stopping, toward a detached building that appeared to house the first part of the exhibition.

The door was wide open. The building, square in form, was full of racks. At first sight, it seemed to me that those racks were full of seeds, and I expected to see interesting varieties of peas, beans, lentils and vetches. On moving closer and looking more attentively, however, I perceived that what I had mistaken for dried vegetables were quite simply the eyes of birds: the eyes of eagles, vultures, parrots, falcons, crows, magpies, starlings, blackbirds, finches, sparrows, titmice and, in sum, every species. One might have thought that they were lead shot of all dimensions, from twelve to a pound to the finest-ground.

Thanks to a chemical preparation, doubtless invented by the owner of the establishment, all those eyes had conserved their coloration, their solidity and, I might almost say, their expression—except that, extracted from their orbits and deprived of their eyelids, the eyes had taken on a ferocious and threatening expression.

Above each rack, a label indicated the bird to which the eyes belonged.

Oh, Coppelius, Doctor Coppelius, fantastic brainchild of Hoffmann, you who were always demanding eyes beautiful eyes, if you had come to Brussels, how easily you would have found there what you sought with so much perseverance for your daughter Olympia![5]

"Messieurs," said our guide, when he thought that we had examined that first collection sufficiently, "would you care to pass into the crows' gallery?"

We nodded our heads as a sign of assent, and followed our guide, who introduced us into the crows' gallery.

No gallery every justified its title more fully. Picture a long corridor, ten feet broad and twelve high, illuminated by windows overlooking a garden, entirely decorated with crows nailed on their backs with their wings extended and their feet and neck drawn out. Those crows formed along the walls the most fantastic and extravagant designs. Some were crumbling to dust, others exhibited all the degrees of putrefaction; others were fresh and yet others were agitating and screeching. There might have been eight or ten thousand.

---

[5] The reference is to E. T. A. Hoffmann's classic story "Der Sandmann" (1816). Hoffmann was a great favorite of the French Romantics, frequently discussed in their *cénacles*.

I turned to Biard, full of gratitude; I had, indeed, never seen anything like it.

"And it's your master who has taken the trouble to trace all these cabalistic figures on the wall?" I asked the domestic.

"Oh, yes, Monsieur, no one touches his crows but him. He wouldn't like it if anyone else put a hand on them."

"But he must have suppliers of crows all over Belgium?"

"No, Monsieur, he catches them himself."

"What! He catches them himself? Where?"

"Up there, on the roof." And he showed me a roof, on which I could indeed see a kind of mechanism, the ingenious details of which I could not make out.

I am a great hunter of birds, although I do not take the love of ornithology as far as a mania, like our worthy native of Brussels. In my youth, I had made decoys and wire snares, so that detail began to interest me.

"Tell, me, then," I said to the domestic, "how your master catches them. The crow is one of the cleverest, subtlest, wiliest and most suspicious of birds that exist."

"Yes, Monsieur, against the old means, the rifle, *nux vomica* and bird-lime, but not with regard to the bass fiddle."

"What! Not with regard to the bass fiddle?"

"Of course, Monsieur. A crow can suspect a man holding a rifle, and even a man who isn't holding anything, but how can he suspect a man who is playing a fiddle."

"So your master attracts crows like Orpheus, by playing a bass fiddle?"

"I'm not saying that, exactly."

"What are you saying, then?"

"Well, I'll explain it to you. My master has a traitor."

"A traitor?"

"Yes, a domesticated crow, Look—that old vagabond strolling over there in the garden." And he pointed out a crow hopping along the pathways. It was a hooded crow, almost white with old age. "He gets up at four o'clock in the morning..."

"The crow?"

"No, my master. As for the crow, does he ever sleep? Day and night his eyes are always open. He ruminates evil. Personally, I believe that he's not a real crow but a demon. So, my master gets up at four, before dawn; he goes downstairs in a dressing-gown; he puts his old tramp of a crow in the middle of the net that you can see up there on the roof on the far side of the garden; he attaches a string to his foot that connects to the net; he picks up his bass and starts to play *Une fièvre brûlante*.[6] His crow screeches; the crows of Saint Gudule hear him, they come down, they see a comrade eating white cheese and a monsieur playing the bass. They don't suspect anything, you understand, those animals. They come down near the traitor, and he more of them descend, the more my master saws away with his bow. Then, all of a sudden, *zing!* He lifts his foot and, *snap!* the net closes, and the imbeciles are caught. There you go."

"Then your master nails them?"

---

[6] The tune in question originated in André Grétry's opera *Richard Coeur-de-lion* (1784), supposedly played by Blondel, and thus a pastiche of Medieval music, but it is nowadays better known because of a series of variations on the theme composed by Beethoven for the piano.

"Oh, then, you see, my master is no longer a man but a tiger. He puts down his bass, detaches his string, runs to the wall, climbs the ladder, takes the crows, jumps down, fills his mouth with nails, takes up a hammer, and *bang, bang!* there's another crow crucified. It goes *caw! caw!* but that only excites him, my master. Anyway, you can see."

"And has your master been suffering from this malady for a long time?"

"Oh, ten years now, Monsieur. It's his life, that man. If he goes three days without catching a crow, he falls ill; if he went a week he'd die of it. Now, would you like to see the tits' gallery?"

"Gladly."

That wallpaper of feathered corpses, the air impregnated with the miasmas of a fry fetor, and the convulsive movements and screeches of the agonized crows were making me feel sick.

We traversed the garden again, and it was then, while looking at the hooded crow with one eye and our domestic with the other, that I perceived the similarity of their movement in the research and punishment of insects. It was evident that the crow had copied the domestic, or that the domestic was imitating the crow. Personally, as the public notoriety of the crow went back a hundred and twenty years and the domestic was only forty, I suspected the domestic of being the plagiarist.

We arrived at the tits' gallery; it was a small detached building located at the opposite corner of the garden, decorated with the wings and heads of housesparrows, embroidered with the wings, heads and tails of tits. Imagine a large gray curtain with yellow and blue designs. Those designs represented wheels, flowers, stars and arabesques—in sum, all the fantasies that an unhealthy imagination can design with the bodies, feet and beaks of birds.

In the intervals of the designs the heads of cats were attached to the wall, mouths open, faces wrinkled, eyes sparkling; those cats' heads surmounted cats' paws, crossed like the bones with which funereal ornamentation ordinarily accompanies skulls.

The heads were surmounted themselves by captions conceived in these terms:

Misouf, sentenced to death 10 January 1846, for having damaged two finches and a blue-tit.

The Doctor, sentenced to death 7 July 1847, for having stolen a sausage from the grill.

Blucher, sentenced to death 10 June 1848 for having drunk from a jug of milk reserved for my breakfast.

"Aha!" I said. "It appears that your master, like our ancient feudal overlords, has arrogated the right of high and low justice."

"Yes, Monsieur, as you can see; he uses it without appeal. He says that if everyone did as he does and destroyed pillagers, thieves and murderers, only mild and benevolent animals would soon remain on earth, and then humans, only having good examples, would become better."

I inclined before that axiom; I respect collectors without understanding them. In Ghent I visited an amateur who collected buttons; well, that appeared ridiculous at first, but ended up becoming interesting. He had divided up his buttons into series, from the ninth century to our time; the collection began with a button from Charlemagne's robe and ended with one of Napoléon's uniform buttons; there were buttons of all the uniforms that had ever existed in France, from Charles VII's archers to the riflemen of Vincennes; there were buttons made of wood, lead, copper, zinc, silver and gold, or rubies, emeralds and diamonds. The material value of his collection was estimated at a hundred thousand francs; it had probably cost him three hundred thousand.

I knew an Englishman in London who collected hangman's ropes. He had traveled all over the globe; he had correspondents, and he had entered into communication with executioners in all four continents. As soon as a man was hanged in Europe, Asia, Africa or America, the executioner cut a piece off the end of the rope and sent it to our collector with a certificate of authenticity, who returned the price of its postage. He had one rope that had cost him a hundred pounds sterling; it is true that it had had the honor of strangling Selim III—a strangulation with which, as everyone knows, English politics was not entirely foreign.[7]

I had just copied the epitaph of Master Blucher, the milk-drinker, when half past nine chimed on Saint Gudule; we only had half an hour to catch the train for Antwerp. I added my tip to the one that Biard had already given when we came in, and we exited the necropolis at a run.

Our guide, full of gratitude, accompanied us, hopping along, as far as the door, and followed us with his eyes, while twisting is neck, as far as the street corner.

We arrived on the platform just as the engine was sounding its departure whistle.

---

[7] Selim III (1762-1808), the reformist Sultan of the Ottoman Empire was, in fact, hacked to death by his assassins—a circumstance that helps to emphasize that this chapter, like the next two, is a tissue of fantasies rather than authentic reportage.

II. Waffles and Gherkins

We arrived in Antwerp at eleven o'clock. In order not to miss the boat, which was leaving at midday, we went to have lunch on the quay facing the boat. At noon, we went aboard. At five past noon we departed, accompanied by a fine drizzle that I believe is particular to Antwerp, given that I have encountered it again on every voyage I have made to that city.

Biard was not without anxiety as to where we would stay in Rotterdam, The Hague and Amsterdam, a ceremony like the one that we were going to attend bringing a great influx of travelers. I am, however, a careful man—and in any case, where is the city in which I don't know anyone?

In 1840 I went down the Rhône, Embarked at Lyon at four o'clock in the morning, I went to sleep between eleven and twelve on deck, in the shade of a tent, gently caressed by the fresh breeze that run over the surface of rivers. That slumber was so pleasant that, partially woken up two or three times by some incident, I had not wanted to open my eyes for fear of waking up entirely. I had therefore remained motionless, my reason suspended above the wave that accompanies the twilight of sleep, when, extracted from my blissful reverie by a third or fourth shock, I felt the half-light of my consciousness penetrated, so to speak, by a few words pronounced in French by female voices with a slight English accent.

I opened my eyes very gently, and, looking around cautiously, distinguished between my three-quarters-closed eyelids a group made up of two young women between eighteen and twenty, a young man of twenty-six or twenty-eight and a man of thirty-four or thirty-six. The two women were charming, not only in their own beauty, but also with the naïve and almost nonchalant grace particular to Englishwomen. The two men were remarkable in their distinction.

There was an argument within the group, revolving around the itinerary to follow: to stop over in Avignon or go on to Arles. It was very serious, and quite embarrassing, for foreigners who had no other guide than Richard.[8] One of the women suggested that they needed the advice of someone who had made the journey through Arles and Avignon.

That desire seemed to be addressed to me. I had traveled along the Rhône several times from Lyon to Marseilles, through each of the two towns. I thought that the moment had come to introduce myself, and that the service I was about to render the society of travelers would enable my boldness to be forgiven.

I opened my eyes entirely and, bowing, said: "If these Messieurs will permit the author of *Impressions de voyage* to enlighten them on this grave matter, I will say to the ladies that it is better to go via Arles than via Avignon."

The two young women blushed; the two men turned toward me with courteous smiles on their lips. It was evident that they knew me before I had spoken to them, and that someone had told them who I was while I was asleep.

---

[8] The signature "Richard" or "J. B. Richard" (the pseudonym of Jean-Marie Aubin) was affixed to a series of travel guides issued between the 1820s and 1850s, coverings various regions of Western Europe, in French.

"And why is that, if you please?" asked the older of the two travelers.

"Firstly, because in passing through Arles you will see Arles, which is well worth the trouble of being seen. Secondly, between Arles and Marseilles, you will have a road free of dust and extremely curious, in which one travels alongside the Camargue on one side—which is to say, the ancient camp of Marius—and the Crau on the other."

"But we need to be in Marseilles this afternoon."

"We shall be."

"We're leaving on the boat to Livorno."

"I'm leaving on the same boat."

"We want to be in Florence for the feast of Saint John."

"I'm expected there at that time."

"How will we get from Arles to Marseilles?"

"I have my caleche on the boat. There are five of us; it holds six. We'll hire post-horses. We'll take a picnic, and I'll be your guide along the route."

The two travelers turned to the two young women, who nodded almost imperceptibly, and the matter was decided. The two couples were n their honeymoon, and during the honeymoon, as everyone knows, the wife has the power of decision.

We made a charming voyage. In Arles we visited the Arenas and bought sausages. In Marseilles we visited Méry and ate with Courty.[9] Eventually, in Florence we

---

[9] Méry is the journalist and novelist whose full name was Joseph Méry (1797-1866), although he usually signed himself only with his surname. He was one of the pioneers of fiction set in the Far East during the 1840s. Courty was a restaurateur

watched chariot races with Monsieur Finzi and the illuminations of Arno with Prince Corsini.

Finally, it was necessary to part. I stayed in Florence and my traveling companions left to tour Italy. We made promises to meet again, exchanging addresses in case either of the gentlemen came to Paris or I went to Holland. On the part of the travelers, the cards were those of Monsieur Jacobson of Rotterdam and Monsieur Wittering of Amsterdam. Contrary to the habit of promises of that sort, those were kept—more than kept, in fact, for Monsieur Jacobson has become my friend, and on one occasion rendered me a service that many friends would not.

Before I left for Holland, therefore, I had written to Monsieur Jacobson in Rotterdam, notifying him of my arrival—which assured me a regal hospitality, first in his home and then in Monsieur Wittering's.

In fact, Monsieur Jacobson is not only a traveler full of intelligence and a banker full of honor but has the heart of an artist. When we see our most charming paintings by Decamps, Dupré, Rousseau, Scheffer and Diaz departing for Holland, he is the one who is taking them from us, so I had scarcely pronounced his name than Biard was reassured.

As for The Hague, Jacquand should have arrived there a week before with his painting of William the Taciturn selling his ship to Jews in order to sustain the war of independence.[10] He ought to have reserved me a

to whom Dumas claimed in an account of his travels in the south of France that Méry had introduced him.

[10] The reference is to the historical painter Claude Jacquand (1803-1878), who preferred to sign himself Claudius Jacquand. He was effectively ruined by the fallout of the 1848

room at the Imperial Court Hotel. We could, therefore, follow the course of the Scheldt tranquilly, and, during the rare moments when the wind and the rain permitted us to go up on deck, cast a glance over the Paul Potters, the Hobbemas and the Van de Veldes that we were going past.

We traversed Dordrecht through a forest of windmills compared with which the mills of Puerto Lapice are mere pygmies.[11] In Dordrecht, everyone had his own mill; they are by the waterside, in gardens, on top of houses; there are small ones, large ones and gigantic ones, mills for children, mills for adults and mills for old men. All of them have the same form, but everyone paints his mill according to his whim; some are gray with white trimmings, reminiscent of widows in semi-mourning; there are brown ones with black trimmings reminiscent of desolate monks, and white ones with blue trimmings reminiscent of Pierrots on a spree. Nothing is more eccentric than those great immobile bodies, nothing more fantastic than all those great rotating sails. Alongside those mills, in their shadow so to speak, are little red houses with green shutters, neat, clean and arching, appearing behind groves of leafy trees, their trunks whitewashed. And all of it passes by with the rapidity of two hundred horses; it is a charming panorama.

On nearing Rotterdam, vessels multiply in their turn; ships gliding over the water compete with the windmills immobile on the ground. They too are of all

---

Revolution and barely survived on the produce of his labor thereafter.

[11] Puerto Lapice in Castille-La Mancha is the presumed location of the windmills that Don Quixote famously mistook for giants.

sizes, three-maters, brigs, sloops, fishing smacks. There are some, especially, that have a very particular appearance, with their large bleached sail and their small blue sail at the top of the mast; one might think them immense sugar-loaves still wrapped in their gray and blue paper, which are being allowed to dissolve in the river—and I say dissolve because as they draw away they seem to be sinking into the water. All of that is alive, active and mercantile; one senses that one is approaching the Holland of old, which is nothing but an immense port where ten thousand vessels swarm every year.

At eight o'clock in the evening the boat stopped at the quay in Rotterdam. Scarcely had a communication been established between the ferry and the shore than I heard my name pronounced. It was one of Jacobson's clerks informing me that his master had departed that very day for Amsterdam, where I was awaited impatiently by his brother-in-law Wittering, in whose house Gudin had been installed the previous day.

More good news! Gudin had come, like Biard and myself, to witness the coronation; he was not only a friend but also a colleague. Gudin is at least as much a poet as a painter; remember the shipwreck victim who no longer has anything but a mast to sustain him and a star to guide him.[12]

We leapt ashore; there was no time to lose, the train for The Hague left at nine o'clock and it as half past eight. We traversed the entire city with the kind of urgency only manifested by people running after locomotives.

---

[12] The painter Jean-Antoine-Théodore de Gudin (1802-1880) was particularly celebrated for his naval scenes, in which he became a virtual specialist.

As in Brussels, we arrived just in time.

Three quarters of an hour later we ran into a hectic celebration, full of noise, dancing, shouting, the sounds of musical instruments, fairground booths, and the stalls of hawkers of waffles and gherkins. Sellers of waffles and gherkins are two industrial specialties that merit the trouble of being recorded here, in view of the fact that those two speculations are entirely lacking in France.

In Holland, one gets drunk with gherkins and hard-boiled eggs, and sobers up with waffles and punch. Anyone who wants to go on the spree simply pauses at the shop selling pickles, puts five sous on one of the tables, takes a fork in his right hand and a hard-boiled egg in his left. Then he pokes the fork into a big bucket in which slices of cucumber the size of an ordinary gherkin are swimming like goldfish. He takes one of those slices, which he devours, and on top of which he immediately adds a hard-boiled egg. And he alternates thus until his stomach cries *enough*—so much the better for those whose gastric capacity is double, triple or quadruple; it costs them no more than anyone else. It is five sous for everyone.

The physicians of all countries have made scientific and moral observations regarding different sort of drunkenness: the drunkenness of eau-de-vie, wine, beer and gin have all been studied; there is only the drunkenness of gherkins on which, I believe, no report has yet been made. I shall try to fill that gap.

Scarcely has the Dutchman got drunk on gherkins than he experiences the need to do foolish things. In consequence, he approaches the establishments of waffle-sellers. Those shops warrant a particular description. They are normally kept by four women, two of an uncertain age, two young and pretty. All four wear the Friesian costume.

The Friesian costume includes a more or less elegant jacket, and a more or less elegant dress; that is not where its originality resides; its originality resides in a double skullcap of gilded copper that clings to the temples on either side. Two little golden ornaments are worn at the exterior extremity of each eyebrow, reminiscent of little fire-irons; two or three curls of false hair are ordinarily attached to those copper plates. A bonnet with flaps is worn over the whole.

In general, that strange assembly of copper, which gives the head the appearance of a gilded skull, and hair growing on the copper, and lace extinguishing overly bright light over all the parts it covers, makes a very agreeable sight.

Those ladies follow the métier that almas follow in Egypt and bayaderes in India, except that they neither dance not sing.

The two woman of a reasonable age sit on an armchair beside the door and an armchair behind the counter; they are encrusted there. The one at the door serves the waffles, the one at the counter serves the punch.

The two young women do...well, it is rather difficult to say what they do, especially after having said what they do not do. The recognize men drunk on gherkins at a glance and beckon to them. When signs are insufficient they emerge from the shop and go after them.

Once inside the shop, the customer disappears into a private booth. A Friesian follows him. Then a plate of waffles and a bowl of punch are brought in. Then the curtains, which separate the passers-by and inhabitants of the shop from the interior of the booth, fall back with an entirely Dutch naivety. A quarter of an hour later, the man emerges, completely sober.

That is what we saw on the evening of the tenth of May, only twenty-four hours after leaving Paris. Thanks to all the turns and twists of the Scheldt, we had covered sixty leagues during those twenty-four hours.

Upon which, having found our rooms ready thanks to the cares of our friend Jacquand, we went to bed to the sound of the most infernal music I have ever heard.

III. Mermaids and Sirens

Memory, the pleasant gift of Heaven by means of which a man may relive his past existence, a magic mirror that reflects of objects while lending them the vague poetry of twilight and the suave contours of distance, it is in me especially that your presence is real, your attraction irresistible! I take up the pen with the firm intention of traversing space as a bird flies, with the sole desire to depart and arrive, but all along the route, memory has left footprints that I rediscover. I no longer belong to myself, but to the past, body and soul. My mind, which wants to travel with lightning rapidity, drifts uncertainly, like a soap-bubble borne away by the wind, and which, while bathing in sapphire, ruby and opal, reflects on its ephemeral globe houses, fields and the sky—which is to say, a eternal world within an instantaneous one.

That is, however, true; I wanted to traverse France and Belgium in a single chapter, to descend the Scheldt, reach Amsterdam and embark for Monnikendam, where we are to find Père Olifus. But already, on the route, I have encountered Biard, the King of the Belgians, the man with the bass, the windmills of Dordrecht, the ships of Ysselmonde, Jacobson's letter, Jacquand, the festivities in The Hague, the slicers of gherkins and the sellers of waffles, and the Friesian woman with golden bonnets; I have paused at every one, at people and things; I have extended my hand, turned my head, slowed my pace; here I am at the beginning of my third chapter, and I am still—where? In The Hague, on the eve of the coronation; I will still need another chapter to talk about the King, the Queen, Amsterdam with its three hundred canals, its thirty thousand flags and its hundred thousand inhabitants.

May my readers forgive me; God has made me thus; let them take me as God has made me, or close the book.

I have not yet lost the hope of arriving at Monnikendam by the end of this chapter...but man proposes and God disposes. Like the paper boats that children put in a stream, which is a river for them, I shall let the course of my story go, at the risk of foundering today and only arriving tomorrow.

I had a letter from King Jérôme Napoléon for his niece, the Queen of Holland. As soon as I arrived, I had transmitted that letter to her, with the result that I was woken up by a messenger from the palace.

I stuck my head out of the feather-bed in which I was buried, and enquired as to the cause of my awakening. The King's aide-de-camp passed me, on behalf of His Majesty, an authorization to take the special train, along with my traveling companions, and sent tickets to watch the coronation from the diplomatic benches.

The special train was leaving at eleven; it was nine o'clock. I thanked the messenger and tried to drag myself out of bed. I say that I tried to drag myself, and that is the appropriate word; it is not easy to extract oneself from a Dutch bed, made in the form of a crate and equipped with two mattresses stuffed with feathers, in which one hollows out one's mold, which closes around you.

It is quite incredible, the variety brought to the accessories and the form of an item of furniture has the same purpose in every country in the world, that of resting the human body. Sedentary individuals believe that one must go to bed in the same fashion everywhere, or very nearly, but they are greatly mistaken.

Put alongside one another an English bed, an Italian bed, a German bed and a Dutch bed, have them studied by a Parisian scholar who has never seen any other kind of bed than a French one, and you will have a volume of conjectures, each more curious than the last, regarding the different uses for which those different items of furniture might be employed. He will assign them different destinations before divining that they are all sleeping machines.

Fortunately, I had familiarized myself long ago with the most extravagant beds, and I had slept perfectly in my Dutch bed. It was not the same for Alexandre and Biard, who had got up at seven o'clock in the morning to go in search of a bath-house. They had hoped that the water my help them recover from the feathers, and the bath from the bed.

They came back at about half past nine, having gone around the Hague three times, visited all the museums and all the junk shops but without having discovered a single bath-house. It is true that the sea is only a league from The Hague.

I had just enough time left to go to the Museum myself.

There was one thing I wanted to see, apart from the Rembrandts, the Van Dycks, the Hobbemas, the Paul Potters and all the masterpieces of Dutch painting; there was, in one of the rooms in the middle of the picturesque museum, a glass case in which several specimens of mermaids were preserved.

The mermaid is a particular product of Holland and its colonies.

As you might or might not know, mermaids are divided into two classes: the siren and the nereid.

The siren is the ancient monster with the head of a woman and the tail of a fish. They are the daughters of Parthenope, Ligeia and Leucosia. If the authors of the sixteenth, the seventeenth and even the eighteenth centuries are to be believed, sirens are not rare. In 1614, in New England in the Occidental Indies, the English captain John Smith saw a siren having the upper part of the body perfectly similar to that of a woman. She was swimming with all possible grace when he saw her from the sea shore. Her eyes were large, although slightly round, her nose well-formed, although a trifle snub, and her ears prettily shaped, although a little long, to which her long green hair gave a character of strangeness that was not without charm. Unfortunately, the beautiful bather turned a somersault, and Captain John Smith, who was beginning to fall in love, perceived that below the navel, the woman was nothing but a fish.

It is true that the fish had a double tail, but a double tail does not replace two legs.

Dr. Kircher observes, in a scientific report, that a siren was caught in the Zuiderzee and dissected at Leyden by Professor Pierre Paw.[13] In the same report he men-

---

[13] This anecdote dates back to the 17th century, and appears in a 1671 article by the Danish physician Thomas Bartholin. The same article relates the oft-quoted anecdote about John Smith's mermaid sighting, which had previously appeared in Georg Stengel's *De Monstris et Monstrosis* (1647), and appears to derived ultimately from a 1628 text in which the engraver Theodor de Bry attached his illustrations to various travelers' tales. The claim to have seen a mermaid appears to have been misattributed by de Bry to John Smith, actually originating, as recently discovered by Vaughn Scribner, from

tions a siren that was found in Denmark, which learned to spin and to predict the future. That siren had long tresses formed not of hair but of fleshy threads. She had an agreeable face, arms longer than those of humans, fingers and toes joined by a cartilage in the form of a goose-foot, round and firm breasts, and skin covered with scales so white and delicate that they could be mistaken at a distance for white fleshy skin. She recounted that tritons and sirens formed a submarine population that, combining the skills of the monkey and the beaver, constructed rocky grottoes in places in accessible to divers, where they lay down on beds of sand, on which they rested, slept and made love.

Jean-Philippe Abelinus reports, in the first volume of his *Théâtre de l'Europe*,[14] that in 1619, councilors of the King of Denmark sailing from Norway to Copenhagen saw a merman swimming in the sea and carrying a bundle of plants on his head. He was thrown a bait in which a hook as concealed. The merman was as greedy, it seems, as a terrestrial human, and let himself be caught for a morsel of lard, into which he bit, and was hauled aboard the ship. Scarcely was he on deck, however, than he started speaking the purest Danish and threatening the vessel with its doom. At the first words he spoke the sailors, as one can imagine, were very astonished, but when from simple words he progressed to threats their astonishment changed into fear. They hastened to throw

---

Captain Richard Whitbourne's *Discourse and Discovery of New-found-land* (1620).

[14] The reference is to *Theatrum Europaeum* by Johann Philipp Abelinus et al. (1685), which can be read on Google Books by anyone who can read German in Gothic script.

the merman back into the sea, making him all sorts of apologies.

It is true that, as it is the sole example of a merman who talked, Abelinus' commentary claims that it was not a triton but a specter.

Johnston recounts that in 1403, a mermaid was caught in a Dutch lake, where she had been washed up by the sea. She allowed herself to be dressed, became accustomed to eating bread and milk, and learned to spin, but remained mute.[15]

Finally, to conclude like a firework display—which is to say, with a flourish, Dimas Bosque, physician of the Viceroy of the isle of Manara, recounts in a letter inserted in Barthole's *History of Asia*,[16] that while he was strolling on the sea shore with a Jesuit, a band of fishermen came running to invited the priest to climb into their boat to see a prodigy. The priest accepted their invitation, and Dimas Bosque accompanied him.

In the boat were sixteen fish with human faces, nine females and seven males, which the fishermen had just caught with a single cast of the net. They were taken ashore and examined minutely. Their ears were prominent, like ours, cartilaginous and covered in thin skin. Their eyes were similar to ours in coloration, form and location, they were enclosed in orbits hidden beneath the brow, were equipped with eyelids and did not have different axes of vision, like those of fish. The nose only

---

[15] I can find no trace of this anecdote prior to Dumas' citation.

[16] Dimas Bosque certainly existed, and was indeed a physician, but I can find no trace of the history of Asia supposed written by "Barthole" and no trace of this anecdote prior to Dumas' citation. The reference to the island of Manara is also enigmatic, and Dumas appears to have made up the anecdote.

differed from a human nose in being slightly flattened, like that of a negro, and lightly cleft like that of a bull-dog. The mouth and lips were perfectly similar to ours. The teeth were rectangular and tightly juxtaposed. They had broad chests covered with extremely white skin, which allowed the blood vessels to be perceived.

The females had round, firm breasts, and some of them were undoubtedly nursing, for on pressing the nipples, a very white and pure milk sprang forth. Their arms, two cubits long, fuller than ours, were unjointed, and the hands were attached to the cubitus. Finally, underside of the belly, at the commencement of the hips and thighs, divided into a double tail like that of fish. Understandably, such a catch caused a great rumor. The Viceroy bought that catch from the fishermen and make gifts of that entire population of tritons and sirens to his friends and acquaintances. The Dutch resident receives a siren for his part, which he sent to his government, which passed it on it to the Museum of The Hague.

You will understand that a veritable siren, an authentic siren, encased and labeled in a museum, a siren that science has declared not to belong to the family of Lazarillo de Tormes or Cadet-Roussel Esturgeon,[17] but is an authentic descendant of the river Achelous and the

---

[17] Lazarillo de Tormes is the central character of the Spanish novella *La Vida de Lazarillo de Tormes y de sus fortunas y adversidades* (1554), which founded the genre of picaresque fiction and formed as a model for other works of that genre, including *Père Olifus*. *Cadet-Roussel Esturgeon* (1813) is a vaudeville signed "M. Delaligne" (Marc-Antoine Désaugiers) in which the central character visits a fair where he encounters a fortune-teller and a series of costumed tricksters.

nymph Calliope,[18] was much more curious than a gallery of crows, even if there were ten thousand crows in the gallery. For after all, one sees crows every day, whereas sirens are becoming increasingly rare.

Thus, not knowing whether I would ever return to The Hague, I did not want to miss the opportunity to see a siren.

In haste as I was to give myself that pleasure, however, I stopped short as I went in.

I knew that it was in the same museum that the complete costume was exhibited that William of Nassau, Prince of Orange, whom history has nicknamed the Taciturn was wearing when he was assassinated in Delft by Balthazar Gérard on 10 July 1584. That historical memory had a positive attraction of me worth as much as the sirens and mermaids of all lands. I therefore asked the guide to show me first the glass case in which William's vestments were contained, and then the cupboard where the cadaver of the mermaid was.

The relic of the founder of the Dutch Republic, the author of the Union of Utrecht, the spouse of Téligny's widow, is to the left of the entrance of the first room; for two hundred and sixty-four years, it has been exposed to the veneration of the people for whom William's last sigh was.

"Lord, have pity on my soul and this poor people!" said the Taciturn, as he fell.

---

[18] In ancient Greece Achelous, the patron deity of the river of the same name, appears to have been widely worshiped at one time as the source of all fresh water; Servius attributed the river to the god's grief after losing his daughters, the Sirens. Calliope was the muse of epic poetry and mother of Orpheus.

The bloodstained doublet, waistcoat and shirt are there, along with the bullet which traversed his chest and the pistol from which it emerged. It is a living and eternal curse against the assassin.

I do not know of anything that urges meditation, reverie and poetry like the sight of material objects. How much there is in Ravillac's dagger and Balthazar Gérard's bullet! Who can say what three inches of iron or an ounce of lead weight in the destiny of peoples! Hazard, providence or fatality; the world blanches upon those three worlds, and the sphinx that watches over them is doubt.

I would return to The Hague purely to see that bloodstained shirt, that pistol and that bullet again.

But it was quarter to eleven, and I only had a few more minutes to myself. I asked to see my siren; I was taken to case no. 449. That case contained three monsters: a faun, a vampire and a siren. It was the siren I wanted; I left the vampire and the faun to one side.

She was desiccated and very nearly the color of a Carib head. Her eyes were closed; the nose was flattened; the lips were stuck to the teeth, which were yellowed; the breast was evident, although depressed; a few sores and short hairs were bristling on the head. Finally, the inferior part of the body terminated in a fish's tail.

There was nothing to say; it was definitely a siren.

Interrogated by me, my cicerone then told me the story of Dimas Bosque, the Jesuit priest, the Viceroy of Manara and the Dutch resident, such as I have recounted it. Then, as I saw that I insisted on having further details, he said: "It appears that you are curious for information about animals of this sort.

I thought my cicerone impertinent to classify as an animal a creature with a woman's head, a woman's hands and a woman's breast, but I did not have time to argue the point with him.

"Very curious," I replied, "and if you can give me any..."

"Oh, not me exactly, but I can tell you where to find some."

"Where is that?"

"In Monnikendam."

"What is Monnikendam?"

"It's a town two leagues from Amsterdam, in the depths of a little gulf of the Zuiderzee."

"And I'll find information about sirens there?"

"Oh, certainly, about sirens and about mermaids, which are even more curious."

"Is there one in the Museum of Monnikendam, then?"

"No, but there's one in the cemetery there; you'll see her husband and her children, which is much more amusing."

"She was married, then, your mermaid? She had children?"

"She was married and had children. It's true that the children deny it, but her husband will tell you everything."

"Does he speak French?"

"Oh, he speaks all languages. He's an old sea-dog."

"And his name?"

"Père Olifus."

"Where will I find him?"

"Perhaps in Amsterdam itself; he has a boat in which he ferries travelers from Amsterdam to Monnikendam. If you don't find him in Amsterdam you'll find him in Monnikendam, where his daughter

Marguerite keeps the hostelry of the Bonhomme Tropique."

"Père Olifus, you say?"

"Père Olifus."

"Good."

I darted a final glance at the siren, of which Biard made a sketch, and we leapt into our cab, saying: "To the railway station."

IV. The Bonhomme Tropique Inn

Holland is the fatherland of railways; from The Hague to Amsterdam the Dutch engineers have not had a single ravine to fill in or a tunnel to dig. Furthermore, the country is always the same: a vast meadow intercut by watercourses, clumps of woodland of the freshest green, sheep buried in their wool, and cows with overcoats.

Nothing is more scrupulously true than the landscapes of the Dutch masters; when one has seen Hobbema and Paul Potter, one has seen Holland. When one has seen Teniers and Terburg, one has seen the Dutch—and yet, those who have not been to Holland go there; even after Hobbema and Paul Potter, Holland is beautiful to see; even after Teniers and Terburg, the Dutch are good to know.

In two hours, we were in Amsterdam. A quarter of an hour later, we climbed the front steps of a charming house situated on the Kaisergratz, and, alerted by the domestic who was waiting for us we saw Madame Wittering, and Messieurs Wittering, Jacobson and Gudin hurrying to meet us.

Madame Wittering was still the charming woman that I had already had the honor seeing three times, beautiful and modest, blushing like a child, a gracious mixture of a Parisienne and an Englishwoman. Her sister, Madame Jacobson, was in London.

For five minutes there was a clicking of cheek-kisses and a gymnastics of handshakes.

Gudin was there, as I said, having arrived from Scotland.

The table was laid.

It is my French habits that caused me to say that the table was laid; in Holland the table is always laid; it is there that a house is hospitable in the full meaning of the word.

Each of us had a room already prepared in that charming house, which was a cross between a château and a chalet. It was a pleasure to see those transparent windows, those shiny doorknobs, the carpets in the drawing rooms, the corridors and the staircases, and to sense the domestics that one never sees but always divines, occupied with neatness, elegance and wellbeing.

While conducting us to the table, Madame Wittering reminded us that the King was making his entrance at three o'clock, and that we had a window from which to watch that entrance in the home of one of her friends. We hastened our meal, and at quarter to three, we went to the house where we were expected.

We had arrived on the eleventh of May; it was a week since I had seen the fourth of May festivities in Paris. At a distance of seven days and fifty leagues, I saw a second festival, which, at first glance, seemed to be a continuation of the first. In Amsterdam, as in Paris, and in Paris, as in Amsterdam, we passed beneath a vault of tricolor flags, in the midst of the cries of the populace—except that the French flags bear the three colors vertically and the Dutch flags bear them horizontally, while in Paris people were shouting: "Down with royalty!" and in Amsterdam, "Long live the King!"

We were introduced to our temporary hosts. There was a further specimen of a Dutch house; it was slightly larger than the Witterings', similarly situated between a canal and a garden, facing the canal with the garden behind. The ceiling was ornamented with beautiful paintings.

In Holland I expected to encounter lacquer furniture and porcelain vases from China and Japan at every step, heaped up in dining rooms and drawing rooms, but the Dutch are like those disdainful proprietors who do not esteem what they have. I saw French shelf-units, a few Saxe figurines, but few screens, few porcelain vases and little in the way of Chinoiserie.

At quarter past three, we heard a great noise that made us run to the widows. It was the beginning of the procession. First we saw the band appear, then the cavalry, than people and carriages mingled together, and finally the National Guard on horseback, clad in plain clothing, with no other weapons than riding-crops and no other distinction than a crimson velvet sashes.

The whole was preceded by two or three hundred workers and children, who were throwing their caps in the air and singing the Dutch national anthem. The remarkable thing is however, that the national anthem of the Dutch—which is to say, the most Republican people on earth—is a hymn to monarchy.

While I was dreaming about all the royal entrances that I had seen in my life, the cortege filed past, and the King came toward us in the midst of a dozen general officers or senior officials of his palace.

He was a man of thirty or thirty-two, blond with blue eyes, to which he was able to give by turns an expression of great mildness and firmness, and a beard that covered the base of his visage. The ensemble of his physiognomy was sympathetic, his salutations affable and grateful.

I bowed as he went past, and, turning round, he saluted me individually with his hand and eye. I could not believe that that double salute was addressed to me, so I turned round to see who had just received that royal honor.

Jacobson understood my movement. "No, no," he said, "it's really you that the King saluted."

"Me that the King saluted? Impossible; he doesn't know me."

"That's exactly why he recognized you. He knows all our faces by heart. He saw a strange face, and said to himself: 'That's my poet.'"

The curious thing is that it was true, and the King told me so himself the following day.

The King was on horseback and wearing an admiral's uniform. A large gilded carriage came next, drawn by eight white horses, each held by the bridle by a valet in livery. At the two sides of the carriage, balanced on the footsteps, pages were recognizable in their red and gold uniforms.

A woman of twenty-five or twenty-six, and two children between six and eight were in the carriage, waving, the children without thinking about anything, the woman perhaps thinking about too much. The woman and the two children were the Queen, the Prince of Orange and Prince Maurice.

It is impossible to see a face more gracious and melancholy at the same time than that of the Queen; she is a woman in all her grace and a princess in all her majesty. I had the honor of being received three times by her during the two days that I stayed in Amsterdam, I have not forgotten a single word of what she said to me. May her people be good and faithful to her, and may God never change her melancholy into dolor!

The cortege passed by, drew away and disappeared. A strange vision, in this epoch when kings seem marked with a fatal Tau.[19] Alas, who is right, them or peoples? That is the great enigma to which Charles I and Louis XVI were sacrificed. The Restoration of 1660 belied the people. The Revolution of 1848 belied the Kings. The future will decide, but I would bet on the people.[20]

Once the cortege had passed, I had nothing more to do in Amsterdam until eleven o'clock the following morning. I therefore took my leave of my hosts, asking them to give me directions as to how to reach Monnikendam.

That whim seemed strange to them. What could I have to do in Monnikendam? I refrained from telling them that I was in search of a mermaid. I simply insisted on going to Monnikendam.

They gave me Wittering's brother to accompany me. Alexandre and I separated; he wanted to go to Brock. Biard wanted to remain with me and declared that he would accompany me to Monnikendam.

Biard, I believe, was slightly ashamed of having been to North Cape, of having seen, from the utmost extremity of Europe, two seas, and of not encountering, in those two seas, a single mermaid. He was counting on my lucky star, having found his own waning.

Having arrived in the port, I set forth—or, rather, asked my guide to set forth, in search of Père Olifus.

---

[19] The Tau Cross, so-called because of its resemblance to the Greek letter, became one of the versions of the crucifix, but it had a reputation long before Christ as a mark sometimes born on the forehead, with a variable symbolism.

[20] All of this paragraph but the first sentence is excised from the abridged version of the text, presumably because of its political sentiment.

The search was fruitless for some time; the boat was there, but its owner was not. Finally, he was discovered in a frightful species of tavern that he visited habitually. He was told that a traveler departing for Monnikendam only wanted to go with him.

That preference flattered him. He consented to quit his grog and advanced toward me, smiling.

"This is Père Olifus," said the man who had set out in search of him at Wittering's request.

I gave the unearther of my man a florin.

Père Olifus perceived the florin, and seeing the price at which I valued him, became more amiable than ever. In the meantime, I examined him with a curiosity in proportion to his importance.

Biard sketched him.

He was, as I had been told, an old sea-dog between sixty and sixty-five years old, having more seal than human about him: white hair and beard, both an inch long, both stiff as a brush; round eyes, of a faience blue, with moist irises; a mouth slit to the ears, displaying two yellow teeth planted vertically like the tusks of a walrus; a mahogany complexion.

He was clad in wide trousers that had once been blue, and a kind of hooded overcoat, on the seams of which a few ornaments could still be distinguished that assigned the coat a Spanish or Neapolitan origin.

One of his cheeks was inflated by an enormous plug of tobacco, as if by a gumboil. From time to time, a jet of black saliva was launched from his mouth with that whistle particular to chewers of tobacco.

"Ah, you're French!" he said to me.

"How do you know that?"

"Well, it's hardly worth of having seen the four continents of the world, Asia, Africa and America, if one can't recognize a man right away. French, French, French! And he started to sing: "*Mourir pour la patrie...*"

I stopped him. "Oh, not that, Père Olifus—something else."[21]

"Why not that?"

"Because I know that refrain."

"Well, as you wish. So you want to go to Monnikendam?"

"Yes."

"And you're determined that it shall be Père Olifus who takes you there—not stupid!"

"Yes."

"Well, you'll be taken there, and without fixing the price yet."

"Why without fixing the price?"

"Because one has eyes, and what one has seen in sufficient. Are you staying overnight in Monnikendam?"

"Yes."

"Well, I recommend the Bonhomme Tropique inn."

"That's exactly where I'm going."

---

[21] The words are from the chorus of *Le Chant des Girondins*, which became the French National Anthem during the Second Republic. The words of the song are by Dumas, from the theatrical version of his 1846 novel *Le Chevalier de Maison-Rouge*, first performed at the Théâtre Historique in 1847. The music was composed by Alphonse Varney, who worked extensively with Dumas in his theatrical endeavors during the relevant period, although the chorus is adapted from a piece by Rouget de Lisle, the author of the *Marseillaise*. Dumas's request for Olifus to sing something else is therefore feigned modesty; when he wrote the passage Dumas could not have known that his composition of the anthem would be a factor in his subsequent banishment by Napoléon III.

"It's kept by my daughter Marguerite."

"I know."

"Ah!" said Père Olifus. You know that? Good."
And he seemed to reflect.

"Well, shall we go, Père Olifus?"

"Yes, yes, let's go." He looked at me. "I know why
you've come."

"You know?"

"I know. You're a scholar, and you want to make
me talk.

"Is it difficult to make you talk, Père Olifus, when
the commencement of the conversation is watered with
tafia, the middle with rum and the end with arrack?"

"Ah! You know the gradation?"

"Oh, in truth, no—that's luck."

"Well, one will talk—but not in front of the children, you understand?"

"And where are the children?"

"You'll see." And he turned in three different directions and whistled. Père Olifus' whistle closely resembled that of a locomotive.

In response to that whistle I saw five big fellows
coming from different directions, heading for a common
center. That common center was Biard, Père Olifus and
me.

"Hey, Joachim, Thomas, Philippe, Simon and Jude"
he shouted, adding in Dutch: "Hurry up! Here's business
for us and your sister Marguerite."

By the name of Marguerite and the fashion in which
Père Olifus talked to the big lads who were advancing
toward us, I understood approximately what he had just
said. "Ah, Père Olifus, is this a specimen of the fine
family that I've been told about?"

"In The Hague, no doubt, at the Museum? I'll have to have a word with that old rogue. Yes, these are my five sons."

"You have five sons and a daughter, then?"

"A daughter and five sons, two of them twins, to wit Simon and Jude; the oldest is twenty-five.

"And all from the same mother?" I asked, with a certain hesitation.

Olifus looked at me. "The same mother, yes, in that regard, for sure. I won't say as much for the side of...but shh! Here's the children, not a word in front of them."

The children passed before me, saluting me and looking suspiciously at their father; it doubtless seemed to them that the old man had already been talking.

"Let's go, lads, to the boat," said Père Olifus, "and let's show Monsieur that we're not out of place on an eighty-footer."

Three of the young men went down swiftly into the boat, while the other two pulled the chain to bring it to shore. We leapt into the rear, where Père Olifus got down, still quite lightly. Then the last two sons, Simon and Jude, followed us, and crew and passengers found themselves complete. It seemed to me that Simon and Jude were never apart, for they busied themselves raising the little mast that was in the bottom of the boat, while the father sat down at the tiller, Joachim detached the chain and Philippe and Thomas, each armed with an oar, steered through the middle of the thousands of boats and ships that were cluttering the harbor.

Once clear of obstacles, we were able to hoist the sail. The wind was good; we advanced rapidly. After ten minutes, we had doubled the small cape that blocked our view, and we were sailing in the open Zuiderzee.

After half an hour, we passed between Tidam and the island of Marken.

Olifus touched me with the tip of his finger. "Look carefully at those tall reeds," he said.

"On the shore of the island?" I asked.

"Yes."

"Well, I'm looking at them."

"That's where I found her."

"Who?"

"Shh!"

In fact, Joachim had seen the movement, had turned toward us, and, shrugging his shoulders rather disrespectfully, had darted a reproachful glance at his father.

"Well, what, children?" he said.

"Nothing."

Silence fell again.

After five minutes, we were in the little gulf, and began to distinguish the village that rose up to our left.

The young men had cast glances southwards several times, and although their gazes were not anxious, they were concerned.

"What's the matter with your children?" I asked. "They seem to be expecting something."

"Yes, they're expecting something they'd rather not see coming."

"What's that?"

"The wind..."

"The wind?"

"Yes, the wind, the southerly wind; and this evening, it'll probably be necessary to watch the dykes. So much the better for us..."

"Why so much the better for us?"

"Yes, we'll be tranquil and we'll be able to chat."

"So it doesn't bother you to talk about..."

"On the contrary, it soothes my heart, but it's as if they'd been given the word to take the side of that slut La Buchold. Right—now I've let the word slip, and they've heard it. See how Simon and Jude are looking at me. They're the youngest, though, they're not twenty. Oh well, they're already like the others."

"Who's La Buchold?"

The young men turned round, frowning.

"Right! Now you've repeated it and you're going to set them off."

In fact, our five sailors appeared to be in a rather bad mood.

I shut up.

We drew nearer to the little village, which, as we advanced, seemed to be emerging from the water.

"Don't seem to be doing anything," Père Olifus said to me, "but look to your left."

I saw a cemetery.

He winked, with a triumphant expression. "That's where she is," he said.

I understood, and this time I contented myself with replying with a slight nod of the head. But our dialogue, although half-mute, had not escaped Thomas, who, doubtless in opposition to the sentiment of satisfaction that his father appeared to feel, uttered a sigh and made the sign of the cross.

"Your children are Catholics, then?" I asked him.

"Oh, my God yes! Don't talk to me about it, they were only able to think of it to make me angry, those fellows. Anyway, I'm wrong to hold it against them; it's not their fault but their mother's."

"Oh! Their mother was..."

"The day when I found her, I left her alone momentarily. *Crack!* In that time, the curé had baptized her."

"Father!" said Philippe, who was the closest to us, turning round.

"It's all right!" he said. "We're talking about Saint John, who baptized Our Lord in the Jordan, and nothing else." Getting to his feet at the same time, he waved a greeting with his cap. "Hey, Marguerite!" he shouted to a beautiful young woman of nineteen or twenty standing on her doorstep. "Prepare your best room and make a good supper; I'm bringing you business."

He added: "Go on ahead and wait for me in your room. While they're at the dykes, I'll come up to you and, while smoking a pipe and drinking a glass, I'll tell you the story."

I made a sign of assent, to which he responded with a sly wink. Having set foot on land with Simon and Jude, we advanced toward the Bonhomme Tropique inn, on the threshold of which our beautiful hostess was waiting for us, with a smile on her lips.

V. The First Marriage of Père Olifus

We were welcomed perfectly by Mademoiselle Olifus. She guided us to a room with two beds, and asked us whether we wanted to be served in our room or to eat in the common room.

The hope that Père Olifus would tell us about his adventures made us opt to be served in our room.

Invited to say what we would like for our supper, we declared that we would leave it entirely to Mademoiselle Marguerite's good will. All of that conversation, of course, was carried out in sign language, but the signs in question, ridiculous between impatient men, become a very agreeable language when spoken by a pretty woman who is smiling at you. In consequence of which, although not a word had been pronounced between us, at the end of ten minutes, we understood one another perfectly.

Père Olifus was not mistaken; the wind continued to blow, increasing in strength; there was nothing to fear, but it was necessary nevertheless, as a precaution, to watch over the dykes. Already, from the window, we could see three of Père Olifus' sons heading in that direction; the other two, Simon and Jude went into a house in which, we learned subsequently, they were paying court to two sisters.

While we were following the movement of the streets and the harbor with our eyes, amid the first shadows of the night, which were about to thicken, our table was set, first with a dish of grilled salmon and a plate of hot hard-boiled eggs. Those eggs, as large as pigeon's eggs, were green and speckled with red; they were lapwings' eggs, which are found in abundance in the month of May, and are much more delicate than hens' eggs.

A bottle of Bordeaux wine stood in the middle of that exhibition of national products, like a slender steeple, vacillating at the slightest shock.

We went to table with a sailor's appetite. Everything was excellent, the wine and food alike. In any case, for us, supper was only an accessory; what we were awaiting with the greatest impatience was the appearance of Père Olifus.

At dessert we heard footsteps on the staircase that were simultaneously heavy and furtive. The door opened, and Père Olifus came in, with a bottle under his arm and his pipe in his mouth, laughing silently.

"Shh!" he said. "Here I am."

"And in good company, it seems."

"Yes, I said: they're Frenchmen, let's go all out, to be strong. I've got a bottle of tafia, a bottle of rum, a bottle of arrack, and here I am."

"In truth, Père Olifus," I said to him, "the more I listen to you, the more you astonish me; you don't speak French like a matelot of His Majesty William II but like a mariner of His Majesty Louis XIV."

"That's because I'm fundamentally French," said Père Olifus, winking.

"What do you mean, fundamentally?"

"Yes, my father was French and my mother Danish; my grandfather was French and my grandmother from Hamburg. As for my children, I can boast that they have a French father and a mother...oh, as for the mother, I won't venture to say what she was. As for them, they're true Dutch—which wouldn't have happened if I'd been there to take care of their education, but I was in the Indies."

"You came back from time to time, though!" I said, laughing.

"That's where you're mistaken; I didn't come back."

"But your wife went to find you there?"

"Yes and no."

"What do you mean, yes and no?"

"That's just where the chaplet gets tangled, you see. It appears that distance is nothing, when one has a witch wife."

"What?"

"Yes, that's it. In any case, I'm going to tell you everything—but first, a glass of tafia; it's the real stuff, this, I can answer for that. Your health!"

"To yours, *mon brave*!"

"So, as I was saying, I'm French, the son of a Frenchman, matelots from father to son, from the race of sea-dogs and sea-cows. I came into the world on the sea, I hope to die on the sea."

"With that vocation, why didn't you go into the navy?"

"Oh, I served in the time of the Emperor, but in 1810, *bonsoir!* I was captured and sent to England, probably to learn English there; that served me later, as you'll see.

"In 1814, I came back here, to Monnikendam, that's where the Emperor had taken me. I was industrious, I did all kinds of wicker-work, out there in the pontoon, and sold it to Englishwomen who came to visit us, with the result that I saved up a small sum, about three or four hundred florins. I bought a boat, became a captain, and amused myself taking travelers to Amsterdam, Purmerend, Edam and Hoorn—all along the coast, in sum.

"That went on from 1815 to 1820. I was thirty-five; people were always saying to me: 'Aren't you going to marry, Père Olifus?' I said: 'No, I'm a mariner, I won't marry until I've found a mermaid.' 'And why do you want a mermaid, Père Olifus?' 'Well,' I replied, 'because mermaids can't talk.'

"It's necessary to tell you that two or three hundred years ago, a mermaid was found washed ashore on the sand; she was taught to curtsy and spin, but no one was ever—never, ever—able to teach her to talk."

"Yes, I know. So?"

"You understand: a wife who curtsies, spins and doesn't talk is a treasure; but the truth is, you see, that I didn't believe in mermaids, and I'd decided not to marry.

"One day—it was the twenty-third of September 1823, I'll never forget that date—there had been bad weather the day before; the wind was blowing from the North Sea. I was coming back from taking an Englishman to Amsterdam, and as I was passing between Cap Tidam and the little isle of Marken, at the place where the reeds are that I showed you earlier, we perceived something like an animal splashing in the water.

"We sailed closer, and he closer we went, the more we thought that we recognized a human being. We shouted: 'Hold on! Courage! We're coming!' But the more we shouted, the louder the racket became. We arrived, and what did we see? A woman, splashing around."

"There was a Parisian in the crew, a joker. He said to me: "Look, Père Olifus, a mermaid; that's exactly what you need.'

"At that word, I should have run away, you see— but not at all. As curious as a porpoise, I kept going, and

I said: 'In truth, it is a woman, who's still in the process of drowning. Necessary to pick her up and take her away.'

"'She's barely dressed,' said the Parisian.

"In fact, she was stark naked. 'Oh, are you scared?' I said to him—and at the same time, I jumped into the water and I took her in my arms.

"She'd just fainted.

"We tried to pull her out of the reeds. I don't know how she'd been caught there, but the plants had formed a knot around her leg, like an unholy sailor's knot. We were obliged to cut the plants.

"We laid her down in the boat, covered her with her cloaks and set a course for Monnikendam.

"We presumed that there had been some shipwreck in the vicinity, and that the poor woman had been pushed toward the coast, where she she'd got tangled up in the reeds. Only the Parisian shook his head. He said that he woman had fainted from fear on seeing us, and he claimed that she was a Nereid, not a shipwreck victim. Then he lifted a corner of our cloaks and looked.

"I looked too, and I confess that I even took pleasure in looking. She was a lovely creature, who appeared to be twenty or twenty-two at the most. Beautiful arms, beautiful throat—except that her hair was tinted green. As she was very white, though, that suited her well enough.

"While I was looking at her, she opened an eye. The eye was green too, but it was no uglier for that.

"When I saw that she'd opened the eye, I let the cloak fall back, while begging her pardon for my indiscretion and telling her that in Monnikendam I'd go to borrow the best dress of the daughter of Burgomaster Van Clief, to give it to her. She didn't reply; I thought it was out of shame; I made a sign to the others not to say anything, but I encouraged them to row.

"Suddenly, the cloaks lifted up, and she braced herself to jump into the water. Imbecile that I was not to let her do it!"

"You held her back?"

"By her green hair, exactly. Then something happened that really ought to have opened my eyes, though; it was that, all alone as she was, she nearly reckoned with all six of us. The Parisian, among others, received a sharp blow in the eye. 'Oh!' he said—he'd never seen anything like it in La Courtille.

"I thought she was a madwoman who was trying to kill herself. I put my arms round her body, and although her skin was as slippery as an eel's, I succeeded in holding her, while my companions tied her feet and hands.

"Once her feet and hands were tied, it was finished; she uttered a few cries, shed a few tears, than decided to remain tranquil.

"There wasn't one of us who hadn't received a clout, but the best one was the Parisian's; he was bathing his eye with sea water every five minutes. If ever you get a black eye, you see, that's sovereign, sea water.

"In brief, we landed. When the find we had made became known, the whole village came running. We carried the woman to my house, and I sent word to Burgomaster Van Clief's daughter asking whether she would be so kind as to put one of her dresses at the disposal of shipwreck victim. What can you expect, when one doesn't know?

"The burgomaster's daughter came, bringing a costume. I sent her into the room where our prisoner was lying on the bed, still tied up. It's necessary to believe that she recognized her as a creature of her species, because she made signs to the young woman to untie her, and when the girl hastened to render her that service she began to look at her with curiosity, to touch her clothes and to lift them up as if to see whether they were part of her body, to look under her dress and inside her corset—to which the burgomaster's daughter lend herself very obligingly, showing her the difference there was between flesh and fabric, undressing and dressing again in order to help her to understand the resemblance there was between them when they were naked, and the difference when they were dressed.

"Coquetry, you see, is a vice natural to the savage woman as to the civilized one, and to the civilized woman as to the mermaid. Ours, instead of trying to flee, instead of continuing to cry out and weep, amused herself looking at dresses and jackets, bonnets and gilded hairornaments—after which, she made signs that she wanted to get dressed. She had seen at once how all that was undone and hastened. Bah! She was almost as adept as if she had been dressing and undressing all her life. When her toilette was finished she looked for water in order to see her reflection therein. The burgomaster's daughter presented her with a mirror; she looked at herself, uttered a cry of surprise, and started laughing like a lunatic.

"It was at that moment that the curé came in and, at hazard, set about baptizing her. Only, when the curé tried to take away her bonnet, she nearly scratched his eyes out. It was necessary to make her understand that it was only for a moment that her head was being uncovered—but she didn't let go of the bonnet or the golden ornaments, which she readjusted as soon as the curé had gone.

"I was dying of the desire to see her, so I went upstairs, asking the burgomaster's daughter whether I could come in, and she opened the door. My five companions were behind me; they were crowded in the corridor. The Parisian came last, with a salt-water compress over his eye.

"I looked for the mermaid and didn't recognize her. I saw a beautiful Friesian, with slightly green-tinted hair, that's all—but green and gold, you know, go very well together.

"The burgomaster's daughter curtsied to me. The mermaid watched what her friend did, and did the same. That's woman, Monsieur—what a hypocritical being she is! She had only made the acquaintance of human creatures two hours ago, and she was weeping, laughing, looking at herself in a mirror and curtsying. Oh, that ought to have enlightened me—but what is written is written.

"I began a conversation with her, by signs. I asked her whether she was hungry. I knew that it's by means of greed that one makes oneself loved by animals. What do you expect? I had the idea, if only out of curiosity, to make that woman love me. She made signs saying yes. Then I brought her watermelon, grapes and pears—all the fruits I could find.

"She knew all that. As soon as she saw them she leapt on them. Except that once she had eaten the fruits she tried to eat the plate, and we had all the difficulty in the world making her understand that it wasn't for eating.

"Meanwhile, the curé had already gone into action. He had explained to the burgomaster's daughter that the mermaid might be a fish, but that she was a fish who resembled a woman too closely to remain with a bache-

lor, with the result that as she finished her meal the burgomaster came to fetch her, with his wife and his other
daughter.

"The two new friends went away arm in arm. Only
the mermaid went barefoot; she hadn't been able to put
on the shoes that had been brought for her. Not that they
were too small; on the contrary—but that part of her ac-
coutrement was the last to which she became accustomed.

"When she arrived at the door of the house she
darted a glance at the sea; perhaps she had a desire to
return to her former domicile, but it would have been
necessary to traverse the entire population that had been
assembled by curiosity. Besides which, it would have
spoiled her nice clothes. The new disembarkee shook her
head and tranquilly made her way toward the burgomaster's house, followed by the entire population of
Monnikendam, who cried: "La Buchold! La
Buchold!"—which, in local dialect, means 'the daughter
of the water.'

"As she had no family name, that name stuck to her.

"I'd said a hundred times that I'd only marry a
mermaid. I'd been served in accordance with my wish.
So, that evening, all the comrades drank to my imminent
marriage with La Buchold. She was young, she was pretty, she had looked at me with her green eyes in a certain
fashion that hadn't displeased me, and she was mute.
Truth to tell, I drank like the others.

"Three months later, she knew how to do everything that a woman knows how to do, except talk. In her
Friesian costume she was the prettiest girl, not one in all
Holland but all Friesland. She had the appearance of not
detesting me, and I was madly in love with her. I had

every right to her, since it was me that had found her; there was no opposition to fear on the part of her parents.

"I married her.

"She was married at the Mairie under the name of Marie La Buchold, Monsieur le Curé having judged it appropriate, in baptizing her, to give her the name of the mother of Our Lord.

"I gave a great dinner, and then a great ball, of which the new Marie did all the honors by signs, drinking, eating and dancing like an ordinary woman, but as mute as a carp. There was only one cry among all the guests; on seeing her so pretty, so gracious and so must everyone said: 'Isn't he a lucky devil, Olifus! Isn't he lucky!'

"The next day, I woke up at ten o'clock in the morning. She was already awake and watching me sleep. I opened my eyes suddenly, and seemed to read on her face a singular expression of mockery and malevolence, but as soon as she saw my gaze fixed upon her, her face resumed its habitual expression, and I no longer thought about the other. '*Bonjour*, my little wife,' I said to her.

"'*Bonjour*, my little husband,' she replied.

"I uttered a cry of despair. Sweat rose on my brow. My wife could talk. It appears that the marriage had cut the net. That happened on the twenty-second of December 1823.

"To your health, Monsieur," said Père Olifus, swallowing a second glass of tafia and thus inviting Biard and me to do as much. "And don't marry a mermaid!"

Then he passed the back of his hand over his lips and continued:

VI. Conjugal Tribulations

"However, as the usage of her tongue only seemed to have come to my wife in order or her to say nice things to me, I consoled myself for not having a mute wife.

"There was even more; for a month I was happy enough. Everybody gave me compliments; there was only the Parisian who, when I boasted of my happiness, responded to me by singing: "Go and see if they're coming, Jean, go and see if they're coming."[22] It's necessary to render him that justice: he never had confidence in La Buchold.

"At the end of a month of calm, I thought I perceived that the weather was darkening. There was still calm now and again, but it was the calm that precedes a storm. As a mariner, you understand, I knew that, and I got ready to face up to it.

"It began with regard to a visit I had made to Amsterdam; she claimed that I had been to visit an old friend who lived on the harbor, that I had stayed there all night, and that if that friend had been mute the day before, there was no reason why she wasn't talking the day after.

---

[22] The French words in question—*Va-t'en voir s'ils viennent, Jean, Va-t'en voir s'ils viennent*—originate from a song by Antoine Houdar de la Motte composed in the 1720s, but they were adapted as a kind of proverb, something said ironically to someone who seems to be waiting for something that will never arrive.

"Oh, it's necessary to tell you that in less than a week, my wife had learned to say everything, and that she could have shown something, after a month, to all the language masters Amsterdam, Rotterdam and The Hague.

"What made me angry about what she'd said about my visit to the port of Amsterdam is that it was true; one might have thought that the witch had followed me, that she'd come into the house and had seen everything that had happened. I denied it until I was blue in the face, but she persisted nevertheless in believing what she wanted and threatening, the next time something similar happened, to make me remember it.

"I took the threat for what a woman's threat is normally worth, and as nothing in the world is more unbearable to me than a sullen face, I cajoled La Buchold so well that the next day, she was no longer thinking about it, or at least had the appearance of no longer thinking about it.

"A fortnight went by tranquilly enough. On the sixteenth day, I took some passengers to Edam. They were to come back to Monnikendam the same evening, but they were painters, they'd found drawings to make; they told me that they'd retain me until the following day. I could have come back and told them that, as they weren't keeping their promises, I wasn't keeping mine, but one doesn't give up good business like that, you understand. Besides which, I had an old friend in Edam, and hadn't seen her since my marriage to La Buchold. As I was passing in the street she had made me a little sign behind her curtain and I'd winked at her in a way that meant: 'Understood; if I have a moment I'll pay you a visit.' I had more than a moment; I had all night.

"Then again, this time, I was tranquil. As my friend had precautions to take, when I visited her before my marriage it was at night, climbing over the garden wall, opening a little door that closed a hedge and climbing in through her bedroom window. No one had ever known anything then about those nocturnal expeditions, and no one would know anything about it now.

"At eleven o'clock, therefore, on a night as black as ink, I made my way to the wall, and climbed over it, to the door and went through it, to the window, to which I climbed up, and at the height of which I found two pretty arms that received me wide open."

"Damn!" said Biard. "You have a way of storytelling, Père Olifus, that makes the mouth water. To the health of the owner of those pretty arms!"

"Oh, Monsieur, rather drink to mine," said Père Olifus, in a melancholy fashion, swallowing a third glass of tafia.

"Bah! What happened to you, then, in that little room where you were so agreeably awaited?"

"It wasn't in that little room, Monsieur, it was when I left."

"Go on, Père Olifus, we're listening. You're narrating like Sterne, go on."

"Well, when I left, it was before dawn, you understand; she had precautions to take, as I told you, and after what had happened to me at the house on my return from Amsterdam, I didn't care to be seen. Well, when I left, after having gone through the little door in the hedge, I found an obstacle in the middle of the path—nothing much, a thread, a piece of string, extended across my path. I had my pen-knife in my pocket; I opened it, and *snip!* I cut the thread.

"But at the same instant, you see, I received a blow from a rod across my back, and quite a blow! 'Wretch!' I cried, and I grabbed the stick—but there was no one there, except a pear-tree to which the rod was fitted by an ingenious mechanism. By cutting the thread, I'd released the rod, and when the road was released, it struck.

"I ran away, rubbing my back. My first thought was that the father or brothers had suspected something, and, not daring to come and attack me head on, had prepared that ambush.

"Anyway, as no one had laughed, no one had breathed a word, and no one had even budged, I went away on tiptoe and went back to the inn.

"At ten o'clock, we left Edam, and half an hour later we were in Monnikendam harbor.

"From the furthest distance at which I could see my house, I saw La Buchold on the doorstep; she was waiting for me with a bad-tempered expression that seemed to me to be an ill omen. I, on the contrary, put on a cheerful expression. Scarcely had I crossed the threshold, though, than she slammed the door behind me. 'Oh,' she said, 'that's a fine way to behave for a man married six weeks.'

"'What way to behave?' I asked, innocently.

"'Oh, he dares to question again!'

"'Certainly,'

"'Shut up and answer.' Her green eyes were sparkling. 'Where were you last night, at eleven o'clock? Say it. Where did you stay from eleven o'clock to five o'clock this morning? What happened to you, when you came out of the place where you'd spent those six hours?'

"'I don't know what you're talking about.'

"'Oh, you don't know!'

"'No.'

"'I'll tell you, then. You left the inn at eleven o'clock, you climbed over a wall, you opened a door, you climbed up to a window, and you went into a bedroom, where you stayed until five o'clock in the morning. At five o'clock in the morning, you left, you received a blow from a stick, and you went back to the inn rubbing your back. Tell me whether any of that isn't true!'

"I denied it anyway. I confess that I didn't have the same aplomb this time as the other; in any case, I was carrying my domination on me, given that I had the mark on the road on my back. While denying it, though, I made eyes at La Buchold. I caught a hand here, a cheek there, and, while still grumbling, she ended up forgiving me, saying: 'Be careful; the next time, you won't get away so cheaply.'

"*Oh*, I said to myself, *the next time, I'll take my precautions so well that we'll see*. She made me a sign of the head that seemed to say: 'Yes, *we'll see!*' One might have thought that that witch La Buchold was reading my innermost thoughts.

"Anyway, once again, we sorted things out.

"A week later, I took some passengers to Stavorin. It was a long journey, and there was no means of getting back the same day. I didn't know what to do with my evening, when I suddenly remembered that I had a friend in the vicinity. She was a pretty miller's wife who lived on the shore of pretty little lake between Bath and Stavorin. When I used to visit her before I swam across the little lake and, as her window overlooked the lake, she only had to reach out and *snap!* I was in her bedroom.

"This time, it was even easier; the lake was frozen. I borrowed a pair of skates. At ten o'clock I left Stavorin; at quarter past ten, I was on the edge of the lake; at ten twenty-five I arrived under the window of my miller's wife. I made the agreed signal; the window opened.

"My marriage was known in the mill, the miller's wife had a strong desire to sulk, but she was an excellent woman, so the dispute didn't last long.

"At six o'clock I took my leave; I was quite tranquil; the lake was absolutely deserted; no one had seen me arrive, no one saw me leave. I pushed off, and *zip!* away I went.

At the third or fourth thrust of the skates, it seemed to me that I could feel the ice cracking underneath me. I tried to turn back, but it was too late. I felt myself carried toward a place where I could hear water splashing; the ice had been broken while I was with my miller's wife; there was a kind of liquid ditch in front of me. I dug my heels in, but in vain, I arrived at the edge of the hole and *bonsoir!* I was in the lake.

"Fortunately, I dive like a seal. I held my breath and searched for the opening. It isn't easy to get your bearings under ice, you know. Finally, I saw a kind of band that was more transparent.

"I was swimming toward the band when I felt something grab me by the leg and drag me into the depths of the water. I had my mouth open to breathe, but instead of a gust of air, I swallowed a mouthful of water. It isn't the same thing. I saw everything turn blue. I heard a ringing in my ears; I understood that if I didn't free myself from whatever was dragging me down, and right away, my goose was cooked. I kicked out with all my strength; I felt the blow strike home; the thing that was dragging me down let go.

"I took advantage off my liberty to get back to the surface. For a further two or three seconds I bumped my head against the ice. Finally, choking and half-dead, almost unconscious, I reached the breach of continuity, as mathematicians say. I put my head out of the water; I breathed through my eyes, nose and mouth at the same time; I clung on to the ice, but the ice splintered as I tried to climb back on to it.

"Finally, by means of a vigorous impulsion, I slid over it on my belly; with the weight distributed over a large area, the ice held. I gave a thrust of the skates. Oh, believe me, no ship running before the wind ever went as fast as I went. I was going at thirty knots, but when I reached the edge of the lake I was out of strength. I fell down and lost consciousness, and when I came to, I found myself in a warm bed and recognized the room in the inn from which I'd departed the previous evening.

"Peasants who were going to market had found me lying on the ground, half dead and three-quarters frozen; they'd put me in their cart and brought me back to Stavorin, where the hostess, who recognized me, had lavished all sorts of cares on me.

"Two hours later, thanks to a bowl of punch that I swallowed while it was still aflame, I was no longer thinking about it.

"Our passengers had concluded their business by ten o'clock in the morning; they were in a hurry to get back, and so was I, for I wasn't without anxiety as to what awaited me at the house. We set forth at eleven o'clock; the wind was good. It's nearly twelve leagues from Stavorin to Monnikendam; we covered them in six hours—that's good going.

"This time, it wasn't on the threshold that La Buchold was waiting for me, it was on the seashore. Her green eyes were shining in the shadow like two emeralds. She made me a sign with her hand to walk in front of her and go into the house. I didn't make any protest, having decided, if she annoyed me too much, to give her one of those petty conjugal corrections that it's said women need every three months if one wants to make perfect wives of them. So I went in and closed the door myself.

"Then, having sat down, I said: 'Well, what?'

"'What do you mean, what?'

"'Yes, what do you want with me?'

"'What do I want with you? I want to tell you that you're an infamous man to do what you're doing at the risk of drowning and leaving your poor wife with a child in her arms.'

"'What! A child?'

"'Yes, wretch, I'm pregnant, as you know very well.'

"'In truth, no.'

"'Well, if you don't know, I'm telling you.'

"'That gives me pleasure,'

"'Oh, it gives you pleasure?'

"'Do you want me to say that it gives me pain?'

"'That's how you reply to me, instead of begging my pardon?'

"'Pardon for what?'

'For running around at night like a werewolf, going to pay court to millers' wives. Is six o'clock in the morning a time for skating, I ask you?'

"'Oh!' I said, 'I've had enough of your spying, and if you don't leave me tranquil...'

"'What will you do?'

"I had a nice Indian bamboo cane, as pliant as a rush, which I used to beat my Sunday clothes. I took it

79

from its corner and I made it whistle in La Buchold's ears. 'That's all I have to say to you, my darling.'

"'Oh,' she said, you're threatening me! Wait.'

"Her eyes launched two flashes of green lightning. She leapt on my bamboo, tore it from my hand was easily as I might have done from those of a child, and, gritting her teeth, gave me a beating. Oh, the Devil, you see, had possessed those arms."

"Bah!" we said.

"I'd forgotten the affair of the boat, when she had nearly thrashed all six of us, as you know. At the first blows I received, though, I remembered; I tried to resist, but it was a hailstorm. I began by threatening, swearing, cursing, and ended up asking forgiveness. I'd had my fill, as they say, and more than my fill.

"When she saw that I was on my knees, she stopped striking. 'There!' she said. 'That's good. That will do this time, if I have to do it again, next time you won't get off so cheaply.'

"'Damn!' I said. 'Unless you kill me...'

"'Shut up, and let's go to bed,' she said. 'You must be tired.'

"I was more than tired; I was worn out.'

"I went to bed without saying anything; I turned my back on her; I closed my eyes and pretended to go to sleep, but I wasn't asleep."

VII. Flight

"You'll understand that I wasn't wasting my time; that life didn't speak to me to be tenable. I was ruminating a means of getting myself out of the claws of La Buchold and avenging myself on her at the same time. I don't know why, but I had an idea that it was her who had organized the business with the road at Edam and had broken the ice of the lake at Stavorin.

"There was more. You'll recall that I had felt something drag me by the leg into the depths of the water, and that I'd only freed myself from it with a mighty kick. Now, I also had it in mind that it wasn't some*thing* but some*one* that had grabbed me by the leg, and that that someone was La Buchold.

"*Any day now*, I said to myself, while ruminating, *I'll know whether it was her.*"

"How?" I said, interrupting Père Olifus.

"Well, you understand, I had skates on my feet. In order to launch the kick, I hadn't taken the precaution of removing my skate. A kick with an ice-skate isn't healthy, especially when the kick is a direct strike. Well, my kick had struck home, and if it was La Buchold who had received that kick, she had to have a trace of it somewhere."

"That's true."

"So I said to myself: *It's necessary to dissimulate, to appear to have forgotten the blow with the stick in Edam, the drowning at Stavorin and the beating in Monnikendam; if it's her, she'll pay for all three at the same time.*

"Having made that resolution, I turned over.

81

"The next day, while she was still asleep, I lifted up the bedclothes, and I looked. She didn't have the slightest trace of a skate on her entire body. Except that, instead of putting on her nightcap, as usual, she'd kept her copper bonnet on.

"*Good*, I said to myself. *If you don't take it off tomorrow, it's because there's something underneath.*

"But I didn't let anything show, you understand. I began to get dressed, and while I was getting dressed, La Buchold woke up. Her first movement was to put her hand to her copper bonnet.

"*Good*, I said, again. *Now we'll see.* But I said that internally, while putting on a semblance of laughing. For her part, and it's a justice to render her, when the first moment had passed, she seemed not to think about it anymore—but the first moment had been rude.

"The day went by without either of us mentioning what had happened the day before; we were like two turtle-doves. When the evening came, we went to bed.

"As the previous night, La Buchold slept in her copper bonnet.

"All night long I had a diabolical desire to get up, light the lamp and pres the little catch that opened up that damnable bonnet, but as if expressly, one might have thought that La Buchold had a fever; she did nothing but toss and turn. I was patient, hoping that the following night, she would sleep more tranquilly.

"The following night arrived; I wasn't mistaken. That night, she slept like a log. I got up very quietly; I lit the lamp. La Buchold was lying on her side. I pinched the catch; the plate opened, and under the plate, above the temple, I saw a line that there was no mistaking. The blade of the skate had cut the skin of the head, and without her accursed green hair, which had deadened the blow, it would have split her skull.

"I was convinced. Not only was it my wife who had prepared the mechanism in Edam, it was my wife who had broken the ice of the lake, and it was also my wife who had grabbed me by the leg with the intention of drowning me. Me drowned, she could have came back to Monnikendam, and as we were, everything passing to the last survivor, inherited from me, the poor little she-cat!

"You'll understand that I no longer had any considerations to preserve with regard to such a creature. My decision was already made. I had put all the money I had into a bag, and with that money I'd embark for no matter what country, and in that country, it mattered little to me what became of me; I'd live tranquil and happy, provided that I was a long way from La Buchold.

"In consequence, determined to put that project into execution, I put the lamp out, got dressed quietly, got my bag out of the cupboard, and went to the door on tiptoe.

"As I put my hand on the key, I felt a claw grip my by the neck and drag my backwards. I turned round; it was that witch La Buchold; she was pretending to be asleep, and she had seen everything.

"'Ah!' she said 'That's what you're doing? After having deceived me, you're abandoning me, and, in abandoning me, you're ruining me! Wait! Wait!'

"'Ah! And you, after having beaten me, you break the ice, after having broken the ice, you try to drown me! Wait! Wait!'

"She took the bamboo cane from the corner of the room. But I picked up a poker from the corner of the hearth. We both struck at the same time, except that I remained standing and she fell. She fell like an inert mass, uttering a cry—or rather, a sigh—and once she was on the floor, she didn't move again.

"*Good*, I said, *she's dead. Too bad! I only did to her what she wanted to do to me!*

"And patting myself to make sure that my bag was secure in my pocket, I ran out of the house, locked the door behind me, threw the key into the sea, and started running through the fields in the direction of Amsterdam.

"Half an hour later, I was on the shore. I woke a fisherman, one of my friends, who was asleep in his cabin. I told him that I was so unhappy with my wife that I'd decided to go abroad that very night. I asked him, in consequence, to take me to Amsterdam, where I'd take the first opportunity to leave Holland.

"The fisherman got dressed, pushed his boat into the sea, and set a course for Amsterdam.

"Half an hour later, we went into the harbor. A magnificent three-master was ready to leave for India, and was preparing to sail immediately. I made a prompt decision. 'In truth,' I said to my friend, 'that suits me, and if the captain's reasonable and doesn't ask too much for the passage, we'll make the voyage together.' And I hailed the captain.

"The captain came to the rail. 'Who's calling from the boat?' he asked.

"'Me.'

"'Who are you?'

"'Someone who'd like to know whether you still have room for a passenger.'

"'Yes, go round to starboard and you'll find the ladder.'

"'It's not worth the trouble—throw me a rope.'

"'Right! You're a sailor, it seems.'

"'Somewhat.' I tuned to the fisherman. 'As for you, friend,' I said to him, 'I want you to drink to my health, and here's ten florins. Oh, damn it, what's this?'

"'What's what?'

"What it was, was that I had just opened my bag, and instead of being full of gold, it was full of pebbles. 'Damn! You can see, my friend,' I said to the fisherman, showing him my bag, that the good will was there, but I've been robbed.'

"'Bah!'

"'Yes, word of honor!' And I emptied my bag into the boat.

"'Well, too bad, Père Olifus,' said the worthy fellow, 'what do you expect? The good intention was there; this won't prevent me from drinking to your health—don't worry.'

"'Hey!' cried a voice from the deck, 'here's the rope you asked for.'

"I shook the fisherman's hand, grabbed the rope and climbed it like a squirrel. 'Here I am,' I said, jumping on to the deck.

"'What about your luggage?' asked the captain.

"'Does one need luggage to be a matelot?

"'Matelot? You said passenger.'

"'Passenger?'

"'Yes.'

"'It was a slip of the tongue, then. I meant: Have you a place for a matelot?'

"'Well, you seem to me to be a good fellow,' said the captain. 'Yes, I have a place for a matelot, and for a matelot, forty francs a month as well, given that I'm a captain in the service of the India Company, and the India Company pays well.'

"'If it pays well, it'll be well served, that's all.'

"The captain didn't say any more, and I didn't reply anymore; the engagement made was worth as much as of all the notaries in the world had certified it. Two days later, we were in the open sea."

VIII. Man Overboard

"The first land we sighted, after having lost sight of the French coast, was the little island of Porto Santo, north of Madeira. Madeira, hidden in a thick fog, only emerged two hours later. We left the port of Funchal to our left and continued on our way. An the fourth day, after having doubled Madeira, we sighted the peak of Tenerife, which showed itself and disappeared in the undulations of the mist, which seemed to be a second sea, beating its flanks with its waves. We passed by without stopping, and came into a green sea that resembled a vast field of cress; thick layers of dark green wrack, turning yellow, covered the surface of the Ocean, forming clusters that the sailors called tropical grapes.

"It wasn't the first time I had made such a voyage. I'd been to Buenos Aires twice and I'd seen what mariners call the blue waters. I therefore found myself in my element again; I breathed entirely at my ease. The ship was a good sailor and traveled at seven or eight knots. Every knot took me another mile away from La Buchold, and I had nothing else to desire.

"We crossed the equator and there was a celebration aboard, as usual. I presented my certificate, signed by the Bonhomme Tropique, and instead of receiving one, I was one of those pouring buckets of water over others.

"The captain was a good fellow; he'd opened the rum-store, with the result that I went to bed a trifle tipsy. Suddenly, I was, as they say, half seas over. I was drowsing, half singing and half snoring, chasing away the cockroaches with my hand which I mistook for flying fish, when I seemed to see a great white figure descend through the hatch and approach my bunk.

"As it came closer, I recognized La Buchold. Perhaps I was still snoring, but I can guarantee that I was no longer singing.

"'Ah,' she said to me, 'after having staved in my skull twice, once with an ice-skate and once with a poker, instead of repenting, instead of doing penance, this is the state you get into, drunkard!'

"I wanted to reply to her, but it was funny; it was her who could talk now, and me who had become mute. 'Oh, it's futile,' she went on. 'Not only are you mute, but you're paralyzed. Try to run away—just try.'

"She could see perfectly well what was happening within me, the accursed La Buchold, and that I was making superhuman efforts to step out of my hammock, but my leg was as stiff as the mizzen mast, and it would have needed the capstan to budge me.

"I made my decision. I lay still, and stayed as motionless as a buoy."

"Fortunately, I was able to close my eyes and not see her; that was a consolation. Unfortunately, though, I couldn't close my ears and not hear her. She said so much to me, she had so much to say, that it ended up droning in my ears without me being able to hear the words. Then I could no longer hear the drone; then I heard the hour chime, and then the voice of the mate shouting: 'Second watch on deck!'

"Do you know what quarter watches are?" Père Olifus asked me.

"Yes," I answered. "Go on."

"So, I was on the second watch. It was me that was being called. I heard that I was being called, but I couldn't move my hands or my feet. Only I said to myself: *You're in trouble, Olifus, you're going to get the lash. Wretch, they're calling you, get up, then, sluggard!*

"All that was inside, Monsieur. Outside, nothing budged.

"Suddenly, I felt someone shaking me; I thought it was La Buchold. I made myself small; I was shaken harder; I didn't budge. Finally, I heard an oath to make the ship split, and a voice saying to me: 'Well, are you dead, then?'

"Good! I recognized the voice of the master helmsman.

"'No, no, I'm not dead! No, Père Vidercome, here I am, only help me to get out of my hammock.'

"'What! You need my help?'

"'Yes, it's impossible for me to move.'

"'I think, God forgive me, that he isn't yet desouled. Wait, wait!'

"And he picked up a broom-handle that was lying there. I don't know whether it was fear that gave me strength, or whether my paralysis had passed, but I was as light as a bird. I leapt out of my hammock and I said; 'There! There! It's that slut La Buchold. Decidedly, she was born for my misfortune, that creature.'

"'Buchold or not, don't let it happen tomorrow,' said the master helmsman, 'or we'll see...'

"'Oh, tomorrow,' I said, putting on my trousers and climbing the ladder to the hatch, 'there's no danger of that.'

"'Yes, tomorrow you'll no longer be drunk. I understand; for today, I'll let it go; the festival of the Bonhomme Tropique doesn't happen every day. Let's go, let's go, on deck.'

"I was there. Never have I seen such a night. It was no longer stars that there were in the sky, Monsieur, it was gold dust. As for the sea, it was wrinkled by a little breeze, such that one wouldn't ask for another to go to paradise.

"That wasn't all. The ship seemed to set the waves ablaze as it cleaved through them. There was nothing to do. The ship was traveling under full sail, royals and studsails in the wind, like a young woman going to mass on Sunday. So I leaned over the side and gazed at the water.

"You can't imagine anything like it, you see. It's said that it's little fish that do that; personally, I prefer to think that it's the good Lord. It was as if there were fifty roman candles all along the hull of the ship. There were endless fireworks bursting in her wake. All that stood out against the somber tint of the waves like a flaming pennant whose long folds were being shaken under the water.

Suddenly, in the midst of those flames, it seemed to me that I saw something like a human form playing. The form became increasingly visible, and who did I recognize? La Buchold!

"There's no need to ask me whether I wanted to jump backwards—but no; stuck to the bulwark of the ship like a dry eel, it was impossible for me to get away from it. On the contrary, while playing in the water, making dives and leaps and floating, there were signs, there was teasing, there were smiles, and I felt my feet quitting the deck, my belly sliding. It was attracting me like a vertigo; I tried to hang on, but I couldn't find anything to grasp; I wanted to cry out, but I no longer had a voice; it was still attracting me. Oh, the accursed siren! I felt my hair standing on end; there was a drop of water on every hair, and I was slipping, slipping, my head dragging my rear, and I felt that I was going where I was going. Accursed siren!

"Suddenly, someone grabbed my trouser-bottoms.

"'Are you mad, then Olifus?' said the master helmsman, dragging me toward him. 'Help, two men! Two strong men! Two solid men! Help me!'

"They arrived—just in time! I nearly dragged them with me. I fell back on to the deck. *Oof!* I was drenched like a soup, Monsieur; I was grinding my teeth; my eyes were rolling.

"'Good!" said the master helmsman. 'When one's epileptic, one says so, at least. 'It's a breach of contract. There! That's a fine thing—a matelot who has attacks of nerves. That's nice. Little Miss Olifus, eh!'

"It's true, Monsieur, I was having convulsions, while saying: 'No, it's not epilepsy, it's La Buchold. Didn't you see her?'

"'What?'

"'La Buchold—she was there, playing in the water and in the fire, like a salamander; she called to me, she attracted me, it was her! Oh, accursed siren!'

"'What's that you're saying about a siren?'

"'Nothing, nothing...'

"You see, Monsieur," Père Olifus continued, "if you make long voyages, it's necessary never to talk to matelots about sirens, or nereids, or mermaids, or mermen, or sea-bishops. On land, it's all right; on land, they joke about it, sailors, but at sea they don't like it; it frightens them.

"As things stood, I had nearly taken a dive, and, but for the master helmsman, I'd have drunk from the big cup. I went to sit down at the foot of the mizzen mast; I passed my arm through the rigging, and waited for dawn.

"When daylight came, it seemed to me that all that was a dream, except, as I had a terrible fever, I understood that there was a foundation of reality to it. Now, the reality seemed quite simple; I had hit La Buchold over the head with a poker; the blow with the poker had been well struck—so well struck that she had died of it—and it was her soul that had come to demand my prayers.

"Unfortunately, there are no chaplains on the ships of the India Company; if there had been a chaplain, I would have had him sing a mass, and all would have been said. Then I thought of another means, a known means.

"I took a nutmeg, and I wrote La Buchold's name on it; I wrapped it up in a piece of cloth, put the whole thing in a tinplate box, inscribed two crosses on the lid separated by a star and, when dusk came, I threw the talisman into the sea, with a *De profundis*, and then I went to lie down in my hammock.

"I was no sooner there than I heard the cry: 'Man overboard!'

"When one hears that cry, as you know, it's for everyone, for on a ship, if it's my comrade's turn today, it will be mine tomorrow. I leapt out of my hammock and I ran on to the deck.

"There had been a moment of confusion. Everyone was saying: 'What's happened? Who's gone overboard? Is it me, is it you, is it him?' But no matter, on a well-run ship there's always a man armed with a knife near the knot of the lifebuoy, or the catch that it's necessary to release in order to drop the buoy into the sea; the man had already done his work, and the buoy was in the ship's wake.

"In the meantime, the captain shouted: 'Helm down; take down the high sails; slacken the halyards and the rigging.' That's a standard maneuver. When a man falls into the sea, the ship has to be stopped, and to stop the ship, if you don't slacken the ropes, you'll have booms broken and studsails ripped, especially if it's running with full sail.

"At the same time, the launch was hoisted on its davits. A strong rope was brought to support it, and the end passed through a loop attached to the davit. In brief, the launch put to sea.

"Meanwhile, everyone was at the stern; it was a true lifebuoy that had been dropped, with a flare to light it; the flare was burning, so that we could see someone swimming, swimming, swimming. When I say that *we* could see, I'm mistaken; there was only me that could see, and no matter how much I said 'Can you see? Can you see?' the others said: 'No, we can't see.'

"Then, looking around, the matelots said: 'That's funny; here I am, here you are, there he is—we're all here. Who went overboard, then?

"Everyone said: 'Not me, not me, not me.'

"'In that case, who shouted *Man overboard*?'

"'Not me, not me, not me.'

"No one had seen, no one had shouted. In the meantime, the swimmer had reached the buoy, and I could distinctly see someone clinging to it.

"'Good,' I said. 'He's got it,'

"'What?'

"'The buoy.'

"'Who?'

"'The man in the sea.'

"'You can see someone on the buoy?'

"'Of course—look.'

"'Well, Olifus, who can see someone on the buoy,' said the master helmsman, 'until now, I thought that I had good eyes, but I'm mistaken. Let's say no more.'

"The boat was at sea and rowing toward the buoy. 'Ahoy the boat!' shouted the master helmsman, 'can you see anyone on the buoy?'

"'No one,'

"'Say, I've just had an idea,' said the helmsman, turning to the sailors.

"'What?'

"'It's that Olifus shouted *Man overboard*!'

"'Oh! No!

"'Well, no one's missing, no one can see anyone on the buoy. It's only Olifus that claims someone's missing, only Olifus can see someone on the buoy; he must have his reasons for that.'

"'I don't say that there's anyone missing, I only say that there's someone on the buoy.

"'We'll soon see—here's the launch bringing it back.'

"In fact, the launch had reached the buoy and had moored it to its stern, so that it was following in its wake. I could distinctly see someone sitting on the damnable buoy, and the closer the launch came, the more distinctly I could see.

"'Ahoy the launch!' shouted the master helmsman. 'What are you bringing back there?'

"'Nothing.'

"'What do you mean, nothing? Can't you see?'

"'Why, what's the matter? One might think that your eyes were about to pop out of your head?'

"In fact, you see, I had just realized what was happening, and I said: *Right, I'm done!* Monsieur, the person who was on the buoy was La Buchold, whom I thought I had thrown into the sea in a tin box. 'Don't bring her back!' I shouted. 'Throw her in the sea! Can't you see that it's a siren? Can't you see that it's a mermaid? Can't you see that it's the Devil?'

"'That's it,' said the master helmsman. 'He's definitely mad. Tie that fellow up for me and inform the surgeon.'

"In a trice, I was tied up and carried to a cot. Then the surgeon came with his lancet. 'Oh,' he said, 'it's nothing—a cerebral fever, that's all. I'll bleed him white, and in three days, if he isn't dead, there's every chance that he'll recover.'

"I don't remember anything more, except that I experienced a pain in my arm, saw my blood flowing, and fainted. But I didn't faint quickly enough not to hear the captain shout: 'No one, right?' and the entire crew reply: 'No one.'

"'Oh, the brigand Olifus. I promise him one thing, and that's to drop him on the first land we encounter.'

"It was on that pleasant promise that I lost consciousness."

IX. Pearl-Fishing

"The captain was a man of his word. When I recovered consciousness, I was indeed on land. I asked what part of the world I was in, and I learned that the three-master *Jan de Witt*—that was my India Company ship—had dropped me off in Madagascar.

"As I had been aboard the Jan de Witt for three and a half months, I found a sum of a hundred and forty francs on my pillow, which was my exact pay for those three and a half months. You can see that the captain was a worthy man all the same; he could have held back a month, since I had no longer been in service for the last month. During that month, when it's impossible for me to say what had happened, we had landed at Saint Helena, doubled the Cape and dropped anchor at Tamatave, where I had been set down.

"As it was not in Tamatave that I wanted to settle, but in India, I enquired of my host about a means of transport. A ship bound for India was an event in Tamatave; my host therefore advised me to make my way to Sainte-Marie, where I would have a better chance. A boat was departing a week later for Pointe-Larrée, and I decided to take passage on it if I was feeling better by that time.

"I had only one fear, Monsieur; there was only one thing that could have made my illness worse, and that was if, by chance, my wife had been disembarked with me.

"The first night, you see, I spent in a mortal panic; at the slightest sound I heard I said to myself: *It's La*

Buchold! and sweat formed on my brow. After that, you understand, there was still a little fever.

"Finally, daylight came. Nothing. I breathed. The second night, nothing again. The third, ditto. The fourth, fifth, sixth, seventh and eighth, nothing. So I was visibly recovering. And when my host came to say: 'Are you in a fit state to leave for Sainte-Marie?' I said: 'I believe so.' And in ten minutes, I was ready.

"Our account was regulated. He didn't want to take anything. I preferred to pay him in gratitude rather than money, given that I was better furnished with the former than the latter, so I didn't insist. We embraced and I embarked for Pointe-Larrée.

"It wasn't without anxiety that I returned to sea. Every time I caught sight of a fish I thought it was my wife. The crewmen wanted to fish on the way, but I begged so much that they couldn't bring themselves to cast a line.

"I was only really tranquil when we arrived at Pointe-Larrée. The sea was La Buchold's element, but having not caught sight of her during the crossing, I said to myself: *Good, she's lost the track.* I decided nevertheless that I would go from Pointe-Larrée to Titingue overland. Land was my element, and it seemed to me that I was stronger there. It's odd—previously, I had thought that the land was only good for taking to the water and for drying fish.

"I therefore made an arrangement with two black guides, who, in exchange for a knife-and-fork I had, which could be separated into two, agreed to guide me from Pointe-Larrée to Titingue. You'll understand that I still wanted to conserve my hundred and forty francs.

"We left the next day; it couldn't really be called going by land, for the route was continually interrupted by rivers and marshes in which we had water up to our waist. From time to time we perceived a few islets of solid ground on which game was swarming. Are you a hunter?"

"Yes."

"We'll, if you'd been there, you'd have enjoyed yourself greatly. Guinea-fowl, turtle-doves, quail, green pigeons and blue pigeons were all flying around in thousands, so that we could procure a princely roast with nothing but our staffs. At midday we stopped under a clump of palm trees; it was time for dinner. I plucked our guinea-fowl, my negroes built a fire, we shook a few trees, which gave us their fruits—the King of Holland has never eaten the like—and we commenced our meal.

"There was only one thing we lacked, and that was a good bottle of Bordeaux wine or Edinburgh ale, but as I'm a philosopher, and know how to do without what I don't have, I went to the stream in order to have a drink anyway.

"Seeing that, one of my guides said: 'That not good water, Mossié.'

"'I know it isn't good,' I replied, 'and of course I'd rather have wine.'

"'He'd like wine better, Mossié?'

"'Well, yes, Mossié would like wine better,' I retorted, impatiently.

"'Well, me go get some.'

"'Wine?'

"'Yes, and new wine. Come, Mossié.'

"I followed him, muttering to myself: 'Joker, if you're putting me on, we'll have a reckoning when we arrive.'

"I said *when we arrive*, you see, because my fellows might have done me a bad turn on the way, whereas once we'd arrived…"

"Yes, yes, I understand."

"So, I followed him. He walked about thirty paces, and then looked around. 'Come, come, Mossié, here's the barrel.' And he pointed at a tree. I was still muttering: 'Joker, if you're putting me on…'"

"Well, it was a ravenala,[23] the tree he was showing you," said Biard.

Olifus looked at him, wide-eyed with astonishment. "You know that?"

"Of course."

"It was a ravenala, as you say, nicknamed the traveler's tree. Well, I'd already traveled a good deal, but I didn't know of that tree, so that when he plucked a leaf, to which he have the form of a glass, and said to me: 'Take that, Mossié, and don't waste a drop', I was still repeating; 'Joker!'

"Monsieur, he struck the tree with my knife and a kind of water came out, you see, or rather a kind of wine, or even a liqueur. I took my hat off to him, Monsieur. After me, the two negroes drank. After them, I had another drink. I could have drunk until the next day, but they told me that it was necessary to resume our route. I wanted to drill into the tree, so much did it pain me to see such a good liquor going to waste, but they told me that I'd find ravenalas all along the route, and that there

_____

[23] *Ravenala madagascariensis*, commonly known as the traveler's tree, is the only species in its genus. The quality attributed to it here is entirely fanciful; the liquid that collects at the base of its leaves, to which it probably owes its name, is foul-tasting and dubiously potable.

are ravenala forests in Madagascar. For a moment, I thought about settling in Madagascar and exploiting one of those forests.

"The next day we arrived in Titingue. My guides hadn't lied to me; all along the route we had found ravenalas, which I had pierced.

"In Titingue, hazard enabled me to meet a rich Sinhalese pearl trader. The time for that kind of fishing, which takes place in the month of March, had arrived, and he had come to search for divers on the Zanzibar coast and among the subjects of King Radama,[24] who are reputed to be the boldest pearl-fishers in the world. He recognized me as a European. He thought that I could help him out; he helped me out marvelously. I offered to let him take me on trial; he accepted. A fortnight later we dropped anchor in the port of Colombo.

"There was no time to lose; the fishing had already begun. We only called in at Colombo and then set sail for Condatchy, which is the island's bazaar. My Sinhalese was one of the principal adjudicators of the fishing. We set forth with a veritable flotilla and had for the island of Mannar, in the vicinity of which the fishing takes place.

"Our flotilla consisted of ten boats each manned by twenty men. Of those twenty, ten formed the crew and ten were divers. Boats of that sort have a particular form, long and broad, with only one mast and sail, and draw no more than eighteen inches of water.

"I was in charge of one of the boats. I'd told my Sinhalese that I didn't know anything about pearl-fishing, but that I was a first-class sailor, and he didn't

---

[24] Radama I was the King of Madagascar from 1810 to 1828.

take long to perceive that I guided my boat in a sure fashion that put the other captains in the shade.

"After three days, however, I perceived that our divers, if they were skillful, could sometimes earn ten times as much in a day as I, their boss, earned in a month. That was because the fishers have a ten per cent interest in the fishing they do, with the consequence that if a fisher is lucky, and finds a rich bank of oysters, he can earn ten, fifteen or twenty thousand livres in a season—which is to say, in two months, while I, in those two months, earned five hundred livres, purely and simply.

Then I started studying what my men were doing. All things considered, it wasn't drinking the sea.

Each diver took a stone between his feet or knotted it around his waist, about twelve pounds in weight. Then, ballasted by that stone, which dragged him down to the sea-bed, he threw himself into the water, holding a bag and a net in one hand, and collecting as many oysters as he could find with the other. When he had no more air, he shook the rope that moored him to the boat, and was brought back to the surface. Every crewman watched a rope, so that the diver had no need to make the signal twice; that was why the crewmen were equal in number to the divers.

"The fishing was excellent, and I only had one regret, which was to have signed on as a boat-captain instead of as a diver. In Monnikendam, I had certain reputation for remaining under water, even though I had been caught out when I had been obliged to find my way under the ice, as you know, in the lake at Stavorin. The only thing that consoled me was that I had a terrible fear, if I dived, of encountering La Buchold—and that, you'll understand, wouldn't have been funny. *Bonsoir* oysters!

I'd rather have remained a boat-captain all my life at two hundred livres a month.

"In addition, that wasn't the only thing there was to fear; the sharks knew the fishing season as if they had calendars, and the quantity of those fish that came to idle around the bay of Mannar during the two months it lasted was incredible. I must say, though, that if there had only been sharks, it wouldn't have stopped me from diving; it was La Buchold.

"Among the divers we had aboard there was a negro and his son. They were two magnificent Africans, who had been given to my Sinhalese by the Imam of Madagascar himself; the son was fifteen and the father thirty-five. They were our boldest and most skillful divers. In the ten or twelve days the fishing has lasted, they had brought back between them almost as many oysters as the other eight fishers combined. I'd formed a friendship with the young black, and, in the midst of his comrades, it was him that I followed particularly in his dives; so, when he emerged from the water, it was always between my legs that he came to deposit his catch, and I kept watch on his behalf. His name was Abel.

"One day, he threw himself in the water. Good. He always spent fifteen or twenty seconds without reappearing, which is enormous, you see. Contrary to his habit, scarcely had he disappeared than he shook the rope, and damn it, the man in charge of the rope was thinking about something else; he had just seen the poor boy jump into the sea. When I said to him: 'Haul, then, imbecile, haul—you can see that something extraordinary is happening down below, haul!' as you might expect, it was already too late; I saw a huge red dot rising toward the surface of the water, broadening out, and then, in the middle of the pool, the child, who was splashing about, with one leg severed below the knee.

"At the same time, the father reappeared; he saw the convulsive face of his child, the blood reddening the water. He didn't weep or cry out, but his face, which was ebony black, went the color of ash. He climbed back into the boat with little Abel, placed him on my knees, cut the rope that attached him to the boat and dived at the exact moment when the shark came to the surface of the water.

"I said: 'Pay attention you others. I know that man; we're going to see something unusual.'

"Scarcely had I fished when, *snap!* the shark, whose dorsal fin had been visible above the water, whipped the sea with its tail and dived in its turn; then there was turbulence in the water, eddies and a frightful chaos., and the boy cried out, his eyes ardent, without thinking of himself: 'Courage, father, courage! Kill, kill kill!' and wanted to throw himself into the sea with his poor leg torn away. Believe me, you'll never see anything like what happened before our eyes; it lasted a quarter of an hour, a full quarter of an hour.

"During that quarter of an hour, he only came up to the surface five times to breathe, and to make a sign with his eyes to his son, as if to say to him: 'Don't worry, you'll be avenged!' and then he dived again, and the sea was immediately tormented as if by a submarine tempest. For twenty paces around there was nothing but a bloody stain; the monster made six-foot leaps out of the water, and its entrails could be seen hanging out of its open belly.

"Finally, the sea began to calm down; it was no longer the man who came up to breathe, it was the animal. Finally, the shark went into its death-throes, turned upside down, thrashed the air with its tail desperately, plunged, reappeared, plunged again, and the we saw something like silver streaks under the water; it was floating to the surface, belly up, as inert and stiff as a wooden beam.

"The shark was dead.

"Then the negro reappeared in his turn, came to take his child in his arms, and went to sit down with him at the foot of the mast.

"The surgeon of a French ship, which was in the bay of Colombo, carried out pour Abel's amputation, and the entrepreneur gave the father the entire share of the oysters he had fished.

"On looking at the shark that had come back up to the surface, and counting its sixty-six wounds, two of which had pierced the heart, I had made the reflection that since once could defend oneself against a shark, and put an end to the shark, one could surely defend oneself against a woman and put an end to the woman, even a mermaid. I was therefore ashamed of my cowardice, and, as the two negroes' share of the pearl-oysters was estimated at more than twelve thousand livres, for ten days of fishing, I was tormented by the idea of making a fortune. In consequence, the first time my Sinhalese came to pay us a visit, something he never failed to do very four or five days, I asked him, as a favor, to exchange my job as a boat-captain for that of a simple diver.

"That request appeared to annoy him. 'Olifus,' he said to me, in Dutch. 'I'm sorry that you've asked me that; you're one of my best boat-captains, and if it's only necessary to double your salary to keep you, I'll double it.'

"'You're very kind,' I replied, 'but you see, I'm Breton by origin, with a Dutchman grafted on top; went something enters my head it enters so deeply that even I can't get it out. I've got it into my head to fish for pearls; that's the way it is and that's the way it will be, and it can't be otherwise.'

"'Can you at least dive?'

"'Oh, I was born in Denmark, the land of seals.'

"'Well, let's see what you can do.'

"'Oh, as for that,' I said, 'it won't take long.'

"In a trice, I stripped off, attached a ten-pound stone to my feet, took a net in my left hand as I had seen the other divers do, not forgetting a knife with a good hilt that I passed through my belt, and had myself moored in the same place as or little Abel. I said to myself: 'Bah! Too bad if La Buchold's there we'll see.' And I leapt into the sea.

"It was nearly seven fathoms deep. I went to the bottom quite rapidly, and then opened my eyes. I looked around; that was the critical moment. No La Buchold, and oysters by the spadeful. I filled my net and I tugged the rope in order to be brought up. I stayed under water for ten seconds at that first attempt.

"I emptied the net at the entrepreneur's feet. 'Well,' I said to him, 'what do you say?'

"'That you're a good diver; that you might, indeed, make your fortune, and that I don't have the right to stop you.'

"That facility in getting what I wanted made me slightly ashamed. I compared the conduct of the boss of the fishery with that of the boss of the boat. I didn't come out of it brilliantly. 'However,' I said to him, 'as you hired me as a captain and not as a diver, you have the right to ask more of me than the others.'

"'No,' he said. 'We'll settle that differently, and, I hope, to everyone's satisfaction. You're a good captain and a good diver; be a captain for me and a diver for yourself. Divers have a right to a tenth of their catch; as you're rendering me services I'll give you a eighth of yours—which is to say that you'll be a captain for seven days and a diver on the eighth, but the totality of what you fish on that eighth day will be yours. Is that agreeable to you?'

"'I should think so!'

"'Well, now, as the season commenced some time ago, let's suppose that our bargain was made seven days ago, and you can begin tomorrow.'

"There was nothing more to say but to thank him. I took his hand and I kissed it.' That's the fashion of giving thanks in those parts.

"I waited for the next day with impatience."

X. Nahi-Nava-Nahina

"I wasn't mistaken," said Père Olifus, after having passed on from the tafia to the rum. "The fishing was excellent; during the six days that I devoted myself to that exercise, I fished up nearly seven thousand francs' worth of pearls and didn't see a shark, or La Buchold.

"The season was finished. I thanked my Sinhalese and offered him my services for the following year. And, having realized my profit, I retired to Negombo, a charming little village surrounded by fields and shaded by cinnamon woods.

"My intention was to employ the whole interval that would elapse between the two fishing seasons in commerce, either in cinnamon-wood, shawls or fabrics. That was easy for me, the dominant population in Colombo, one of the island's capitals, only a few leagues from Negombo, now being the Dutch population.

"I began by buying a house in Negombo. That was no great expense; for three hundred francs I had one of the nicest in the village. It was a charming cabin made of bamboo-stems linked together by coconut fiber ties; it only had one floor and three rooms—but three rooms were as many as I needed. In exchange for five hundred francs I had one of the most comfortable dwellings on the island. The furniture consisted of a bed, four mats, a mortar for crushing rice, six earthenware dishes and a coconut rasp.

"I had already settled on the kind of commerce that I wanted to undertake; it consisted of buying European fabrics in Colombo and bartering them with the Bedaths.[25]

"I'll tell you what the Bedaths are.

"The Bedaths members of are a savage tribe who hide in the forest, who live independently, who have no King and who nourish themselves by hunting. Those fellows have no need to buy houses, given that they have no towns and villages, not even a simple cabin. Their bed is the foot of a tree surrounded by thorny branches; if an elephant, a lion or a tiger tries to get through the hedge they have made the noise wakes them up, they climb their tree, and from there they thumb their noses at the lions, tigers and elephants. As for snakes, there are hooded cobras, kraits, vipers and cat-snakes, four nasty kinds of reptile that can kill a man like a fly, but they mock them, because they have charms against their bite. There is only the giant species, which has no venom, to be sure, but can swallow a man as we swallow an oyster, about which they have to worry, but you'll understand that insects twenty-five or thirty feet long aren't common. In brief, they have no houses, and they can do without them.

"This is the fashion of trading with them. When they have need of some manufactured object, such as iron of fabrics, they approach towns or villages, deposit wax, honey or ivory in an agreed place; they write in bad Portuguese on a leaf what the desire n return, and it is brought for them.

---

[25] I have retained the original text's spelling of this word, although this account, like almost all the other details of the island of Ceylon, is slavishly derived from Robert Percival's *Account of the Island of Ceylon* (1803), where the name of the tribe is rendered as Bedaha or Vaddaha.

"I therefore put myself in communication with the Bedaths, and made exchanges for ivory.

"In the meantime, I had cultivated a society. I frequented, in particular, a worthy Sinhalese man, an enthusiastic player of draughts, who was a trader in cinnamon-bark. He had ruined himself ten times over at the game, and had remade his fortune ten times in order to ruin himself again. He was perhaps the man who knew the spices of the island better than any other, and at the mere sight of a cinnamon-tree, he could say: 'Good, that's the real counoundou'—which is to say, the best kind. It's necessary to tell you that there are ten species of cinnamon-trees in Ceylon, and even the most expert and mistake them, but he was never mistaken. How did he recognize them? Was it the form of the leaf, which resembles that of an orange-tree? Was it the perfume of the flower? Was it the little yellow fruit, almost as large as an olive? I have no idea. As long as he could find a cinnamon tree for you, trip off the outer bark, split the inner, dry it out, roll it up in coconut matting, put his name on the bale, that was enough; no one even asked to see a specimen.

"As soon as he had money in his pocket he made it ring, and wanted to play draughts, with his opponent already found.

"Now, you might or might not know that the Sinhalese are fanatical gamblers. When they have no more money they stake their furniture; when they have no more furniture they stake their houses; when they have no more houses they stake one, two or three fingers..."

"One, two or three fingers?" I interrupted.

"Exactly! The loser places his finger on a stone; the winner has a little hatchet with which he cuts it very skillfully at he agreed phalanx. One isn't obliged to stake the entire finger, you understand, one can wager a phalanx. The loser dips his finger in boiling oil, which cauterizes the wound, and he carries on playing. My neighbor Vampounivo had three fingers fewer on his left hand; he had stopped at the thumb and index finger, but I can't guarantee that they haven't joined the others by now.

"Between him and me, you understand, it never went that far; I respect my person too much; I wagered a pearl or an elephant tusk against a share of cinnamon; I won or I lost, and it was finished.

"One evening, when we were playing our game of draughts, I suddenly saw a beautiful young woman appear on the threshold, who came in and threw her arms around Vampounivo. She was his daughter; she was sixteen, and had only been married five times as yet.

"It's necessary to tell you that in Ceylon, couples can separate after a trial marriage; the period of trial lasts between a fortnight and three months. Now, the beautiful Nahi-Nava-Nahina—that was the name of Vampounivo's daughter—had made five trials, and, always discontented with her husbands, had always returned to the parental home.

"I saw that they had family affairs to talk about, and left them discreetly.

"The next day, Vampounivo came to look for me. His daughter had asked him two or three times who the European was who was playing draughts with him when she had come in, and he wanted to introduce me to her.

"I've already told you that Nahi-Nava-Nahina was a superb woman; she had struck me at first sight, and I had produced the same effect. The facility that one has in Ceylon of taking one another on trial and quitting one another if you didn't suit one another seduced me most of all. After a week we were in accord; she would make a sixth trial, and I would make a second.

"The conjugal ceremony is prompt and easy to accomplish among the Sinhalese; one discusses the dowry; an astrologer fixes the day of the marriage; the families of the two spouses gather; they sit down around a table in the middle of which there's a pyramid of rice placed on coconut leaves; everyone fills their hands from the pyramid. After that testimony of intimacy, the bride approaches the groom; each of them has made three or four balls of rice and coconut. They exchange balls, which they swallow like pills. The groom offers the bride a piece of white cloth, and all is said.

"The affair was soon concluded. For my part, I gave my father-in-law four elephant tusks and he gave me a bale of cinnamon bark. An astrologer fixed the day of our marriage. When they day came we are the handfuls of rice, after which I swallowed two balls that the charming Nahi-Nava-Nahina had prepared for me. I gave her a piece of cloth as white as snow, and we were married.

"The custom in Ceylon is that the spouses are conducted to the conjugal chamber separately, the wife first and the husband afterwards. That is done to the sound of sistrums, drums and tomtoms, with a part of the population accompanying the newlyweds.

"I had arranged the nuptial chamber as best I could. At ten o'clock in the evening, the young women came to take the beautiful Nahi-Nava-Nahina, who went to the house after darting ne last glance at me. Oh, what a glance!

"I was dying of the desire to follow her, but it was necessary to give the young women time to take the bride to her bed and lie her down in it, so I stayed for another half hour in her father's house; he proposed a game to pass the time. Oh yes, I was enthusiastic to play!

"Finally, my turn came. I set forth at a pace that my companions had all the difficult in the world in following. On the threshold I found the young women who were dancing, singing and, in sum, making the devil of a racket. They tried to stop me passing. Well, yes, I would have passed through a massed battalion.

"I went up to the bedroom; all light had been extinguished, but I could hear a slight respiration, as soft as a breeze, coning from the alcove. I closed the door and bolted it. I got undressed. I lay down.

I was thinking that Nahi-Nava-Nahina's first five husbands were very difficult fellows, when all of a sudden I heard a voice that made a shiver run through my entire body. 'Ah!' said that voice, at first, modulating a sigh.

"'Eh!' I replied, lifting myself up on my two fists.

"'Well, yes, it's me,' replied the same voice.

"'What, you, La Buchold?'

"'Of course.'

"At that precise moment, Monsieur, a ray of moonlight passed through the window and illuminated us like a reflector.

"'My love,' La Buchold continued, 'I've come to tell you that for two months you've had a son, whom I call Joachim, after the name of the saint that presides over the day on which I gave birth.'

"'I had a son two months ago!' I exclaimed. 'But how did that happen? We've only been married nine.

"'You know, my love, that there are premature births, and that physicians recognize that children born at seven months are viable.'

"'Hmm!' I said.

"'For a godfather,' she continued, I chose Burgo-master Van Clief, in whose home, as you know, I spent three months before our marriage.

"'Ah!' I said.

"'Yes, and who had promised to raise him.'

"'Aha!'

"'What are you trying to say?'

"'Nothing. It's all right, good for Master Joachim. What's done is done. But why the devil are you meddling with what's happening in Ceylon, when I'm not interfering with what's happening in Monnikendam?'

"'Ingrate,' she said, 'so that's how you receive the testaments of love that are given to you! Have you seen many women who travel four thousand leagues to spend a night with their husband?'

"'Ah! So you've only come to spend a single night with me?' I asked, softening slightly.

"'No more, alas,' she replied. 'How do you think I can abandon the poor innocent back there?'

"'That's true.'

"'Who has no one but me.'

"'You're right.'

"'And this is how you receive me, ingrate!'

"'But it seems to me that I haven't received you too poorly.'

"'Yes, because you mistook me for someone else.'

"I scratched my head. What had become of that other? That worried me a little. But for the moment, what worried me more, I confess, was La Buchold.

"I thought that the best thing to do, since she hadn't mentioned the blow with the poker, was not to say anything about it; that since she wasn't breathing a word about the nutmeg, it was to maintain silence on the matter; and finally, since she was promising to go at daybreak, to be as amiable as I could toward her as long as it was dark.

"That resolution taken, there was no further discussion between us. At about three o'clock in the morning, I went to sleep.

"When I woke up, I was alone—but there was a din outside the door. It was the father of the beautiful Nahi-Nava-Nahina, who had come with all his relatives to compliment me on my wedding night.

"You'll understand that before opening the door, my first concern was to worry about what had become of the beautiful Nahi-Nava-Nahina. I was not too reassured on the poor woman's account, knowing La Buchold as I knew her.

"I called out in a low voice, not daring to call out loudly: 'Nahi-Nava-Nahina! Beautiful Nahi-Nava-Nahina! Charming Nahi-Nava-Nahina!' and it seemed to me that a sigh responded to me. That sigh came from a little cabinet adjacent to the bedroom.

"I opened the little cabinet and I found poor Nahi-Nava-Nahina bound hand and foot with a gag over her mouth, neatly laid down on a mat.

"I ran to her; I untied her and took off the gag; I tried to explain the matter to her, but, as you can understand, I found a furious woman. She hadn't heard what La Buchold and I had said, because we had been speaking in Dutch, but she had understood anyway.

"I did what I could, but there was no means of appeasing her. She told her family that she was even more discontented with her sixth trial than the other five; that European husbands treated their wives even worse than Sinhalese ones, and that she wanted to quit a house in which one spent the first night of one's marriage bound and gagged, lying on a mat, while her husband, next door…anyway…that's not important…

"She stirred up her father, brothers, nephews, cousins and second cousins against me to such an extent, that, seeing that it was impossible for me to remain in Negombo after such an adventure, I made the decision to return the bale of cinnamon-bark to her father while letting him keep the four elephant tusks, and to go and seek my fortune in another part of India. I hastened to realize my petty capital, therefore, which amounted to ten or twelve thousand livres, and having found a ship that was sailing for Goa, I embarked on it a week after my second marriage—a second marriage that, as you've seen, had turned out singularly."

Père Olifus uttered a sigh, which proved the profound memory that the beautiful Nahi-Nava-Nahina had left in his mind, and, having swallowed a glass of rum, he continued.

XI. The Auto-da-fé

"During the week I had been forced to spend in Negombo after my marriage I had been greatly tormented. The Sinhalese, when they take against a man, sometimes have a singular fashion of taking revenge on him. In Italy, people arrange to have their enemy stabbed; in Spain one does that oneself; in either case the thing always has inconveniences. Pay a man to strike the blow?—that man might denounce you. Strike yourself?—you might be seen. But in Ceylon, a land of ancient civilization, people are more advanced than in our poor Europe. In Ceylon, one kills one's man by accident.

"It is, in general, with the aid of some accident that one gets rid of one's enemy.

"It's necessary to tell you that Ceylon is the native land of elephants. In Ceylon, one encounters elephants as one encounters ducks in Holland. Ceylon furnishes the entire world with ivory and the whole of India with elephants.

"Now, elephants, as you know, are animals full of intelligence, who fulfill all functions out there, including that of executioner, and in that case, they learn the role so well that they proceed according to the program that is given to them. When a criminal is condemned to be quartered, they tear his limbs off one by one, and then kill him. When death is ordered, they pick up the victim with their trunk, throw him in the air and catch him to their tusks. When there are attenuating circumstances, they lift the condemned man up, again with their trunk, whirl him round three times as a shepherd dies with a sling, and throw him into the air; if he doesn't encounter a tree and doesn't fall on harder ground, he sometimes gets way with a broken leg, a mangled arm or a dislocated neck. Thus, I noticed that it's rare in Ceylon for an elephant to go past a cripple, a one-armed man or a hunchback without making him a little sign of recognition.

"Now, you understand that everyone has his elephant and every elephant has his mahout. One invites some mahout or other to smoke a pipe of opium, or chew a plug of betel or drink a glass of eau-de-vie, and one says to him: 'I'd give ten, twenty, thirty, forty or fifty rupees to the man who came to tell me that such-and-such is dead.' You insert the name of the person you want to destroy, of course.

"'Really?' says the mahout.

"'Word of honor,'

"'Put it there, and if I learn of his death, I promise to be the first to inform you.'

"A week later, someone informs you that an elephant, on going past a worthy man who didn't say a word to it, has suddenly entered into a fury, has seized him with its trunk, and, in spite of the protests of its mahout, has thrown him up so high, so high, so high that he was dead before he came down.

"The same evening, the mahout is found dead drunk, and when interrogated, he says that he is drunk on despair.

"The next day, the dead man is buried in the local manner—which is to say that a tree is uprooted and hollowed out, the body is placed inside, the empty space is filled with pepper, and it's left there until permission is obtained to burn it.

"That, in consequence, is what I was afraid of. So, for the week that I remained in Negombo, whenever I saw an elephant in one direction, I said 'Right!' and went the other way.

"I was therefore quite content when I felt a nice little brig beneath me, traveling at eight knots, going along the Malabar coast.

"Three weeks after my departure from Negombo I disembarked in Goa.

"I had embarked on a Portuguese ship and I saw that the captain was in such a hurry to arrive that he even put on full sail in bad weather, and in ordinary weather he released so many studsails, that I couldn't help asking him the cause of such great celerity. He replied to me that he was a good Catholic, and that he believed that it would be a good thing for his salvation if he could arrive in time to witness the 1824 auto-da-fé.[26]

"It's necessary to say that in Goa, auto-da-fés only take place every two or three years, understandably, but they are the most beautiful. Monsieur, that demon of a captain did so much and so well that, with God's help, we arrived three days before the ceremony.

"Thanks to him, I found lodgings with a Portuguese family on the very day of my arrival. To begin with, I had wanted to arrange full board, with meals, but the

---

[26] In fact, the last auto-da-fé in Goa took place in 1773, and the Inquisition was abolished there the following year, although a brief revival, during which no auto-da-fés were held, resulted in a second abolition in 1812. Such auto-da-fés became a standard motif in French popular fiction, however, introduced into travelogue romance as early as Simon Tyssot de Patot's *Voyages et aventures de Jacques Massé* (c.1715; included in *The Strange Voyages of Jacques Massé and Pierre de Mésange*, Black Coat Press, ISBN 978-1-370-9) and frequently reproduced thereafter, often anachronistically.

captain, who was a worthy fellow, told me to wait, because Portuguese habits might not suit me.

"In fact, on the day of my arrival, having being invited to dinner with my hosts, and having seen them eat all the dishes anyway, even the soup, I resolved to eat separately henceforth, and that evening, I ran around so effectively that I found a little house for rent on the harbor, which, although it was admirably situated, had one story, and a charming garden, was offered to me at two rupees a month—which is to say, a little over five francs."

"Say, Biard," I said, turning to my companion, "What if we were to go to Goa?"

"Ha ha!" Biard replied, like a man who relishes a proposal.

"Go to Goa, go to Goa," said Père Olifus. "It's a beautiful country where one can live for next to nothing. There are superb women—but be careful of the troa and the Inquisition."

"What is the troa?" I asked.

"Let me tell the story," said Père Olifus. "It will get to that in due course. Having rented the house, as in Negombo, it was necessary to furnish it; that wasn't expensive either. Except that as I had all my petty fortune in gold, I was obliged to have recourse to public money-changers, whose estate, which is very lucrative, is to give foreigners frightful copper coins in exchange for their gold and silver. I therefore had to have recourse to them two or three times in the same day, and had to put my hand in my pocket two or three times, with the result that, as every time I put my hand in my pocket I was seen to pull out five- or ten-florin coins, in no time at all the rumor spread through the small ruined city that Goa is that a nabob had arrived there. So, that evening, I had visits from two or three noble ladies or demoiselles, who sent me their domestics, as is customary, to ask for alms while they waited in a palanquin at the door in case I desired to see them. I was still very tired from my voyage, so I contented myself with sending them all that remained of my copper coins, about two or three rupees, which confirmed in their minds the idea that I was a rich merchant.

"The next day, I visited the city: the churches—which are very beautiful, especially that of Our Lady of Mercy—the royal hospital, which is situated on the river and which I first mistook for a palace; the Place Sainte-Catherine; the Rua Drecha, a perpetual market in which one finds everything one needs: furniture, garments, vegetables, utensils of every sort, males and female slaves, with regard to which one cannot be mistaken, since they are sold stark naked; the statue of Lucretia, who provides enough water through the her self-inflicted would to slake the thirst of the entire city; and the trees planted by Saint Francis Xavier, which, thanks to their sacred origin, have never been touched by the ax or the pruning-hook. I went home convinced that the best commerce to adopt among all those available was that of merchant in fruits.[27]

"This is how commerce is carried out in Goa. One buys fifteen beautiful girls in the bazaar at twenty or

_____

[27] Much of this passage, and all the other details relating to Goa, including the account of the properties of troa, is paraphrased from Joseph de La Porte's *Le Voyageur français* (1774), whose description of Goa—which is internally dated 1742—begins with his account of the Inquisition and the auto-da-fé. La Porte's seems to be the only text mentioning the presumably-fictitious marvelous statue of Lucrece [Lucretia].

twenty-five écus apiece; one puts an elegant costume on their body, rings on their fingers and in their ears, a basket on their head, and fruits in the basket, and at eight o'clock in the morning one releases them in the city. Rich young men, who like fruit and conversation, invite them in and chat with them. There are some among them who can empty their basket eight or ten times a day. As, every time they empty their basket it earns a rupee for her master, who only gives them what he pleases, given they they're slaves, you can see that the commerce in question makes a rather tidy profit.

"What struck me at first was that the streets seem to be entirely populated by slaves, half-breeds and Indian natives. From time to time, it is true, one sees a palanquin passing by, carried by negroes, but so strictly closed that one cannot distinguish the person inside, who, for her part, has loopholes through which she can see everything easily.

"I complained on the first day about that absence of women, which saddens and impoverishes the streets of Goa, but I was told that in two days' time, on the Field of Saint Lazarus, I would see the best there were in the city. I asked what the Field of Saint Lazarus was, and the reply I obtained was that it was the place where the auto-da-fé would take place.

"It was very difficult, I was told, unless one had highly-placed connections, to obtain reserved places, and for the other places it was necessary to queue for a long time in advance; but I was believed to be rich, as I've said, and everyone offered me places. They were not ashamed to let me have those places for two or three pagodas, lowering the price when I haggled, and I ended up obtaining one beneath the Viceroy's box for two rupees.

"The celebration was held on Saint Dominic's Day, he being the patron saint of the Inquisition, and I can say that on that day, with the possible exception of myself, no one in Goa went to bed. There was nothing but dances, songs and serenades in the street, and one could see that something was about to happen, as I heard said twenty times during the day, that was very agreeable to God.

"I had my reserved place in the circle that had been set up around the auto-da-fé; I as therefore able to enjoy, one after another, all the details of the spectacle.

"First I saw the condemned emerge from their prison; there were about two hundred of them.

"I asked how long the celebrations would last; such a large number of victims demanded at least a week. But the person I asked, who was a rich Portuguese merchant of the city, shook his head sadly and replied that the tribunal of the Inquisition was relaxing its zeal every day, and that, among that entire crowd of pagans and heretics, only three had been condemned to be burned, the others having escaped the rigors of the Holy Office and had only been sentenced to fifteen years, ten years, five years or two years in prison, and some merely to make honorable amends whose only punishment would be to witness the torture of the three wretches judged sufficiently culpable to be burned.

"I asked to see those who were destined to be burned; my obliging interlocutor replied that nothing was easier than to recognize them, given that they had the portraits depicted on their long black robes, placed on burning pyres with flames rising all around them, and devils dancing in those flames. Those who were condemned to prison, instead of flames rising from the hem of the robe to the girdle, had, on the contrary, flames descending from the girdle to the hem; those who were only making honorable amends and whose only punishment was to witness the execution, wore black robes striped with white, with no flames ascending or descending.

"All the condemned were taken to begin with to the prison of the Jesuit church, where sharp remonstrations were administered to them, after which the judgment was read to each of them, which they all doubtless knew already, thanks to the robe in which they were clad. Then, the mass having been heard and the judgment read, the funeral procession headed for the Field of Saint Lazarus.

"My spice-merchant had not lied, and this time I would have been wrong to complain. All the noble women, all the rich women and all the elegant women of Goa were there, assembled in a space as large as that of an ordinary bull-ring; all the steps were loaded to the point that one thought they were about to give way. In the middle rose the pyre, with a stake carved with three faces; on each of those faces was an iron ring to maintain the condemned, and opposite each ring an altar had been set up surmounted by a cross, in order that the patient could enjoy the happiness of seeing Christ at the final moment.

"My spice-merchant and I had great difficulty reaching our places, but we finally succeeded, at the exact moment that, for their part, the condemned entered the place of execution through a door curtained in black and sown with silver tears.

"When they came in, hymns rose up on all sides, and the women began to rotate magnificent rosaries in their hands, some of amber and others of pearls, while darting glances right and left over their veils. I believe that I was recognized for the man who was known as the rich pearl-trader, for not a few of those gazes paused on me. It is true that, as I was below the Viceroy's box, I might well have mistaken a good many gazes directed at him for my own account.

"The ceremony commenced. The three patients were taken under the arms and they were assisted to climb the pyre. They had difficulty doing it; as you'll understand, it isn't amusing to be burned alive. Finally, half-aiding and half-aided, they reached the platform. They were secured to the rings by iron chains, in view of the fact that ordinary ropes would have been rapidly consumed—and then, no doubt, the patients would have leapt from the pyre to the ground and started running around the ring, on fire, which would have been a general scandal for everyone and a particular misfortune for their souls, given that they would be thinking about a good flight and not a good death; but thanks to the iron chains that maintained them by the feet, the waist and the neck, there was no danger of them making a single movement.

"Except that, as there is always a weakness in the most ingenious arrangements, in default of that danger there was another, which was that the relatives of the condemned might bribe the executioner and, in passing the chain around the neck, the latter might give it an extra twist and strangle him. Then, you understand, the spectacle loses almost all of its interest, since one sees a cadaver being burned instead of a living individual. That day, however, the executioner was a conscientious man, and everyone could be assured that the condemned were very much alive, given that, over everyone's prayers, they could be heard screaming for mercy for more than ten minutes.

"When the ceremony was over, everyone went to fill a little bag with ash from the pyre; that ash has, it appears, the same privilege as the rope of a hanged man, and brings families good luck.

"As I had just finished filling my bag like everyone else, I felt someone slip a piece of paper into my hand. I turned round. An old woman put her finger over her lips, pronounced the single word: 'Read!' and drew away.

"I remained nonplussed for a moment, and then, un-folding the note, I read: *This evening, at ten o'clock, you will be awaited in the garden of the third house to the right of the pond. The house has green shutters; two co-conut palms rise up at its door. Climb over the wall and stop under the* sad tree,[28] *where the same duenna who has brought you this note will collect you.*

"I turned back to the duenna; she had paused some distance away. I made her a sign of acceptance with my hand; she responded with a bow and disappeared."

---

[28] *Nyctanthes arbor-tristus*, the night-flowering jasmine, also described by La Porte.

XII. Doña Inès

"I knew approximately where the rendezvous was. From the top of the wall of the old city, I had surveyed all of the environs, and I had noticed, as a charming promenade, the edges of that little pond, where all the rich Portuguese had pleasure houses surrounded by gardens. As for the species of tree known as the 'sad tree' because it only flowers by night, I was familiar with it, having seen one in the garden of the house I had rented.

"At half past nine I left Goa; I had three or four pearls in me, beautiful enough that the gift of them—if, perchance, I had to make a gift—would not be scorned. At hazard, I placed a Sinhalese dagger under my waistcoat, and resolved to run the risks of my nocturnal excursion bravely.

"At quarter to ten I arrived at the little house, which I recognized perfectly from the description I had been given. I made a circuit of it in order to find a part of the garden wall that I could scale without too great a difficulty. When I found a door, the thought occurred to me that, in order to spare me the trouble of climbing over the wall, the door might perhaps have been left unlocked. I wasn't mistaken; on being pushed, it yielded, and I found myself in the garden.

"Once inside, it wasn't difficult to find the place where I had to wait. Guided by an admirable perfume, after a few moments I was lost in the dense shadow that the sad tree projected all around it. Its flowers, which open at ten o'clock at night and close again before dawn, were shaking their embalmed calices, and among the multitude of flowers with which it was covered, a few, detaching themselves like snowflakes, fell around me and invited me to lie down on their suave carpet.

"Although, as you've been able to see, I'm not very poetic by nature, I couldn't help surrendering to the charm of that beautiful night, and if I have one regret at the hour at which I'm telling you about it, it's talking to you about it as the old sea-dog that I am and not as the poet that you are, or the painter that your comrade is."

Biard and I bowed. "In truth, Père Olifus," I said to him, "you're wrong to apologize for yourself. You tell a story like Monsieur Bernardin de Saint-Pierre."

"Thank you," replied Père Olifus, "for, although I don't know Monsieur Bernardin de Saint-Pierre, I presume it's a compliment that you're paying me. I'll continue, then.

"I had been waiting there for about a quarter of an hour when I heard a rustle of cloth and the sound of footsteps, after which I perceived a form that was approaching furtively. I called out swiftly; my voice reassured my guide, who then came straight toward me, threw me the end of a belt, of which she held the other end, and, starting to walk in front of me, guided me in the direction of the house without saying a single word.

"Apart from two or three windows where the light from inside was filtering through the interstices of the blinds, the house was completely in shadow, and all the darker because, painted red, its contours could not be distinguished in the obscurity of the night. Once the threshold was crossed, the obscurity deepened. Then the duenna, pulled the belt toward her until she encountered my hand. She took my hand, made me climb a staircase, traverse a corridor, and, pulling a door that allowed a flood of light to emerge from its opening, she shoved me into a room where a woman of twenty or twenty-two, perfectly lovely, was lying on a mattress covered with a magnificent Chinese fabric and supported by a bamboo bed.

"In the middle of the room, whose air was refreshed by a huge fan hanging from the ceiling, and which seemed to be flapping of its own accord, stood a table laden with pastries and conserves.

"In those days, I was young, I was a handsome fellow, and not timid—quite the contrary. I made my compliments to the lady; she received them like a woman who, after all, had gone in quest of them. I sat down beside her.

"In Ceylon and Buenos Aires I had learned, as best I could, to jabber a little Spanish; Spanish and Portuguese are similar. Then too, in addition to the language of words, which is sometimes not understood, there is the language of gestures, which is always understood.

"She showed me the snack that had been waiting for me for an hour; I told her that if the snack had been waiting for me for an hour it was necessary not to keep it waiting any longer. We went to table. In accordance with the habit of intimate encounters in Spain and Portugal there was only one glass. Port and Madeira were sparkling in two carafes, one like a ruby, the other a topaz. I'd already tasted both liquids; I found those first rate, and I was about to start on the pastries and the jam when the duenna suddenly came in, greatly alarmed, and whispered a few words in her mistress' ear.

"'What's the matter?' I asked.

"'Nothing,' replied my beautiful hostess tranquilly. 'It's my husband, whom I believed to be in Gondapour for another three or four days, and who has arrived like a bombshell. He never does otherwise, the frightful half-breed.'

"'Aha!' I said. 'And is he perchance jealous, your husband?'

"'As a tiger.'

"'So that if he finds me here...'

"'He'll kill you.'

"'That's good to know,' I aid, taking out my dagger and placing it on the table; I'll take precautions.'

"'Oh! What are you doing?' she said.

"'Well, you see, there's a proverb that says that it's better to kill the devil than for the devil to kill you.'

"'Oh, it's not necessary to kill anyone,' she said, laughing, and showing me as she laughed, pearls compared with which those I had in my pocket seemed black.

"'Why is that?'

"'I'll take care of everything.'

"'Oh, very well then.'

"'Except, go into that cabinet; it gives access to a terrace. Don't lose sight of what's happening here. If my husband takes a step toward the cabinet, which isn't probable, go on to the terrace and jump down to the ground; it's no more than twelve feet high.'

"'All right.'

"'Go! I'll do my best to make sure that his return doesn't change our plans.'

"'So much the better.'

"'Don't worry. Go; I can hear his footsteps on the stairs.'

"I threw myself into the cabinet. Meanwhile, she threw the porcelain plate and silver cutlery that might have given away my presence out of a window. Then, taking a little bag embroidered with silver out of her bosom she took a little bottle out of it containing a green liquid and poured a few drops on the pastries at the summit of the pyramid—after which she got up and went half way to the door. At that moment, the door opened.

"The man she had called a frightful half-breed was a magnificent Indian, with a complexion the color of Florentine bronze and a short, thick beard. He was wearing a rich Muslim costume, although he was a Christian, or very nearly."

Père Olifus interrupted himself. "Oh, Monsieur, I don't know whether you've studied women, but, terrestrial women or mermaids, I believe that the lovelier they are, the more they're false and hypocritical animals.

"That one, who was as beautiful as an amour, smiled at her husband the same smile that she had been smiling at me the moment before. In spite of that smile, however, the newcomer seemed very preoccupied. First, he looked around, and then he sniffed, like an ogre in search of fresh flesh. It seemed to me that his eyes fixed upon the cabinet. He took a step in my direction; I took two steps back. He touched the handle of the door; I let myself down from the terrace into the branches of a bushy tree. I saw a kind of black shadow lean over above my head; I held my breath, and the shadow disappeared. I breathed out, and, climbing up again quietly, my head was soon level with the terrace. It was empty.

"Then, curiosity gripped me to see what was happening in the room I had just quit. I climbed back on to the terrace with the agility and skill of a mariner, and I advanced on tiptoe in order to see, if possible, through the door that had been left ajar.

"The two spouses were at table side by side, the wife holding the husband amorously enlaced in her arms, while the husband was tucking into the little cakes over which his wife had sprinkled the green liquid.

"The husband had his back to me; the wife, relative to me, was in profile; she perceived a portion of me face, doubtless through the gap in the door, and winked at me in a fashion that meant: 'You'll see what's about to happen.'

"In fact, almost at the same moment, the husband started raising his glass and drinking fanatically to the health of his wife. Having drunk the toast, he commenced a little song, which finished with a great orchestra of plates and bottles, which he struck with his knife. Finally he got up and started dancing like a bayadere, draping himself with his napkin.

"Then his wife got up from the table, came to the door behind which I was hidden, watching that strange spectacle, opened the door and said to me tranquilly: 'Come.'

"'Come…come…' I replied. 'That's charming, but…'

"'Let's go, then!' she said, pulling me by the hand. 'When I tell you to come…!'

"I shrugged my shoulders and followed her.

"In fact, her husband entirely absorbed in the character he had adopted for his dance, continued his solitary ballet, making all sorts of graceful gestures with his napkin. Then, as the napkin was very restricted for draping his gracious poses, which ought to have been half-veiled, he unwound his turban and started using it as a shawl while he danced.

"In the meantime, his wife had led me to the bed on which she had been lying when I came in, and at each protest that I raised she shrugged her shoulders. When I saw that, I didn't make any more

131

"After dancing for three quarters of an hour, the husband, who also seemed to have enjoyed himself greatly, was snoring like an organ-pipe.

"I took advantage of the circumstance to ask for an explanation of the little drop of green liquid poured over the pastries, as I suspected strongly that the husband's great passion for vocalization and choreography stemmed from that.

"Those drops of green liquid were troa."

"Very good, my dear Monsieur Olifus," I replied. "Now, explain to me what troa is. You've said, like the skillful narrator that you are, that you'd render me that service when the time and occasion warranted it; I believe that the time and occasion have arrived."

"Monsieur, troa is a herb that grows abundantly in India. The sap is extracted while it is still green, or the seed is reduced to powder when it is ripe; then the sap or the powder is mixed with the food of the person from whom one wants to be rid temporarily. The person then becomes self-absorbed, sings, dances and goes to sleep, without any longer seeing what is happening around her, and when she wakes up, as she has completely lost her memory of what has happened, one tells her any lie one pleases, and she believes it.

"That is what troa is—a very convenient thing, as you can see; so be assured that the women of Goa always carry on their person troa juice in a bottle, or troa powder in a sachet.

"At five o'clock in the morning, my beautiful Portuguese asked me to help her carry her husband to his bed; then, as day was about to dawn, we took our leave of one another, promising that we would see one another again.

"I had had the idea momentarily of making a cargo of troa and sending it to Europe with a detailed account of the virtues of the merchandise, but I was assured that it deteriorated on passing overseas, which caused me to renounce my speculation—which I believe, however, would not have been bad.

"In the meantime, my speculation in fruits prospered; my ten slaves brought me, on an average day, six rupees of net profit—between thirty-six and forty francs in our money, which is an enormous income in Goa, where everything is very cheap. so my friend the spice-merchant let slip before me a few words about an alliance with his daughter, Doña Ines, a charming young person, raised devoutly in the Convent of the Annunciation, whom I had already seen in his home once or twice.

"Doña Inès was very beautiful, and appeared very modest. I was beginning to weary of my Portuguese lady, who was gradually gleaning all my pearls. Then, you see, I was born for marriage before women had taken away my taste it. I therefore gave myself wholeheartedly to the proposals of my friend the spice-merchant, and Doña Inès was taken out of the convent, this time with the intention of bringing us together.

"Doña Inès was still the beautiful and modest young woman that I had seen and noticed previously, except that her eyes were red. I enquired as to the cause of that redness, which indicated the shedding of abundant tears, but I was told that Doña Inès was so innocent that when mention had been made of her leaving the convent, she had dissolved in tears.

"I consulted her about the cause of the dolor, and the charming creature did, indeed, tell me that she had no aspiration toward marriage, and that she was truly chagrined to be leaving her convent, in which she generally found everything she could desire.

"I started to smile at that charming innocence, and as I had no doubt that marriage would have the same effect on her as a voyage has on the traveler—which is to say that it seduces by the novelty of its sights—I didn't worry any more about those regrets or their cause.

"My marriage to Doña Inès was therefore decided by common accord between my friend the spice-merchant and myself; we settled the conditions of the dowry and three weeks later, having fulfilled all the preparatory formalities, we were married in great pomp at the cathedral.

"I shall not dwell on the marriage ceremonies; they are almost the same as in France. Furthermore, Doña Inès seemed to have forgotten her convent. She was as cheerful as decency could permit, and when the moment for us to withdraw had come, she asked me with a charming modesty for permission to retire to her bedroom, only asking me for quarter of an hour's grace in order to have time to undress and go to bed.

"A quarter of an hour is a long time at certain moments, but after all!

"In any case, to help me to be patient, there was a little snack, well prepared and neatly set out on China plates; there was a bottle of Sanlucar Muscat shining so brightly in its crystal prison that I set about drinking philosophically to the health of my beautiful wife. I had never drunk such wine, Monsieur, although I know wine.

"I started eating a few fruits. I was a merchant of fruits, as you know, but I had never eaten such fruits.

"The wine was nectar, the fruits ambrosia.

"Then again, all that had a slightly stimulating taste, a little aperitive acid that would have enabled me to eat all night, if, at the first glass of wine and the first banana I hadn't felt so full of joy and content that I started to sing a sea shanty.

"Monsieur, it's necessary to tell you that I never sing, having a voice so false that it horrifies me whenever I try to song he slightest refrain. Well, that evening, Monsieur, it seemed to me that I was singing like a nightingale, quite naturally, and I took such a great pleasure in hearing my own voice that my legs became itchy, my feet were sketching flip-flops and breezy steps, and I felt that I was floating above the ground, as if, instead of having drunk a glass of Muscat, I had drunk a barrel of inflammable air.

"In short, the temptation became so strong that I started dancing and beating time with a knife on the bottom of my plate, which resonated like a tambourine, and I saw myself dancing in a mirror, and was content with myself; and the more I saw myself, the more I desired to see myself, until, by dint of singing, my voice faded away, by dint of dancing, my legs grew weary, and by dint of looking at myself, I no longer saw anything but blue and pink flames, and by dint of jubilation, I went to lie down on a big sofa, thinking myself the happiest man in the world.

"I don't know how long I slept, but I woke up with a charming sensation of coolness in the soles of my feet. I held out my arms; I felt my wife beside me; I thought that it was to her that I owed the sense of wellbeing in which I found myself, and believe me, I was grateful to her for it!

"'Ah!' she said, with a long sigh.

"Monsieur, the intonation of that sigh reminded me so strongly of the sight that I had had before in Negombo on the night of my wedding to the beautiful Nahi-Nava-Nahina, that I shivered from head to toe.

"'What!' I cried.

"'I only said *ah!*' she said.

"At that moment, Monsieur, I became as cold as ice; my teeth chattered, and between my chattering teeth I murmured: 'La Buchold! La Buchold!'

"'Well, yes. La Buchold, who has come to announce to you, my little husband, that you're the father of a second son, as handsome as the amours, who will be six months old tomorrow, and whom I've called Thomas, in memory of the day when I came to prevent your marriage with the beautiful Nahi-Nava-Nahina. He was held over the baptismal font by the engineer of dykes, the honorable Van Brock, who has promised to be a second father to the dear child.'

"'In truth, my dear wife,' I said to her, 'the news is pleasant, I agree, but since I've already waited five or six months to learn it, I could have waited another five or six days, at least.'

"'Yes, I understand,' said La Buchold. 'At least I haven't disturbed your wedding night with the beautiful Doña Inès.'

"'Well, since it's necessary to tell you, you've done exactly that.'

"'Ingrate!'

"'What, ingrate?'

"'Yes, since, on the contrary, I've been diligent in preventing you from being unworthily deceived.'

"'What do you man, unworthily deceived?'

"'Certainly, unworthily deceived. Didn't your wife ask you for a quarter of an hour to go to bed?'

"'Yes.'

"'And while the quarter of an hour elapsed, didn't you drink a glass of Sanlucar Muscat and eat a banana?'

"'Indeed, I believe I recall that.'

"'And from that moment on, what do you remember?'

"'Nothing.'

"'Well, my dear friend, in that wine there was troa juice, and on that banana there was troa powder.

"'Damn!'

"'With the result that, while you were sleeping like a drunkard and snoring like a Kaffir...'

"'What?'

"'Your chaste spouse...'

"'Eh? My chaste spouse…'

"'A very devout person who went to confess every week to a handsome Franciscan throughout her time at the convent...'

"'Well? My chaste spouse…'

"'What do think she was doing all that time?'

"'Was she confessing, by chance?' I cried.

"'Exactly. Look.'

"And she led me to an opening in the partition, which permitted me to see what was happening in the bedroom.

"Monsieur, what I saw was so humiliating for a husband, especially during his wedding night, that I took hold of a bamboo that happened to be there, as if by a miracle; I opened the door and I rained down blows of the bamboo on Doña Inès' confessor, who ran away screaming like the men I had seen burned on the third day of my arrival.

"As for my wife, I tried to reproach her for her conduct, but with the greatest composure she replied:

'That's all right, Monsieur; complain to my father, and I'll complain to the Inquisition.'

"'And of what will you complain, Madame Slut?' I demanded.

"'That you interrupted my religious exercises by striking a holy man who, for three years has been known to be my confessor. Go, Monsieur; you're a heretic, and as I can't live with a heretic, I'm returning to my convent.'

"And with those words, she went out, as proud as a queen.

"As for me, merely at the word *heretic*, you see, fear had gripped me; I saw myself already clad in a black robe, painted with rising flames; I felt myself already attached by the feet, neck and midriff to the stake in the Field of Saint Lazarus, with the result that I didn't think twice; I took my old savings, added to them two or three thousand livres that I'd put by in the fruit business since my arrival in Goa, and, recalling that I'd seen a ship about to depart for Java in the harbor that day, I had myself taken there immediately, abandoning my house, garden and furniture to whoever wanted them.

"Fortunately, the ship was waiting to emerge for a little easterly breeze and the ebb tide. I arrived on board with the breeze in one hand and the tide in the other. I agreed with the captain ten pagodas for my passage, and I had the satisfaction, as the first rays of drawn bleached the summits of the churches of Goa, of sensing the wind and the tide that were gradually drawing me away.

"The precaution was not unnecessary; two years later, I was burned in effigy on the Field of Saint Lazarus."

XIII. Intercalation

I have told my readers that the book I am publishing at this moment is very personal; in addition to my memories, it includes certain quotidian events that will be memories in their turn, and I am distributing in my story not merely the sum of talent that God had been kind enough to grant me, but also a portion of my heart, my life and my individuality.[29]

That is why, today, I shall talk about something other than Père Olifus, and I shall leave our worthy seeker of adventures sailing over the dark and mysterious Indian Ocean, in order to follow the soul in flight of a friend sailing at this moment over the far more somber and far more mysterious ocean of eternity

I had spent the evening at the premiere performance of the drama *Harmental*.[30] It was the fortieth time, I believe, that that proof of the struggle of mind against matter, of isolation against the multitude, had been imposed on me: a terrible gamble that has cured me of any other kind of gambling, for I wager there, not only a sum of money that the boldest of gamblers cannot wager, but

---

[29] Perhaps oddly, in view of the excision of the first three chapters, this "intercalation" is preserved in the abridged version of the novel, where the second of its two chapters is subdivided into two, as it was in the original serial version.

[30] The drama *Le Chevalier d'Harmental*, credited to Dumas and Auguste Maquet, with music by Alphonse Varney, had its première at the Théâtre Historique on 26 July 1849. It was based on an 1842 novel of the same title, known in English as *The Conspirators*.

also the portion of renown conquered during twenty years on the vast literary plain where so many men glean but where so few harvest.

And take note that when a man falls in the theater, he does not fall from the height of the work he has just given, but from the height of twenty, thirty or forty successes that he has had—with the result that the more success he has had, the deeper is the abyss, and the more risk he runs of being killed outright in consequence.

Well, the efforts that an entire audience makes to push from the summit to the base of his renown, efforts that I have studied when they operated upon my colleagues, I had the courage to study when they operated on me.

It is a curious thing, I swear to you, for the heart that God has covered with a triple layer of steel strong enough to support it, that struggle in which a work comes alone to throw down a challenge to eighteen hundred spectators, a hand-to-hand struggle with them over six hours, yielding, and sometimes, like an athlete wearying of getting to his feet again, making the public yield in its turn, and holding it down, panting, under the knee until it cries mercy and asks the name of its unknown conqueror...

Or too well-known, for, in that knowledge, anticipated or not, the secret is very often contained of the fervor of the public at premiere performances.

In fact, remember it well, the public of premiere performances is a public apart, composed of elements that assemble without amalgamating, and which one only finds united on that day; but a public that is nevertheless always the same, and which you recognize at every solemnity of that sort, in its ensemble and in its details, no matter how poor a memory you have for faces and sensations.

These are the elements of which the audience of a premiere performance is made up:

Five or six hundred men and women of the world, a portion of whom have taken care to book seats early and have obtained them at the box office price, and the other portion of whom have left it too late and have got them from ticket touts. The members of the latter portion are extremely annoyed at having paid fifteen, twenty, thirty or as many as fifty francs for a five-franc seat. That fraction of the public, therefore, is not content to have five francs' worth of distraction; they want fifty francs' worth.

That latter fraction is further subdivided, into people who have not come for the spectacle, but have come in order to be there, some of them because Madame *** or Mademoiselle X is coming, and who could not get a place in Mademoiselle X or Madame ***'s box, and, desiring to see Madame *** or Mademoiselle X in order to exchange some signal or other, imperceptible for anyone else, but only perceptible for themselves, was compelled to make that expense in order to come: an expense often exorbitant, and which, in this blessed epoch of universal penury, reduces the person who has made it to regulation cigars for a month, and dinner at the English tavern for a week.

That, therefore, is a first section of the public, composed of six hundred people, three hundred of whom are indifferent and three hundred in a bad mood. Let us pass on to the others.

Thirty of forty journalists, friends or enemies of the author or authors, more enemies than friends, who will have a great deal of wit if the piece fails, given that they will pick up a part of the fallen wit with which to make projectiles, whereas, if the piece succeeds, they will only have their own wit.

Thirty or forty dramatic authors, whom the excessively continuous success of two of their colleagues humiliates in their pride, who applaud without bringing their hands together, while murmuring to their neighbor: "It's frightful! It's detestable! Always the same means, the same plots, the same threads"—with the result that they applaud very quietly and murmur very loudly.

Thirty or forty artistes from neighboring theaters, who have not come to see the play but to see how it is performed by the artistes who fill the same employment as them, and who almost always choose the rare moments when the audience falls silent to emit the most judicious observations on the art of the actor, accompanied by commentaries on the fashion in which they have played, in some circumstance and with greater success, a role analogous to the one that the actor on stage is playing—except that their role was much finer, with the consequence that it is naturally implied that it required a much greater talent to play it.

Thirty or forty demoiselles, part-sluts and part-artistes, who are always making debuts and are never taken on. They do not come for the play or the actors; they always come for the spectators, floating during a tableau or two from the forestage to the orchestra stalls and from the orchestra stalls to the balcony, and end up by sitting down; then telegraph lines are established, the three principal signals of which are the lorgnette, the fan and the bouquet; when the play is over, all that they have seen of it is the dress of the amorous woman and the fabric of which that dress is made. Three days later, if the fabric is pretty, they will be seen at another premiere in a similar fabric

Two or three hundred bourgeois who come with the conviction that the modern theater is a tissue of immoralities, who have brought their wives with great difficulty and left their daughters sulking at home, who search in five or six tableaux for the immoralities thy have been promised, and who, not finding them, are ready to murmur that they have been cheated. They are formed of a good enough dough, which allows itself to be kneaded by interest; they render to the author in tears and laughter the advances he has made to them; the author rarely has to complain of them.

Finally, three or four hundred children of the people, without bias or prejudice, who have queued for two hours, with their bread under the arms and their sausage in their pocket, who say Dumas bluntly, Maquet bluntly, Historique bluntly, who come to amuse themselves, who applaud when they are amused and whistle when they are bored. They are good judges; they are the intelligent part of the society, for their intelligence is nor obscured by hatred, envy, vanity, interest or frivolity.

Add to that fifty claquers, who only seem to be there to make people say, every time they applaud: "Down with the claque!"

That, therefore, is a premiere performance audience, the areopagus before which the genius of all epochs appears; that is the Briareus with two thousand heads and four thousand arms, against which, for the fortieth time, I struggled that evening with my habitual tranquility, but with an even greater sadness than usual.

I say greater than usual, because nothing is sadder, I repeat, than the contest, even when victorious, that one is obliged to sustain against the malevolent portion of the public that one finds at every premiere performance, re-acting against laughter, reacting against tears, ever ready to charge full tilt, at the first sign of weakness that it perceives, or thinks it perceives, in front of it.

Then, all of that society flows away, leaving you more isolated the greater the success is. All those friends who have gone away, forgetting to shake your hand, all those lights going out even before the last spectators have gone; the curtain that goes up again on a cold and empty stage; the theater whose soul has just flown away and which is no more than a cadaver; the night-light that shines all alone, replacing all those fires; the silence that success all those noises—that, believe me, is enough to cause the most real silence, the most profound discouragement.

How many times, my God, even on the days when the sadness is only superficial, when the discouragement does not descend to the heart, how many times, after my finest, noisiest, most uncontested successes, after *Henri III*, after *Antony*, after *Angèle*, after *Mademoiselle de Belle-Isle*, how many times have I come back alone, on foot, heart swollen and eyes humid, ready to shed the bitterest of my tears, while half the spectators were saying: "How happy he must be at this moment."

Well, I went home alone that evening, as I said, even sadder than usual, when I found my son waiting for me at home, and who said to me: "Our poor James Rousseau is dead."[31]

---

[31] Pierre-Joseph Rousseau (1797-1849), who preferred to call and sign himself James Rousseau, was a novelist, journalist and writer of vaudevilles who numbered among Dumas' many collaborators. Dumas wrote a eulogy for him published in *Le*

I bowed my head without making any response. For some time, the same words resonated around me.

Mademoiselle Mars is dead, Joanny is dead,[32] Frédéric Soulié is dead, Madame Dorval is dead, Rousseau is dead.

There is a time of life, the first age, the portion of existence gilded by the dawn, which flows without anything similar coming to sadden it. The sound of the death knell seems to be incapable of reaching our ears. All the voices that speak to us address sweet words to us, all murmurs are birdsong; that is because one is still climbing the beautiful mountain of life, so cheerful on the face that one is climbing, so arid on the side that one descends.

Salutations to you, then, melancholy hour when, having arrived at the summit of the mountain, one pauses to make a halt in life, when the eye overlooks simultaneously the florid slope that one has just climbed and the desolate slope that one is about to descend, and when, along with the first north wind of winter, the first echo of the tomb reaches you, which tells you that your mother, a relative or a friend has just died.

Then, say adieu to the frank joys of this world, for that echo will no longer quit you, and that echo will vibrate, perhaps once a year at first, then two, then three; you will be like the tree from which the first storm of summer removes a single leaf, and which says: "What

---

Constitutionnel, of which the next chapter might be a reproduction.

[32] This reference is presumably to the writer of vaudevilles Joanny Augier; if so, it casts doubt on the Bibliothèque Nationale's speculative record of the date of his death as "1855?"

does it matter? I have so many leaves." Then the storms succeed one another, and then comes the autumnal wind, and then the first frosts of winter. The tree is bald, its branches naked, and, a fleshless skeleton, it only waits itself, in order to disappear from the surface of the soil, for the noise of the woodcutter's ax.

In any case, is it not a benefit of heaven, that successive abandonment in which all those we have loved and all those who have loved us leave us? It is not better, when one leans toward the earth oneself, that it is from the earth that the most familiar and most cherished voices come? Is it not consoling that when one marches inevitably toward an unknown world, that one is sure of at least finding there all the memories that, instead of following us, have preceded us?

"Our poor James Rousseau is dead," my son had said to me.

Let us say now to what memory of my life the man whose death had be announced to me was attached.

XIV. James Rousseau

I was eighteen years old: no future, no education, no fortune. I was second clerk to a provincial notary and I detested the notariat. I was getting ready to solicit the position of tax-collector in some village, where my life would pass obscure and unknown, when at the head of a small town a league from Villers-Cotterêts, named Corcy, I perceived, coming from the extremity of a path that I was following, three people whose paths I would necessary cross in thirty or forty paces.

Those three people were a young man of my own age, a young woman of twenty-five or twenty-six, and a little girl of five.

The young man was completely foreign to my memories; the other two individuals, the young woman and the little girl, were mingled with the earliest events of my life. The young woman was Baronne Capelle. The little girl was Marie Capelle, later Madame Lafarge.[33]

---

[33] The reference is to the wife and daughter of Guillaume Capelle, an administrator who served under the Empire and the Restoration, but had to flee the country during the July Revolution of 1830; he was sentenced to life imprisonment and his property was confiscated but he was pardoned in 1836 and returned to France. Contemporary readers would, however, have been far more familiar with the name of Marie Lafarge, née Capelle, who became notorious in 1840 when she was convicted of murdering her husband by arsenic poisoning, on forensic evidence that seems extremely dubious with the aid of hindsight (and, indeed, would have been refuted at the time by Frédéric Raspail, had he managed to get to the court in time). Hers was the first sensational trial tracked by the Parisi-

My God, who would have thought then, on seeing that beautiful young woman and that laughing child, one scarcely preceding the other in life, one charming, the other promising to be, that for the mother, premature death awaited in the future, and for the little girl a misfortune worse than death?

A warm ray of June sunlight filtered through tall trees, and caused the shadow of leaves to tremble on the radiant faces and white dresses of the mother and the child, slightly agitated by the breeze that runs through the woods as evening approaches.

I said that I knew that young woman; I did indeed know her by virtue of all the good sentiments of my heart, friendship and gratitude.

I was an orphan at three; her father had become my guardian. In addition to my mother and sister, who remained to me, I found a second mother and three more sisters at the Château de Villers-Hellon. I return to the past and I salute you with my hand, Hermine and Louise; I have not seen you for twenty years, my sisters; I am told that you are still young, still beautiful; I tell you from the bottom of my heart, so religious in its memories, that you are still love loved.

Oh, I often think about you; when my eyes, fatigued by the ardent sun that burns the life of a poet, pierce the radiance of my Midi, and come to repose on the blue

---

an popular press, and established the extreme importance of such reportage for newspaper circulation. Following her conviction, she wrote her memoirs in prison. Dumas subsequently wrote an account of the case in 1866, but did not know when he wrote the present story that Napoléon III would eventually order her release from prison, shortly before her death in 1852 from tuberculosis.

horizon of my young years, I see you again, such as you were, perfumed flowers of my earliest childhood, leaning over the water's edge like lilies, mingled with the bushes like roses, lost in the long grass like violets. Alas, you no longer think about me; the wind has carried me away into another world than yours and mine; you no longer see me, and because you have forgotten me, you think that I have forgotten you.

That is who the young woman and the little girl were, then who were coming toward me at about four o'clock in the afternoon on a beautiful day in June—which is to say, coming toward a poor child whose future, in all eyes, was much more humble and obscure than theirs. Let us now say who the young man was on whose arm Madame Capelle was leaning, and who was dressed as a German student.

He was the son of a man whose name will remain fatal and illustrious in the history of monarchies, of a man who was the friend of Anckarström and de Horn, the son of the Comte de Ribbing; he was the man that you all know under the name of Adolphe de Leuven, a name that was later to sign some of the finest and most productive successes of the Opéra-Comique and the Vaudeville.[34]

---

[34] Adolphe de Leuven (1802-1884) was a prolific playwright, librettist and theater director, associated with the Opéra-Comique for nearly half a century. His father, Adolph Ribbing (1765-1843) had been implicated in the assassination of King Gustav III of Sweden in 1792, of which Jacob Anckarström was convicted. Ribbing was also sentenced to death for his part in the crime, but was pardoned and became an exile in France, where he adopted a Frenchified version of his mother's maiden name.

I joined those three persons, who had a collective age of forty-six years, exactly the age that one of them is today.

Madame Capelle introduced me to her cavalier; we were two youths of the same age, That day we commenced a friendship that no day since, somber or happy, has altered; we still greet one another with the same joyful smile, the same sympathetic heartbeat with which we greeted one another twenty-five years ago.

I am bound to say, even in these times of equality, alas, that Adolphe de Leuven is a man of letters, but most of all a gentleman of letters. He was exiled with his family, obliged to remain within a radius of twenty leagues from Paris. Paris was forbidden to his family, proscribed by the Bourbons of the elder branch. But, young as he was, he had touched the soil of the capital with his feet; he had dipped his lips in its intoxicating cup, where one drinks hope at first, then glory, and then bitterness; as yet he had only tasted the hope.

He had tried to work for the Gymnase, where he knew Perlet, the excellent actor whom all men between thirty-five and forty remember, and a beautiful young woman whose name blossomed like a rose, Fleuriet, who died poisoned, it is said.

All these names were quite unknown to me, a poor provincial, having only left my native town to make one excursion to Paris in 1807, and all of whose memories were limited to seeing again, as if through a cloud, a performance of *Paul et Virginie* by Michu and Madame de Saint-Aubin.

And yet, in the middle of all that, those tall beeches of the forest of Villers-Cotterêts, planted by François I and Madame d'Étampes, under which Henri IV and Gabrielle sat, those great beeches with their somber foliage, their dense shadow, their long murmurs, have not remained mute for me.

The poets of that epoch were Demoustier, Parny and Legouvé. All three had passed under the cool moving vault of that great park, felled today like all great things; and when I ran under that vault as a child, chasing butterflies or picking flowers, it happened more than once that I stopped to read the verses that their hands had written on the silvered bark, and which public veneration preserved from any mutilation.

The first verses I read, therefore, I did not read in books; I read them on trees, where they seemed to have grown as fruits grow and as flowers grow. And more than once, like the vibration of a harp animated by the wind and the finders of a musician causes a solitary, mute lute lost in some corner or suspended from a wall, I had cast into the midst of that creation my first inexperienced and discordant poetic cries.

So when, sitting near one of those old trees bathed by the age-old shadow that shaded both of us, we, whose fathers had been born at the two extremities of society and hazard had brought together in order to influence one another's destiny; when, instead of that humble and tranquil future of a provincial employee, de Leuven lifted a corner of the veil that hid the life of Paris from me; when, with the confidence of youth, a gilded robe that every day of maturity crumples and tarnishes, he showed me the struggle, the noise, the renown; those spectators applauding, the sublime delights of success, so dolorous that their enjoyment resembles torture and their laughter groans; my head fell into my hands and I murmured:

"Yes, yes, you're right, de Leuven, it's necessary to go to Paris, because Paris is all there is."

The sublime confidence of a child in God. What did we lack, in fact, for going to Paris? Him, liberty; me, money. He was exiled, I was poor.

But we were both nineteen years old; nineteen years of age is liberty, it is wealth; it is better than all of that, it is hope.

From that moment on, I no longer lived in reality, even in dreams, like a man who has looked at the sun and who, with his eyes closed, still sees the dazzling star. My eyes were fixed on a goal from which they could turn away momentarily, but to which they returned after each deviation more obstinately than ever.

After a year, the Comte de Ribbing's exile was revoked. Adolphe ran to bring me the news; he returned to Paris with his father and mother. I was then the only one in exile. From that moment on my poor mother has no rest. The word Paris was in all my conversations, all my caresses, all my kisses.

I have recounted elsewhere how that ardent desire was realized; how, in my turn, I came to Paris and how I got down from the diligence at a small hotel in the Rue des Vieux-Augustins with fifty-three francs in my pocket and, as confident and proud as if I possessed Aladdin's marvelous lamp, which was featured the Opéra at the very moment of my arrival.

After three months, my mother had realized what she was able to realize, perhaps a hundred louis, and had come to join me. I had a salary of twelve hundred francs. My mother's hundred louis, reinforced by that twelve-hundred-franc salary, lasted two years. Then the struggle commenced.

I had no sooner bumped into the first intelligences I had encountered than I had perceived that I knew nothing, neither Greek, nor Latin, nor mathematics not any foreign language, nor even my own language, nothing of the past, nothing of the present, about the dead or the living, history or society; so, at the first shock, my self-confidence collapsed—but God permitted that the will remained, and that hope flourished in the bosom of that will.

Meanwhile, de Leuven, my introducer into the real world and the fictional world, had not abandoned me. We had set to work.

Oh, for the moment my ambition was not great. It was a matter of putting together a vaudeville for the Gymnase. Well, after two hours of brain-racking work, we looked at one another; we looked at one another and were forced to confess that we were impotent to complete that work, utterly trivial as it was, on our own. One day, de Leuven proposed to me that we associate ourselves with one of his friends, a charming singer linked with Désaugiers, whose reputation for wit was proverbial. In addition, he knew all the directors in Paris, read marvelously, and "stole" committees.

Like him, I recognized our insufficiency; I accepted the offer he made. The same evening, we read our vaudeville to our future collaborator, on whose face I followed anxiously all the impressions that it translated. It was de Leuven who read; I was unable to read, so impressed was I.

"That's good," he said, when de Leuven had finished. "It's necessary to apply ourselves to that, there might be something to be done with it."

In fact, under the pen of our collaborator, more experienced than ours, the sentences were rounded, the couplets sharpened, and a few sparks sprang forth here and there is the dialogue—and at the end of a week, the work was finished.

We, or rather our collaborator, asked for a reading at the Gymnase, and obtained it. We were refused unanimously. We asked for a reading at the Porte-Saint-Martin; we got six black balls and two white ones. We read at the Ambigu-Comique; we had a resounding reception.

It was a great disappointment, not for my dramatic pride—I had never known what the aristocracy of the theater was—but for my pecuniary calculations; the further my mother and I advanced, the more we were impeded. I had, however, obtained a promotion in my office; I had fifteen hundred francs a year instead of twelve. Also, less of a novice in some matters than others, while the three of us were having great difficulty composing a vaudeville together, I had made a child of my own all alone. Now, the advent in the world of Alexandre fully compensated for the augmentation of twenty-five francs a month that I owed to the liberality of the Duc d'Orléans. The glory that my third of the vaudeville would have brought me was doubtless not to be disdained, but the first authorial rights of that third, I must confess, were awaited by my pocket with the same impatience as the first smiles of renown by my head.

Now, the author's rights for a vaudeville put on at the Ambigu were twelve francs a night and six francs' worth of tickets, which added up, per evening, the tickets being sold at half price, to five francs each. On those future rights, an excellent man, Porcher, who has done more for the dramatic authors of Paris than Monsieur Sosthènes de la Rochefoucauld, Monsieur Cavé or Monsieur Charles Blanc have ever done, lent me fifty francs one day when there was nothing in the house to eat. That loan of fifty francs was the first money I earned with my pen. What Monsieur le Duc d'Orléans' cashier paid me out every month, I earned with my writing.

Finally, the great day arrived. Our vaudeville was performed, and was a critical success. A critical success at the Ambigu in 1826, you understand? Which brought me, for my share, fifty francs!

The piece was entitled *La Chasse et l'Amour*.

As for our collaborator, his name was James Rousseau.

What a strange coincidence it is that at a distance of twenty-five years, also on the evening of a success, my son Alexandre, an infant scarcely whimpering in 1826, was waiting at home to tell me: "Our poor James Rousseau is dead."

During those twenty-five years, poor James Rousseau, what had life been for you, so good, so intelligent and so loving?

I shall describe it.

Do you not think that centuries are like men, that they have their foolish youth, their serious maturity and their somber old age? A foolish youth, indeed, that of the eighteenth century, with its Regency, Monsieur d'Orléans, Madame de Berry, Madame de Prie, Monsieur le Duc, Madame de Châteauroux and Richelieu; a serious maturity that saw the emergence of the reputation of Maréchal de Saxe, Monsieur de Lowendhal, de Chevert, who won the battles of Fontenoy and Raucoux; a somber old age that began with the wars in Canada, the Treaty of Paris, the gangrene of the King that infected royalty and concluded with the massacres of l'Abbaye, the scaffolds of the Place de la Révolution and the orgies of the Directoire.

It was the same in our nineteenth century. Waterloo had made it sad to begin with, like an orphan child; but the Restoration, a good enough mother, all things considered, soon returned its insouciance and folly. From 1816 to 1826 date the last flashes of French gaiety, the last songs of Le Caveau,[35] the songs of singers, which did not yet have the pretension of being the songs of poets, songs signed Armand Gouffé, Désaugiers, Rougemont, Rochefort, Romieu and Rousseau.

In that period, Potier, Brunel and Tiercelin flourished. Tiercelin performed *Le Coin de Rue*, Brunet *Jocrisse maître et Jocrisse valet* and Potier *Je fais mes farces*. It was, in fact, a time of farces; that tradition of the wit of the old legal fraternity we men of forty have seen die gradually, sigh by sigh and gasp by gasp, as one watches an old man die of exhaustion and consumption.

People still dined in that epoch; there were artistic restaurants that discussed cuisine gravely with Messieurs Brillat-Savarin and Grimod de La Reynière as Monsieur de Condé discussed it with Vatel. There were chefs, some with Cambacérès, others with d'Aigrefeuille; their names were Borel and Beauvilliers. Today, people still eat in restaurants, but they no longer dine there.

Then, not only did they dine, but they also supped, another tradition of the last century that is almost extinct in ours. Who can say what French wit has lost by the suppression of that charming repast, made by candlelight at the hour when dreams are made, at the hour, in sum,

---

[35] Strictly speaking, the Societé du Caveau, the ancestor of modern "glee clubs," disappeared in 1739, but its tradition survived and was revived continually by imitative organizations and "Le Caveau" survived in France as a collective term. It is not entirely surprising that Dumas might have thought it dead and gone in 1849, but his announcement can now be recognized as premature.

when all cares, worries and business affairs, those phantoms of the day, have vanished?

Romieu, Rousseau and Henri Monnier were ardent suppers;[36] young and having a great appetite more often than a full purse, living the vagabond life that is characteristic of both the Bohemian and the student, they had no need for a restaurant's sign to bear a name illustrious in the pomp of cuisine to pitch their tent there. Any dive would do; they sat down before a pâté, a cutlet or boiled fish, they ordered Pouilly for want of champagne and Beaugency for want of Chambertin, They sang *La Treille de sincerité, Plus one est de fous plus on rit, Qu'on est heureux d'n'avoir pas le sou!* and emerged at two o'clock in the morning, warmed by wine, laughter and song, and the "farces" commenced.

Those farces, for the generation that followed us, are only known in the state of legends; there is the legend of the Chinese lantern, the legend of the two ugly men and the legend of the porter whom one asks for one's horses, all that mingled with cats attached to bells, broken street-lights and stretched ropes—nocturnal epi-

---

[36] Rousseau's supper companions were Auguste Romieu (1800-1855), who went on to enjoy a successful career in the civil service but achieved an odd kind of lasting fame as a practical joker by virtue of Dumas' *Mémoires*, and Henri Monnier (1799-1877), who built an enduring reputation as a satirist in prose, performance and illustration. Dumas did not know when he wrote the present account that while he was exiled in the early days of the Second Empire, Romieu would be rewarded for the support he gave Napoléon III with the government posts of Director of Fine Arts and Inspector General of the Crown Libraries, while Monnier would become one of the principal caricaturists and vaudevillians of the Second Empire.

sodes that almost always ended up with the jokers at the local commissariat. But the police commissaires were appropriate to their era; they had been practical jokers themselves in their day; a paternal reprimand was usually the sole punishment for those frequent infractions of municipal police regulations; everyone had his favorite commissaire, to whom he asked to be taken.

Rousseau had adopted the commissaire of the Odéon quarter. Six times in the same week, every might from Monday to Saturday, he was recommended to that worthy man, who, finally weary of always being woken up at the same hour by the same man for the same cause, seemed to get annoyed the sixth time.

Rousseau listened to the remonstration with great composure and a profound humility. Then, when the magistrate had finished, he replied: "That's fair, Monsieur le Commissaire. Tomorrow, I'll have myself taken elsewhere. You should at least be able to sleep on Sunday."

That joyful life lasted as long as the Restoration did; it was a good time for whoever had wit, and Rousseau had so much of it, especially over dessert, that everyone knew Rousseau, even though he had not had anything printed except *La Chasse et l'Amour*, because all the charming articles that appeared in the *Figaro*, the *Pandore* and the *Journal Rose*, which all those suppers and dinners furnished lavishly, never identified him; they were written communally, as they were consumed communally.

The July Revolution arrived; it was a bomb thrown into the flock of songbirds; politics took possession of some, business affairs of others; art absorbed a few. Romieu became a sub-prefect, Monnier an actor; Rousseau remained alone and isolated.

From that moment on, the suppers ceased.

A distich observes that it was Romieu's absence that brought about the cessation of the suppers, since his return to Paris after four years' exile in the provinces, caused the revival of the habit there. This is the distich whose support we are advancing:

> *When Romieu returned from Monomotapa,*
> *Paris, no longer supping, returned to supper.*

Romieu came back with the reputation of an excellent sub-prefect. There was a story of a lesson given to children who were unable to break a street-lamp. There was the fable of the clockmaker and his watch. But all that proved something that had not been demonstrated until then, which is that one could be a man of infinite wit and nevertheless make an excellent sub-prefect. That was demonstrated so clearly that Romieu left again, as a prefect.

As for Rousseau, maturity had come, and without taking anything away from his charming wit or his excellent heart, it had added something to his reason. He was still the man of dessert, the singer full of verve, the joyful drinker, but he was also a man of daily labor. The practical jokes had ceased with the suppers. Police commissaries, changed with the July Revolution, did not know his name, famous among the commissaires of the Restoration. He was appointed as the editor of the *Gazette des Tribunaux*. He was the one who recounted in that excellent newspaper, with a verve unique to him, all the stories of vagabondage, drinking dens and thefts in which every actor acquired a character, an appearance, almost a face.

In 1839, I believe, Rousseau married. Rousseau, as you can see, settled down completely. He did more than that, and went to live in Neuilly.

From that moment on there was no more insouciance in that life, once so insouciant, not more idleness in that previously idle existence. Rousseau had understood that, philosophical when he lived alone, he could support privations, but that he did not have the right to impose those privations on the wife whose existence he had united with his own. And yet, in spite of the labor, in spite of the fixed monthly retribution of that labor, life has its exigencies, and Rousseau found himself even poorer than in the times when, in default of money, gaiety remained. In those days, Rousseau no longer sang *Qu'on est heureux d'n'avoir pas le sou!* In those days, Rousseau did not even take the omnibus; he went to Paris on foot, came to see me and asked: "You're still well in with the Duc d'Orléans, aren't you?"

I knew what that signified. I nodded my head, and I gave him, from the cash-box of my dear and excellent Prince, a bond of hundred, two hundred, or three hundred, according to his needs. Asseline did honor to that bond, and Rousseau called back at the house, shook my hand and said: "Oh, I'll have you on the day of my death in order to bury me."

Poor Rousseau, he did not know how truly he spoke!

The Prince was killed; a great and facile resource was lacking for Rousseau. But for want of the Prince, the Ministers remained.

When need made itself too keenly felt in the household in Neuilly, I saw Rousseau again.

"How do you stand with the Minister of Public Education?" he asked.

"Good when Monsieur de Salvandy is the Minister, but not good when it's Villemain or Cousin." And when it was Monsieur de Salvandy, I put in a good word for Rousseau, and Monsieur de Salvandy honored it by virtue of princely tradition. When it was Villemain or Cousin, I opened my drawer and said: "Take what you need, my friend." And Rousseau did not hesitate to take from my drawer as I would have taken from his if Rousseau had had a drawer and I had needed to take something from it.

Do not believe, moreover, that that happened often—scarcely once every two years, once a year at the most.

The February Revolution arrived; Rousseau's salary was reduced from three hundred francs to a hundred. No more Prince, alas, and no more Ministers. Then, on top of that, a cruel malady, a malady of the lungs, with which the physicians could not reckon, choking that interrupted his breathing and damaged his voice.

It was then that one could see all that there was of devotion and courage in that heart, so good, and that soul, so loving, Suffering and obliged to stop every five steps to catch his breath, Rousseau left every morning to go to his office at the *Gazette*, sometimes pretending to have ten sous in his pocket to take the omnibus in order not to worry his wife, and, not having those ten sous, making the journey back and forth on foot.

That lasted for more than a year. I went for more than a year without seeing him.

Poor friend! He knew full well what repugnance I would have had today in asking of those who are there, and he did not want to ask anything of me for fear that I might not have it.

Finally, one day, he came; there was no means of waiting any longer.

"Do you know the Minister of ***?" he asked me.

I did not, but for James to come to me the need had to be so urgent that I did not hesitate.

"I don't know him," I said, "but he must know me, and I'll write to him."

And I wrote to the Minister of ***, to ask him for help for poor James Rousseau, man of letters, dramatic author and journalist.

Rousseau dined with me, shook my hand and took the letter away.

One morning, I received a note from the Minister of ***. He asked me for information about Monsieur James Rousseau. That evening, as I have said, my son was waiting for me when I returned home, to announce the fatal news to me.

I took up my pen and I wrote to the Minister of ***.

Monsieur le Ministre,

The only information I can give you about Monsieur James Rousseau is that he died this morning, without help.

This is how Rousseau had died.

He had come to Paris on foot, going to the Rue du Harlay, where the office of the *Gazette des Tribunaux* is. Having arrived at quarter past ten, he had gone into the editorial office and was reading the newspapers there when he suddenly uttered a sigh, stood up, extended is arms, opened his mouth, vomited a quantity of blood and stammered: "A sudden apoplexy! I'm not unfortunate." Then he added: "My poor wife!" And he fell to the ground face down.

He was dead.

He had five sous in his waistcoat pocket, and that was all he possessed.

You are right, Monsieur L****, men of letters do not die of starvation; they even have a superfluity, since when they die, one finds five sous in their pocket.

At two o'clock in the morning, Alexandre was at Neuilly. He took our poor friend's widow the first consolation that she did not have to take care of anything, that all the sad details that follow the death of a beloved person would be our concern, that of his friends. Quick off the mark as Alexandre was, however, other friends had already taken the initiative; they were the reporters of the *Gazette de Tribunaux*, who claimed the pious honor of placing the body of their colleague in a dwelling that would belong to him eternally.

No, Monsieur L****, men of letters do not die of starvation, but they are carried home on the stretcher of paupers, because the five sous they have in their pocket cannot bring them home in a cab.

No, men of letters do not die of starvation, but if you go to the funerals of men of letters, you will see the bailiffs waiting for the body to be lifted up to seize their belongings, and you can say to them what I said to them:

"Why not seize the body, Messieurs; the will give you seven francs for it at the École de Médecine?"

O poor, ill-organized society, in which the living cannot find a loaf of bread, the dead cannot find a tomb and people wait for the cadaver of the husband to be carried away in order to pillage the widow's home!

Be tranquil, poor wife, weep and pray in peace, poor widow. When you enter that sad dwelling to which you have been carried unconscious, you will find there—and it is me who tells you this—every item of furniture in the place where you left it. Only our friend will be lacking; but he too you will find out there, in the charming cemetery where we have laid him down, near the road, like a tired traveler resting and waiting.

May God grant you peace in life! May God grant him mercy in death.

XV. A Suttee

"Man proposes and God disposes; it is for the navigator most of all, that that proverb, the most veridical of all proverbs, seems to have been made.

"We set sail from Goa in the first days of June, the epoch in which winter commences. Now, whoever has not seen the tempests of the Malabar coast has not seen anything.

"One of those tempests cast us up in Calicut, and whether we liked it or not, we had to stay there.

"What is convenient about winters in India, however, is that they are not accompanied by the slightest chill, but only by winds, clouds and lightning, which enables fruits to ripen as well in winter as in autumn. Furthermore, those who are weary of winter do not have far to go to find another season. They only have to cross the Ghat mountains, which run from the north to the south. In two days, instead of being on the Malabar coast, they find themselves on the Coromandel coast, and instead of being soaked by the winter of the Persian Gulf, they are roasted by the summer of the Bay of Bengal.

"Furthermore, I'll tell you that nothing is as beautiful as that coast, strewn with palm trees and coconut palms, ever green and ever plumed, and which lie down in high winds like the arches of bridges. Nothing is as beautiful as those plains, those grasslands, those steams, those lakes, where towns, villages and country houses are mirrored, and which extend from Cape Comorin to Mangalore.

"When I saw that we were on that coast, and the captain told me that there would be impossibility of putting to sea again for three or four months, I made my decision, and as I was already three-quarters Hindu, I decided to settle in Calicut, with all the more tranquility because, Calicut being in the hands of the English, who are Protestants, I had nothing to fear from the diabolical Inquisitors of Goa. In any case, ten leagues from Calicut I had Mahé, which is a French trading post, and on which I could rely.

"What struck me immediately was the length of the ears I encountered. I had thought until then that I had ears of a rather fine dimension, and I owed that ornament to the liberality with which my father and mother had always put into pulling them in my youth, but I perceived that my own ears had not acquired a quarter of the volume that human ears can attain. That comes from the fact that the ears of children in Calicut are pierced as soon as they come into the world, and from that moment on the ingenious parents put a rolled and dried palm leaf into that opening, which tends incessantly to unroll and dilate the hole excessively, with the result that there are some such ears through which one can pass a fist. You can understand how proud the individuals who possess that kind of beauty are; they are the dandies of the region.

"My first concern, on setting foot on land, had been to obtain a Nair—which is to say, a kind of Janissary—in order to visit the city and its surroundings and to guide me in the locations and the purchases that I had to make.

We therefore headed toward Calicut, but we were caught on the way by such a hurricane that I was force to take refuge in a Malabar pagoda. It was the same one that Vasco da Gama had visited four hundred years before. As the interior of the temple was garnished with images, Vasco and his companions had mistaken the pagoda for a Christian church, and as men clad in calico, thus resembling priests in non-ceremonial garb, poured water and ashes over their heads, that confirmed them further in their belief.

"However, one of de Gama's companions, anxious at seeing all those idols with strange faces, and not wanting to compromise his salvation, accompanied his prayer with the restriction: 'Whether or not I am in the Devil's house, it is to God that my prayer is addressed.'

"As I am something of a pagan, however, I did not pray either to God or the Devil. I waited for the rain to stop, and that is all.

"I had always heard mention of a commercial detail customary in Calicut and which, at the moment of establishing some kind of shop there, could not fail to preoccupy me. A creditor who encounters his debtor, I had been told, had only to trace a circle around him that the latter, I was assured, could not emerge from it on pain of death before the debt for which he had been imprisoned had been paid. There was more. Once, according to what I had always been assured, the King himself had encountered a merchant whom he had been putting off from day to day for three months; the latter drew a line around the King's horse, and the monarch remained as motionless as an equestrian statue until the sum required to liquidate his debt ad been brought from the palace.

"The adventure was true but it had taken place in remote times, and the law just cited had almost fallen into disuse.

"A law that still subsisted, however, although the English had declared that Hindu women were no longer forced to submit to it, was the one ordering wives to burn themselves on the bodies of their husbands. Now, as I was destined to witness the various firms of auto-da-fé that were carried out on that occidental coast of India, I was no sooner established in Calicut than it was announced that a Brahmin had just died and that his wife had decided to burn herself on his tomb. I arrived, therefore, just in time to witness a suttee.

"It was a rather curious spectacle for a European, which that European could hardly miss, especially when he was endowed with a wife who, instead of burning herself on his tomb, would certainly have lit a fire of joy on the day of her husband's death.

"I therefore retained my Nair definitively for a month. He was an intelligent fellow, who struck a bargain with me for half a faron per day, which is five or six sous, and who took charge of reserving me a place for the spectacle.

"The day of the spectacle fell on the following Sunday, and the ceremony took place in a plain a quarter of a league from the city. The pyre, composed of the most combustible materials and the most flammable wood, was, I dare not say built, but established in a ditch, with the result that the hearth presented a hole like that of a crater.

"The cadaver of the husband was laid on the pyre, embalmed in a fashion to await the wife without deteriorating too much in the meantime.

"At the appointed hour—which is to say, about six o'clock in the morning—the Brahmin's widow, barefoot and bare headed, her body covered in a long white robe, emerged from the conjugal dwelling to the sound of flutes, drums and tomtoms and was escorted in great pomp to her husband's pyre.[37] Once outside the city, she sound an English official on the road and a dozen men placed there by the governor of Calicut.

"The officer approached her and said to her in the Hindustani language, which I understood perfectly: 'Is it voluntarily that you're dying?'

"'Yes,' she relied, 'it's voluntarily.'

"'In case your relatives are forcing you to do it, I'm here to bring you help; ask for my support and in the name of my government, I'll take you away with me.'

"'No one is forcing me, I'm burning myself of my own free will, so let me pass.'

"As I've said, I was close enough to those who were speaking to hear the dialogue, and I confess that I was struck by admiration at the sight of such resolution. It's true that the widow was speaking to a Christian, before whom she was glad to parade her religion, and that all the diabolical Brahmins were deafening her by chanting their litanies in her ears.

"So she continued firmly on her way to the pyre. Having arrived at the edge of the ditch, which was beginning to blaze, she was surrounded by the Brahmins, who made her drink a liquid that seemed to give her strength. My Nair told me that the man who was making her drink that liquid, and who was pushing her most vigorously, was her uncle.

"At any rate, the Brahmins stood aside and the poor woman, after having said her farewells to the audience

---

[37] The following description of the poor widow's fate is expanded from an account by Auguste Wahlen of a "suttie" that took place near Bombay in 1822, contained in his *Moeurs, usages et costumes de tous les peuples du monde* [Mores, Usages and Customs of All the Peoples of the World] (1845).

and distributing her jewelry among her friends, took four steps back in order to get a run-up, and, in the midst of the priests' cries of encouragement and to the sound of the infernal music, she launched herself into the furnace.

"Scarcely was she there, however, than she found the atmosphere a trifle warm, it seems, and, in spite of the opium she had drunk, in spite of the chanting of the protests and in spite of the musicians' tomtoms, she uttered loud screams and emerged from the fire more rapidly than she had gone into it.

"It was then that I admired the foresight of the good Inquisitors of Goa, who set up a stake in the middle of the pyre and sealed an iron ring to that stake in order to retain the condemned.

"Furthermore, at the sight of that widow who was thus failing in all her duties, it is necessary to render justice to the audience; everyone uttered cries of indignation and raced to intercept the fugitive in order to push her back into the flames.

"In particular, I had before me an adorable little Calicutian girl of ten or twelve, who was furious, and who declared that when it was her turn to burn herself, she would not behave in such a fashion; so she cried out with all her might: 'Into the fire with the renegade! The fire! The fire! The fire!'

"As everyone was uttering the same cry except me, the English officer and his twelve men, who were doing everything they could to reach the victim, but who, as you can imagine, were easily repelled by that furious population, the 'renegade,' as my pretty little Calicutian girl called her, was caught, lifted up, brought back to the ditch and hurled into the midst of the flames. Then, immediately, everything that could be found of faggots, logs, bundles of twigs and dry leaves was thrown on top of her—which did not prevent her from casting aside all that flaming scaffolding and emerging from the furnace for a second time, and going with the strength of despair, a living conflagration, parting the crowd, to plunge herself into a little stream that was flowing fifty paces from the pyre.

"You can imagine the scandal. Nothing like it had ever been seen—so, at least, the witnesses said. My little Calicutian girl, especially, could not get over her astonishment that a wife could forget her duty to her husband to that extent, to the point that she could only proffer the words: 'Oh, me…! Oh, me…! If it were me…!'

"So she ran with everyone else to the stream in which the half-burned culpable wife had taken refuge. I followed her, for I already felt a profound admiration for her.

"As we arrived at the edge of the stream, the poor creature shouted: 'Help me, Englishmen! Help me!'

"Then, as the Englishmen, pushed back on every side, could not help her, she perceived her uncle, the same one who had urged her to burn herself. 'Uncle!' she cried. 'Help' Have pity on me! I'll quit my family, I'll live like an accursed, I'll beg!'

'Well, so be it,' aid the uncle, slyly. 'Let me wrap her in this damp cloth and I'll take her back to the hut.' And so saying, the uncle winked, as if to say to the Brahmins: *Let me do it; once she's in the sheet, her affair will be settled.*

"Doubtless she had seen the wink too, and understood it, for instead of trusting her uncle she shouted: 'No, no! I don't want to! Go away! I'll go on my own" Leave me alone! Leave me alone!'

"But the uncle did not want to be belied; he had doubtless answered for his niece and he was determined that she would keep her word. He therefore swore to his niece, on the waters of the Ganges, that he would take her back to the house.

"That oath is so sacred that the poor woman believed it. She lay down on the damp sheet, in which her uncle rolled her up like a mummy. Then, when her arms and legs were trapped, he loaded her on to his shoulder and shouted: 'To the pyre! To the pyre!'

"Indeed, her started running toward the ditch, followed by the entire population, who were shouting; 'To the pyre! To the pyre!'

My little Calicutian girl was at the peak of admiration. When the Brahmin had pronounced the sacred oath she had scourged him momentarily with the name of pariah, but when she saw that the oath had no other purpose than to deceive his niece and that he was breaking his oath, she clapped her hands and shouted: 'Oh, the honest man! The worthy man! The saintly man!'

"I didn't understand very clearly how a saintly, worthy and honest man could break his oath, but the little Hindu girl said it with such conviction, and there was so much grace and naivety in her entire person that I ended up agreeing, in spite of myself, with the aid of masculine pride, that a poor widow was decidedly very guilty to hesitate thus over burning herself on her husband's body. So I joined my acclamations with the general acclamations of the crowd when I saw that honest uncle, that worthy uncle, hurl his wretched niece back into the furnace, this time so well wrapped up that, no matter what efforts she made, the flames had reckoned with her in five or six minutes.

"My little Calicutian girl was greatly enthused. That conjugal devotion, preexistent in the heart of a young girl, touched me to the extent that I asked her who she was and what she was called.

"She told me that she was called Amarou, which is a very pretty name, as you can see, and that her father belonged to the caste of Vaishyas, which is to say, that of directors of agriculture and commerce. Amarou's father was therefore in the third class, only having above him the class of Rajahs and that of Brahmins, and below him that of Sudras. The position that he occupied in Calicut corresponded to that of harbor master. He was a man who might be very useful to me, and as my Nair knew him it was agreed that he would introduce me to him the following day."

XVI. The Brahmin's Slippers

"The result of my visit to the father of the beautiful Amarou was that I decided to establish myself in Calicut and found a commerce in spices there.

"My first concern was to buy a house. Houses are even cheaper in Calicut than in Goa. It's true that the most solid house in Calicut is made of dried earth and is only eight feet tall. So, for twelve écus I found myself the proprietor of a house that was ceded to me by the seller with three snakes attached to the property.

"I told him that I didn't much care for snakes and that my first care would be to wring their necks, but he advised me to refrain from such an imprudence, In Calicut, snakes fulfill the function that cats fulfill in Europe, in killing rats and mice, with which the houses are infested.

"I asked that reptiles I had just acquired be introduced to me, so that I could make their acquaintance. In fact, that was important for me and in order that we should understand one another, so that I would not be an intruder in the house. My vendor whistled, and they came like dogs.

"After two or three days, thanks to a few bowls of milk of which I had generously made them a gift, we were the best of friends. However, I confess that the first few times time I found one or other of them in my bed on lying down or waking up, that familiarity inspired a certain repugnance in me. I gradually got used to it, though, and soon did not give it another thought.

"The commerce to which I devoted myself particularly was that of cardamom, a kind of pepper, which is only found here in the shops of apothecaries, but of which all the islanders of the Indies could not be fonder. During my sojourn in Ceylon I had learned the value of that foodstuff, and I decided to make it my principal branch of speculation.

"I had arrived in the rainy season, which is a good time for preparing ground where cardamom is to be planted. The preparation is, in any case, easy; during the winter, a veritable forest of grasses grows in the vicinity of Calicut, which serves to fertilize the ground in which one can plant or sow; one sows or plants, and four months later, one harvests.

"I therefore consolidated a large quantity of land in the vicinity of Calicut and I began my clearance, not, as one does in that regions by bringing in twenty Sudras who, distant from their master's eye, do their best to cheat him in the employment of their day, but by supervising everything personally. In order that the surveillance in question should be more active, I began by building four cabins in the four corners of my plantation, which was easy for me and not expensive, given that I had a large quantity of coconut palms of my land, and, as everyone knows, that tree is a gift of Heaven for those climes, since one can built houses with its wood, cover them with its leaves, weave mats with its bark, nourish oneself on its pith, make wine with its buds, make oil with its nuts and sugar with its sap.

"Now from that wine, by passing it through a still, I composed a kind of eau-de-vie with whose aid I could do whatever I wanted with my Sudras.

"Thus, my harvest felt the effects of my distributions of *tari*. Nothing similar to my ten or twelve arpents of cardamom had ever been seen in Calicut. Not only was my crop abundant but of the finest quality, and I resolved, when I saw the result, to devote five or six years to that exploitation, at the end of which, my fortune would be made, especially if I went myself to sell what I had harvested in Ceylon. For that, it was purely and simply a matter of chartering a small boat, and of going to Ceylon at the end of summer, when I would have a sufficient cargo. Now, two crops ought to be sufficient for me to load a boat, and one obtains two crops a year in Calicut.

"In the meantime, I continued to visit my old friend Nachor and my young friend the beautiful Amarou. I had not forgotten that the father could be very useful to me with regard to patents, customs rights etc., and, I confess, the great devotion to her conjugal duties that the daughter had exhibited on the famous day of the suttee had touched my heart profoundly.

"Now, Papa Nachor was not a simpleton; he had seen me paying cash for everything I bought or hired. He had no doubt, given the way I undertook my exploitation, that I was in the process of making my fortune—with the result that he received me as a man who desires that the man he is receiving should find the house pleasant, in order that he might come back as often as possible.

"I went back so often and so well that, after six or eight months, save for the consent of the beautiful Amarou, which I had believed that I had read more than once in her eyes, everything was almost decided between Père Nachor and me.

An event that might have had the most deplorable consequences led, on the contrary, to a more rapid conclusion of the matter than perhaps any of us desired, but which the modesty of the beautiful Amarou prevented from leaving transparent. One day when I had invited the father and daughter to visit my plantations and, expecting to spent the entire day on the plain, had gallantly organized four snacks in my cabins, the beautiful Amarou, who was directly following the slave who was beating the two sides of the path with a stick in order to drive away venomous reptiles, uttered a loud scream. A little green viper of the most terrible species, whose bite in always mortal, had launched itself out of a clump of grass and had attached itself to the end of her scarf.

"I had seen the viper strike, I had heard the scream, and with a blow of the staff that I had in my hand I had struck it so fortunately that I had made it let go; then, as I was wearing boots, I had crushed its head with a thrust of my heel.

"But the beautiful Amarou was in no better state for having avoided the danger, Instead of dying of the venom, she seemed ready to die of fright. Falling back over one of my arms like a beautiful water lily, she was as pale and quivering. I lifted her up and, holding her to my breast, I carried her to the cabin where lunch was waiting for us. In any case, the charming child, who was scarcely twelve years old, weighed no more in my arms than a dream or a vapor; only her heart, beating against mine, testified to her reality.

"Once inside in the cabin and once a thorough search had been made the beautiful Amarou began to be somewhat reassured, and consented to eat a few grains of rice, but when it was necessary to set forth again, the same fear took possession of her, and she declared that she had decided not to walk on foot any more.

"Nothing could have been more agreeable to me than such a declaration. I offered her the same mode of transport that had brought her to where she was. She looked at her father, who gave her a sign that she could accept. I took Amarou in my arms again, and we resumed our course.

"This time, as she feared weighing too heavily, she had put an arm around my neck, which brought her face close to mine, her hair close to mine and her breath close to mine, all things that, it appeared, were not sorry to be in close proximity, given that they mingled gradually, and the more they mingled, the closer they came. At the first cabin I hoped to be loved; at the second I was sure of being; at the third, Amarou made me the confession of her love; at the fourth, our marriage was agreed, and it only remained to fix the date.

"It was Nachor who fixed that date.

"Nachor was a prudent man; he had seen the crop under foot, but he wanted to see it in storage. He therefore fixed the ceremony for the month of July.

"That epoch suited me well enough; it was the one in which I counted on expediting my little boat—or, rather, of steering it myself—to Ceylon, and I was not sorry to leave behind me someone who would watch over the laboring and the planting of my field. Given the fear that she had of green vipers, Amarou was incapable of fulfilling the function of inspector, but Nachor had proved that he knew it, and when he had the interests of his only daughter to look after, there was no doubt that those interests, which would naturally be mine, would be attended to perfectly.

"Now, it was the end of May; I was not, therefore, condemned to a long wait.

"Nachor and Amarou followed the Hindu religion. It was agreed that we would marry in accordance with the Brahmin rite. In consequence, everything being settled between us, I went in search of a Brahmin to request Nachor on my behalf for Amarou's hand. That is the custom and I did not see any inconvenient in conforming to it.

"I did not have any acquaintances among the Brahmins. Amarou indicated to me the great rogue who had rolled his niece in a sheet after having made a false oath on the waters of the Ganges and had thrown her into the furnace in spite of her screams and supplications. I had nothing against him except deeming him a rather bad relative, but as the mission that he had to fulfill on my behalf with respect to Nachor did not make him my uncle, that did not matter to me.

"On the agreed day, therefore, he left my house to go to Amarou's, and came back twice, at different intervals, under the pretext that he had always found evil omens on his route. The third time, however, the evil omens had disappeared in order to give way, on the contrary, to the most fortunate auspices, It was no longer a matter of anything but choosing a day agreeable to Brahma, when he came back to tell me that Amarou's hand had been granted to me.

"I replied that all days were good for me, and that, in consequence, Brahma's day would be mine. The Brahmin chose the Friday.

I had a momentary desire to quibble; you know that we have prejudices against Friday, but I had boasted that all days were good for me and I did not want to take it back, so I replied: "Go for Friday, as long as it's next Friday."

That blessed Friday arrived; the ceremony was held in Nachor's house. At about five o'clock in the evening I went there. We presented one another reciprocally with betel. We lit the Homan fire with ravasitou wood.[38] The great vagabond of a Brahmin, still the uncle of the burned woman, took three handfuls of rice and threw them over Amarou's head. He took three others that he threw over mine, after which Nachor poured water into a large wooden bowl, washed my feet, and then extended his hand to his daughter. Amarou put her hand in her father's. Nachor dripped a few drops of water on it, deposited three or four coins in it, and presented Amarou to me, saying: 'I have nothing more to do with you. I hand you over to the power of another.'

"Then the Brahmin took out the veritable marriage bond—which is to say, the *tali*, an kind of ribbon from which a golden head is suspended—out of a bag. He showed it to the company, and then handed it to me so that I could attach it to my wife's neck.

"When the ribbon was knotted, we were married.

"But the custom is that the festivities last five days, during which the husband has no right over his wife. So, during the first four days, I was so well kept in sight by young men and women that I was scarcely able to kiss the beautiful Amarou's little finger. I tried to express to her by my gaze how long the time seemed to me; she, for her part, made eyes that seemed to say: *it's true that it isn't short, but patience, patience!*

"And on the basis of that promise, I was patient.

---

[38] References to "feu Homan" lit with "bois ravasitou" (which the original of the present text misrenders as *ravistou*) in connection with Brahmin religion can be found in a number of early-nineteenth-century French works of proto-anthropology, having been widely popularized by a supposedly educational survey of *La botanique historique et littéraire* [Historical and Literary Botany] (1810) by the Comtesse de Genlis.

"Finally, the fifth day dawned, elapsed and ended. Night came and we were escorted to my house. In the first room a meal had been prepared. I did the honors of it to my friends while my wife was undressed and put to bed. Then, after a moment, when I thought that no one was paying attention to me, I slipped toward the bedroom door, gladly abandoning the rest of the house to my guests, provided that they abandoned to me the small room where the beautiful Amarou was waiting for me

"At the door, however, I was astonished to stumble over something. I put my hand to the objet that had tripped me up and found a pair of slippers.

"A pair of slippers at Amarou's door! What did it mean?

"That preoccupied me momentarily, but I soon threw the slippers aside and tried to open the door.

"The door was locked.

"I called out in my softest voice: 'Amarou, Amarou, Amarou,' still thinking that she would come to open it, but although I could hear very well that there was someone in the room, and two people rather than one, no one answered me.

"You will understand my anger; if it had not been for those diabolical slippers, I would still have been able to doubt, but as I was in no doubt, I was about to start shouting at the top of my voice when I felt someone grab my arm.

I turned round and recognized Nachor.

"'Damn it,' I said, 'you've arrived at a good time. You can help me render justice to your slut of a daughter.'

"'What do you mean?' said Nachor.

"'I mean that she's locked in with a man, neither more nor less.'

"'With a man?' exclaimed Nachor. 'In that case I disown her as my daughter, and if it's true, you can put her in prison or even kill her, that's your right.'

"'Ah! So much the better! I'm glad that's my right and I'll take advantage of it, I can guarantee that.'

"'But what makes you think that?'

"'The noise I can hear in the room of course, and these slippers.' And I pushed the proof of conviction into Nachor's leg with my foot.

Nachor picked one slipper, and then the other, and looked at the attentively. He cried: 'Oh, blessed Olifus! Oh, fortunate husband! What a privileged family ours is! My son-in-law, thank Vishnu and his wife Lakshmi, thank Siva and his wife Parvati, thank Brahma and his wife Saraswati; thank Indra and his wife Shachi, thank the tree Kalpa, the cow Kamadhenu and the bird Garuda. A holy man is deigning to do for you what he would ordinarily only do for the king of the country; he is sparing you the trouble that you are going to take, and in nine months, if the eight gods of India do not turn their gaze away from us and your wife, we shall have a Brahmin in our family.'

"'Pardon me!' I cried. 'I have no wish to have a Brahmin in my family. I'm no idler, and the trouble that our holy man is taking, I can take perfectly well myself. I'm not the king of a country and, in consequence, I don't regard it as an honor that a priest locks himself up with my wife on our wedding night. I won't thank either the bird Garuda or the cow Kamadhenu, nor the tree Kalpa, nor Indra, Brahma, Siva or Vishnu, and I'm going break the back of your vagabond of a Brahmin, who burned his niece after swearing by the waters of the Ganges that he was going to take her back to the house.'

"And so saying, I leapt on a bamboo, determined to put my threat into execution. But at the cries of Nachor, the whole wedding party came running, on seeing which I threw away my bamboo and leapt into a cabinet, the door of which I closed behind me.

"There, I could give free rein to my anger. I threw myself down on the floor, covered with mats and rolled around, swearing and blaspheming in a fine manner. While rolling, swearing and blaspheming I found myself between arms that hugged me, and against a mouth that kissed me.

"That didn't astonish me overmuch. Among my slaves of the fourth class—which is to say, the class of Sudras—there was a pretty girl of fourteen or fifteen that I had sometimes found in my bed, like my serpentine rat-catchers, and who I encountered, I must say, with much more pleasure.

"That fidelity to my misfortune, on the very evening when I had completely forgotten the poor girl, touched me. 'Oh, my poor Holaoheni,' I said to her, 'I believe that there's a veritable curse upon me and my wives. So I swear henceforth not to marry again, and, when I have a beautiful mistress like you, to limit myself to her. So, here." And I returned the kiss that she had given me.

"'Ah!' she said, after five minutes.

"'What!' I cried. 'That's not Holaoheni! Who is it, then? Oh my God, my God, can it be, again…?'

"And that familiar sweat, which I had already observed in three similar circumstances, passed over my brow.

"'Well, yes, ingrate, it's me again; it's always me. It's me, who never wearies of being rejected, insulted, deceived, and who comes back every time I have good news to tell you.'

"'Good!' I said, riding myself of that conjugal embrace. 'Known, the good news! You've come to announce to me that I'm the father of a third son, haven't you?'

"'Whom I've called Philippe, in memory of the day when I came to tell you that your third wife was deceiving you. Alas, today I had no need to inform you, you've already perceived it yourself, my poor friend!''

"'Well, I cried, impatiently, that's fine, but now I've got three sons on my hands, and it seems to me that's quite enough.'

"'Yes,' said La Buchold, 'and you'd like a daughter. 'Well, today's the twentieth of July, Saint Marguerite's Day; hope that by the recommendation of that good saint, your wish will be granted.'

"I uttered a sigh.

'Now, my love,' she continued, that when one has a family like mine, one can't be absent from the house for long; and if I didn't have the very honorable Sire Van Tigel, senator of Amsterdam, who has promised to love and protect our poor Philippe as if he were his own son, and who is looking after him and his brothers in my absence, I wouldn't have been able to pay you this little visit.'

"'So you're going,' I said.

"'Yes, but before I go, let me give you some advice.'

"'Go on.'

"'You're bearing a grudge against that poor Brahmin, who, believing that he's doing you a service...'

"'Yes indeed.'

"'Avenge yourself on him, that's only just—but avenge yourself adroitly, as one avenges oneself in this land; avenge yourself without risk. You owe it to your wife and children.'

"'I don't say no,' I said. 'The advice is good. But how can I avenge myself?'

"'Oh, my God! You know what the Gospel says: *Seek and ye shall find.* Seek and ye shall find. You have a boat ready laden, a good cargo, which is worth two or three thousand rupees in this country, double that that in Ceylon and triple in Java. Go to Trincomalee or Batavia, and I promise you a guaranteed sale. Adieu, my love, or rather *au revoir*; for you'll force me, I'm afraid, to make another one or two voyages to the Indian Sea. Fortunately, I'm like Mohammed, and when the mountain doesn't come to me, I go to the mountain. By the way, don't forget to light a candle to Saint Marguerite at the first opportunity.'

"'Yes,' I said, distractedly. 'Don't worry…I'll try to conserve myself for you and for our children…and if I encounter a chapel to Saint Marguerite on my route...ah! I've found it!'

"I expected La Buchold to ask me what I'd just found, but she had already gone.

"What I had found was a vengeance.

"I summoned one of my slaves, who was renowned for his manner of charming snakes, and promised him ten farons if he brought me a green viper before dawn. Half an hour later, he brought me the requested reptile in a box. It was the best there was of the species, a veritable emerald necklace. I gave him twelve farons instead of ten, and he went away recommending me to the eight great gods of India.

"As for me, I began by gathering on my person all the money, jewels and pearls I had. I went on tiptoe to my wife's bedroom, and opened the box that contained my viper directly above the Brahmin's slipper. The animal, finding a niche that seemed made for it, coiled up tranquilly within it, and I went to join my little boat, which was bobbing in the harbor with its cargo of cardamom.

"It's true that I was abandoning a house that was worth twelve écus and furniture worth eight, but in truth, on great occasions it's necessary to know how to support a small loss.

"My crew, who had been warned that they might receive the order to set sail at any moment, was quite ready. We only had to raise anchor, therefore, and hoist the sail, which we did without drums or trumpets.

"When dawn broke we were already more than ten leagues from the coast.

"I never heard any mention of my great vagabond of a Brahmin, but it's probable that he's now cured forever, and for another twenty years, of the mania of leaving his slippers at the door when he goes in somewhere.

"My word!" said Père Olifus, looking at the cadaver of his second bottle, "I believe that the rum has let us down, and it's time to go on to the arrack."

XVII. The Fifth and Final Marriage of Père Olifus

As you will understand, the narrator had not watered the narration of his first four marriages with a bottle of eau-de-vie and a bottle of rum without the memory of the past, mingled with present libations, casting some emotion over his story. So Biard and I were convinced that if he had yet to recount a sixth or seventh marriage, we would be obliged either to appoint ourselves guardians of the bottle of arrack or to postpone until the next day the conjugal odyssey of the Ulysses of Monnikendam.

Fortunately, he reassured us himself, in passing, after having drunk a mouthful of arrack, wiping his lips with the back of his hand, saying to us in the tone of a man making an announcement: "The fifth and final marriage of Père Olifus!"

Then he continued, in is ordinary voice:

"So, I had departed with my little boat, no bigger than a fishing-smack, with a crew of six, in the hands of the good God, determined that we would double Cape Comorin and, if the wind was good and the sea calm, leave Ceylon behind and go to Sumatra or Java—I didn't care which of those islands, since the further I went toward the Pacific Ocean, the more certain I was of selling my cardamom.

"On the seventh day after our departure we sighted Ceylon; with the aid of my telescope I could even make out the houses of Port de Galles—but bah! The wind was fresh, and we still had nearly a month of good weather. I turned my head away from that devil of an island that was attracting us and set a course for Achem, launching my nutshell across the Indian Ocean with as much philosophy as if it were the finest three-master in Rotterdam.

"All went well for the first five days, and even afterwards, as you'll see; but toward the second watch of the sixth night, a small accident nearly sent us all to fish for pearls on the bed of the Bay of Bengal.

"During the previous nights, it had been me who held the tiller, and everything had gone marvelously, but we were a long way from land; not a rock or a sandbank was signaled on our route; thanks to our short mast and the scant sail our vessel was carrying, we ought to be able, especially by night, to escape the eye of pirates, piercing as it might be. I put the most skilful of my men at the tiller and went below deck, lay down on my bales and went to sleep.

"I don't know how long I had been asleep when I was suddenly woken up by a loud noise that came from above my head. My men ran from the poop to the prow; they were shouting—or, rather, howling—and in those howls I distinguished both prayer and oaths. What I saw most clearly in all that was that we were in some kind of danger, and that the danger was great. The greater the danger was, the more it demanded my presence, so, without asking what it might be I ran to the hatch and launched myself on to the deck.

"The sea was magnificent, the sky starry, except for one point, where an enormous mass, almost suspended about our heads, and ready to fall upon the boat, interrupted the light of the stars by virtue of its opacity. The eyes of all my men were fixed on that mass, all their efforts had the goal of avoiding it.

"But what was that mass?

"A scholar might have set about trying to solve the problem and would have been swallowed up before having found it. I didn't have that pretention.

"I leapt to the tiller and put the bar full to port. Then as there passed doubtless sent by a good God, a nice little gust of north-north-westerly wind, I received it in my foresail and aft sail at the same time, which caused our vessel to leap like a frightened ram—with the result that when the mass fell, instead of falling directly on top of us, as it threatened to do, it shaved our poop and it was us, in our turn, who found ourselves on the mountain instead of being in the valley.

What had nearly crushed us was an enormous Chinese junk, with its belly bulging like that of a calabash, which had come upon us without warning.

"I had learned a few words of Chinese, as many in Ceylon as in Goa; perhaps they weren't polite, but they were certainly among the most energetic. I picked up my loud-hailer and sent them like a volley at the subjects of the sublime emperor.

"To our great astonishment, however, no one responded.

"It was then that we perceived that the junk was floating inert, as there was no one on deck to steer it. No light was showing either in the portholes or the binnacle; one might have thought it a dead fish, the cadaver of Leviathan. Not to mention that not a single sail was hoisted.

"The thing was sufficiently extraordinary to merit our attention. We knew that the Chinese were reputed to be very indolent, but no matter how indolent they were, it surely wasn't their habit to go to the devil so tranquilly. I understood that something unusual had happened to the vessel or the crew, and as we had no more than an hour and a half or two hours o wait until daylight, I maneuvered in such a way as to sail in convoy with the junk, which wasn't difficult, as it was rolling like a bale and there were no precautions to take, except not to collide with it. A simple sail that we conserved was sufficient to preserve us from that accident.

"Gradually, daylight arrived; as the obscurity was dissipated, our eyes tried to recognize some movement on the immense machine, but not a single man budged. Either the junk was empty, or its crew was asleep.

"I approached as close as I could. I pronounced all the Chinese words I knew. One of my men, who had been in Macao for ten years, spoke, called and shouted in his turn; there was no response. Then we resolved to circle around the junk to see if the same silence prevailed to starboard as to port.

"There was the same silence—except that, to starboard, a climbing-rope was hanging down. I maneuvered in order to get as close as possible to the enormous hull; I succeeded in grabbing hold of the rope and in five minutes I was on the deck.

"It was evident that something had happened that was not pleasant for the inhabitants of the junk; broken furniture and scraps of cloths lay around, with bloodstains here and there; everything indicated a fight, and a fight of which the Chinese had got the worst.

"While I was scanning the deck, it seemed to me that I heard stifled plaints coming from the interior. I tried to go down below decks, but the hatches were sealed.

"I looked around and saw a kind of crowbar at the foot of the capstan that seemed marvelously suited to my purpose. In fact, by weighing upon it, I forced the trap of one of the hatches, and daylight penetrated into the space below.

"As the daylight penetrated, more distinct plaints reached me. I went down with a certain hesitation, I confess, but half way down the ladder I was reassured.

"On the lower deck, arranged like mummies and tied up like sausages, were some twenty Chinese, gnawing at their gags and grimacing to various degrees, according to whether nature had given them with a more or less patient temperament.

"I went to the one who seemed to me to be the most important. He was bound with thicker cords and was chewing a larger gag: honors worthy of a lord.

"I untied him and removed his gag as best I could. He was the owner of the junk, Captain Ising-Fong. He began by addressing his sincere thanks to me, at least as far as I could comprehend, and then urged me to help to untie and take the gags off his companions.

"In less than ten minutes the operation was terminated.

"As each man was liberated he ran into the hold, where he disappeared. I was curious to see what they were going to do in such a hurry in the bottom of the ship, and I saw that the unfortunates had staved in a barrel of water and were drinking from it.

"They had not eaten or drunk anything for three days, but as they had suffered even more from thirst than from hunger, it was the thirst that they were concerned to slake first. Two of them drank so much that they died of it; a third ate so much that his stomach burst.

"The story of the unfortunate junk, which had seemed so incomprehensible at first, was, however, quite natural. Boarded at night by Malabar pirates, the crew had been captured after a brief resistance; it was that resistance of which we had seen traces on deck. Then, in order not to be disturbed in their commercial visit, the pirates had bound and gagged the crew and lain them down, the captain at the head, below decks—after which, they had loaded up everything that it had been their pleasure to take, spoiling or drowning a fraction of what they had been unable to carry away. Then, doubtless in the hope of making a second trip to the junk, they had taken down all the sails that might have enabled it to make headway, and had left it becalmed. It was in that state that it had nearly fallen on our heads

"You will understand the joy of the captain and his crew on being freed by us, or rather by me, from their disagreeable situation, after three days of anguish. A rope-ladder was lowered to my men, four of whom came up on deck, while the other two moored the smack to the poop of the junk, where it seemed no bigger than a launch in tow to an ordinary brig.

"When the smack was moored, the last two men of my crew came to join us. It was a matter of helping the Chinese crew to get under way again. The subjects of the sublime emperor are neither the bravest not the most skilful mariners on earth, with the result that they uttered loud cries and waved their arms, but would have made no progress if we had not done their work.

"When the work was done, the wounded bandaged, the dead thrown into the sea and the junk under sail, they decided that, the cargo having been taken aboard the pirate ship, it was pointless to continue their route to Madras. In any case, Captain Ising-Fong decided to re-trace his route. He had had been taking a cargo of cardamom to Madras, and I was laden with cardamom myself, but you will understand that the first thing the pirates had visited was Captain Ising-Fong's cash-box. As it was not in a condition to pay me the eight thousand rupees at which he evaluated my cargo, it was agreed that we would sail in convoy to Manila, where Captain Ising-Fong had a correspondent and where, in consequence, thanks to the credit he enjoyed from the Strait of Malacca to the Strait of Korea, we could conclude our bargain.

"As I had no preference for any place in the world, and, especially, nothing in particular against the Philippines, I accepted the proposal, on the sole condition that I would be consulted regarding the maneuver, given that I had no wish to make the acquaintance of the pirates.

"Captain Ising-Fong, whether out of self-respect or mistrust, made a few difficulties at first, but when he had seen that, thanks to my maneuvers, his machine, which had previously been rolling like a barrel, began to cleave through the water like a fish, he folded his hands over his belly, started bobbing his head up and down, pronounced the double syllable *hi-ho* two or three times—which means 'marvelous'—and no longer bothered with anything.

"In consequence, we crossed the strait of Malacca without incident, traversed the archipelago of the Arambas, similarly without incident, and having doubled the little island of Corregidor, placed like a sentry at the entrance to the bay, we went into the Pasig delta and dropped anchor, as night fell, opposite the customs depot."

XVIII. The Bezoar

"Captain Ising-Fong had not made me a vain promise, and on the day of our arrival he took me to his correspondent, a rich cigar manufacturer, who offered either to pay me the eight thousand rupees in cash or to give me merchandise of equal value, at an exchange rate that he alone could furnish, in view of the extent of his commerce and the multiplicity of his business affairs.

"In fact, the Philippines can be regarded as the world's warehouse; there one finds gold and silver from Peru, diamonds from Golconda, topazes, sapphires and cardamom from Ceylon, pepper from Java, cloves and nutmeg from the Moluccas, camphor from Borneo, pearls from Mannar, carpets from Persia, benzoin and ivory from Cambodia, musk from Lequios, fabrics from Bengal and porcelain from China.

"It was up to me to make a choice from all those goods and to select out those that appeared to offer the most reliable and prompt profit.

"In any case, as there was no urgency, given that I had already realized a rather nice profit on my cardamom, I decided to spend a few days in Manila and to study, during my sojourn in the Philippines, which branch of commerce might be the most fruitful for a man who, having commenced with four hundred francs, had thirty thousand livres in cash to invest in commerce.

"My first concern was to visit the two cities: Manila, the Spanish city and Bidondo, the Tagalog city.[39]

---

[39] The following description is paraphrased from the description of Manila and Bidondo contained in Jean-François de La

"The Spanish city is composed of convents, churches, retreats and rectangular stone houses, devoid of any
order, with high thick walls, loopholes pierced at random
and gardens that isolate them from one another, populated by monks, nuns, Spaniards in cloaks having themselves carried around in makeshift palanquins or march-
ing gravely, cigar in mouth, like old Castilians in the
days of Don Quixote de La Mancha. So the city, which
could contain a hundred thousand inhabitants but actually contains eight thousand, is profoundly dreary.

"What I needed was not there, and, after having visited Manila, shaking my head disdainfully, I decided to
make the acquaintance of Bidondo.

"The following day, therefore, having had my
chocolate, I headed for the plebeian city, and as I approached it, the sounds of life reached me that had been
completely absent from the tomb known as Manila. I
breathed more freely, and found the verdure cooler and
the sun more luminous, so I hastened to traverse the for-
tifications and the drawbridges of the military city, and,
like a man emerging from underground, I suddenly
found myself cheerful, joyful and light, on what is
known as the Stone Bridge. There life commenced, or
rather, from there onwards, like was flourishing.

"The bridge was cluttered with Spaniards on palanquins, half-breeds running on foot armed with large par-
asols, creoles followed by their domestics, peasants

Harpe's *Abrégé de l'Histoire générale des voyages* [Abridge-
ment of a General History of Voyages] (1835), which is based
on accounts originally given by the voyager Jules Dumont
d'Urville. All the literary flourishes added by La Harpe are
reproduced and further enhanced by the author of the present
text.

coming from neighboring villages, Chinese merchants and Malay laborers. There was a noise, a racket, a turbulence that was a pleasure to behold for a man who could have believed himself dead after having been buried for two days in Manila.

"Adieu, therefore, to the somber city, adieu to the tedious houses, adieu to the noble lords and bonjour to the joyous suburb, *bonjour* to Bidondo with its hundred and forty thousand inhabitants, *bonjour* to the elegant houses and the busy population; *bonjour* to the quay where the pulleys were grating, where bales were rolling, from the four corners of the world, where Chinese junks were moored with pirogues from New Guinea, Malay proas and European brigs, corvettes and three-masters. There are no categories, exclusions or castes there; a man's worth depends on what is he is, is assessed according to what he has; he is recognizable at first glance by his costume before his accent is recognized.

"Malays, Americans, Chinese, Spaniards, Dutch, Madagascans and Indians are incessantly cutting through the indigenous flood, the ocean of Tagalogs, men and women, that formed the population of the island when the Spaniards conquered it, in which one recognizes the men by their almost-Norman costume, a shirts that hangs like a blouse over cotton trousers, cravat in the Colin style, felt hat with frayed edges. buckled shoes, chaplet worn around the neck and scarf like a plaid; the women by their hair retained by a high Spanish comb, their veil floating behind, the white canezou extended over their bosom leaving naked the portion of the body that extends from the underside of the breast to the navel; by the stockings rolled down to the ankles, the multicolored socks rolled over the stockings, the imperceptible slipper that leave the foot almost naked, by the cigar always suspended from their lips, and which, through the clouds of smoke it spreads, renders their eyes even more ardent.

"Ah! That was what I needed. *Bonsoir* Manila and long live Bidondo! So I only went back to Manila in order to have all my luggage brought to Bidondo.

"The correspondent of my Chinese captain applauded my decision, which, according to him, was that of a man of common sense. He had a house in Bidondo himself, to which he came on Sunday to rest from the tedium of the week. He even offered me a kind of small outbuilding dependent on that house, which overlooked the quay, but I only wanted to accept it as a tenant, and it was agreed that, in exchange for the sum of thirty rupees a year—about eighty francs—I would enjoy and dispose of it, as we say in Europe, with its fixtures and fittings.

"At any rate, after three days of observation, I perceived that the principal industry of the Tagalog is cockfighting. It is impossible to go from one end to the other of the Bidondo quay without bumping into ten, twenty or thirty circles formed around two plumed champions to which are attached the destinies of two, three, four or five Tagalog families; for not only does a Tagalong family that possesses a well-bred cock live on its produce, but also relatives and neighbors who wager on behalf of the cock's owner, living as he does thanks to the cock. The woman has tortoise shell combs, golden chaplets and glass bead necklaces; the man has money in his pocket and a cigar in his mouth.

Thus, the cock is the spoiled child of the household; a Tagalong mother does not take care of her children but her cock; she polishes its plumage, sharpens its spurs. As for the husband, in his absence he does not confide it to anyone, even his wife; if he goes out he carries it under his arm, goes with it to attend to his affairs and visit his friends; if he encounters and adversary on is route, challenges are exchanged and bets laid; the owners crouch down facing one another, pushing their cocks to the combat, and a circle is formed, in the middle of which the two most ferocious human passions, gambling and fighting, contend.

"Oh, believe me, it's a fine life, life in Bidondo.

"Another kind of industry exists among the Tagalogs that bears some resemblance to the search for the philosopher's stone, which is that of bezoar-seekers. Now, as nature has made the Philippines the warehouse of all the poisons in the world, it has also placed in the Philippines the bezoar, which is the universal antidote."

"Pardon me!" I said interrupting Père Olifus. "Since you have pronounced the word bezoar, I wouldn't be sorry to know something about it. I've heard a great deal of talk of the bezoar, especially in the *Mille et une nuits*; I've seen the rarest stones, I've seen a balas-ruby, I've seen a raw garnet, I've seen a carbuncle, and I've searched hard and I've never seen a bezoar, and no one has ever been able to show me the slightest particle of it."

"Well, Monsieur," Père Olifus replied, "I've seen one, I've touched one, I've even swallowed one—without which, as you'll see, I wouldn't have the honor of drinking a glass of arrack to your health at this moment."

And Père Olifus did indeed pour himself a glass of arrack, which he drank in a single draught to Biard's health and mine.

"Ah!" he went on. "So, we were saying that not only does the bezoar exist, but there are three kinds of bezoar: the bezoar that is found in the intestines of cows, the bezoar that is found in the intestines of goats and the bezoar that is found in the intestines of apes.[40]

"The bezoar that is found in the belly of a cow is the least precious. Twenty grains of that bezoar isn't equivalent to seven grains that found in the belly of a goat, just as seven grains of the bezoar found in the belly of a goat isn't equivalent to a single grain of one found in the belly of an ape.

"It's especially in the kingdom of Golconda that one encounters the goats that produce bezoars. Are they a particular species? No, for among two kids from the same mother, one produces bezoars and the other doesn't. The herdsmen only have to touch the belly in a certain fashion to know the situation with regard to that kind of fecundity on the part of their goats; through the skin they can count in the intestines the number of stones they contain, and learn, without ever being mistaken, the value of those stones. One can therefore purchase bezoar on the hoof.

"However, a businessman from Goa had carried out a curious experiment during the time when I was living on the Malabar coast. He bought four goats carrying bezoars in the mountains of Golconda; he transported then five hundred miles from the place of their birth, opened two of them immediately, and found the bezoars still in

---

[40] The differentiation between the kinds of *bézoard* [bezoar] produced by various animal species is found in more than one French reference book of the eighteenth century, but the present author probably adapted the passage alleging that the one produced by apes is the most precious from the thirtieth volume that was added posthumously to the Comte du Buffon's enormous *Histoire naturelle*, where it is credited to Jean-Baptiste Tavernier's 1678 account of his *Voyages*.

the body but diminished in volume. He killed one ten days afterwards. When the animal was autopsied, it was recognized that it had been carrying bezoar, but that the bezoar had disappeared. Finally, he killed the fourth at the end of a month, and that one had no trace of the precious stone, which had vanished completely—which proves that in the mountains of Golconda there is a particular tree, or a special herb, to which cows and goats owe the formation of the bezoar.

"So, were saying that one of the industries of the Tagalogs is hunting the monkeys that carry bezoar, as precious relative and compared to the other bezoars as diamond is to rhinestone, paste or rock-crystal. A single ape bezoar is worth a thousand two thousand or three thousand livres, given that a pinch of grated bezoar mixed in a glass of water can serve as an antidote to all the most terrible poisons of the Philippines, and even the Javanese Upas.

"Now, it is incredible how much use of that poison there is from Luzon to Mindanao, especially in times of cholera, since, the symptoms being similar, people generally take advantage of epidemics, husbands to get rid of their wives, wives to get rid of their husbands, nephews their unless, debtors their creditors, etc., etc., etc.

"But the race that abounds in Bidondo is the Chinese. They possess the finest quarter, on the banks of the Pasig; their houses are constructed half in stone and half in bamboo; they're beautiful, well-ventilated, sometimes ornamented with paintings on the exterior, with stores and shops on the ground floor—and what stores! what shops! You see, it makes the mouth water just to go past them, not to mention that heaps of Chinamen are sitting outside the doors, nodding and winking at the passers-by…enough!

"As I'd saved the life of a Chinese captain, a Chinese crew and a Chinese junk, I found myself highly recommended in Bidondo. In addition, Captain Ising-Fong's correspondent, the man who had rented me the house I lived in, carried out his principal commerce with the subjects of the sublime emperor. The first Sunday when he came to Bidondo was entirely devoted to me. He asked me whether I was a hunter. At hazard, I told him that I was. So he told me that he had arranged a hunt with several of his friends for the following Sunday, and that if I wanted to join it, I needn't worry about anything, because I would find a complete hunting outfit when I arrived at the friend's country house.

"I accepted gladly.

"The hunt was to take place going up the Pasig, in the environs of a charming interior Lake named Laguna. The following Saturday we left Bidondo in a boat equipped with six vigorous oarsmen—and it requires no fewer, I assure you, to go up the Pasig.

"Anyway, that excursion was charming; not only did the two banks of the river offer the most varied aspect, but in addition, to our right and our left, the pirogues going up and downstream offered the most gracious scene that one can see.

"After three hours of navigation, we made a halt at a little fishing village whose inhabitants go in the evening to sell the produce of the day's fishing in Bidondo, and which mirrors in the water its rice-fields, swaying in the wind, its clumps of palm-trees, its sheaves of bamboo an its sharp-roofed huts that resemble suspended cages.

"That halt had the goal of allowing our oarsmen to rest and to have something to eat ourselves. When the meal was over and our rowers had rested, we resumed

201

our route. Eventually, as the sun was setting, we saw Lake Laguna, which is thirty leagues around, resplendent before us, like an immense mirror. We came into the lake at about seven o'clock; two hours later, we were in the home of the correspondent's friend.

The correspondent's friend was a Frenchman named Monsieur de La Géronnière. For fifteen years he had been living on the shore of Lake Laguna, in a charming property named Hala-Hala. He received us with an entirely Indian hospitality, but when he discovered that I was European, of French origin, and had exchanged a few words in the language that, outside his family, he only had the opportunity to speak once a year, the hospitality changed into a veritable celebration.

"All that was all the better because I didn't play the hidalgo, the aristocrat, the braggart; I said: 'You're doing me honor; I was a poor matelot in Monnikendam, a poor boat-owner in Ceylon, a poor merchant in Goa; I have rough but frank hands; it's take it or leave it,' And he took Père Olifus for what he was—which is to say, a worthy man who doesn't give anyone the cold shoulder.

"In the evening, I was faithful to my principle; which is to say that I didn't show a cold shoulder to either the bottle or the bed. I'd been asked to recount my adventures, and they'd had the greatest success, except that they had pushed a funny idea into the head of my Chinese correspondent, which was to marry me off for the fifth time—but I declared to him that I was firmly determined, in my wisdom, not to trust women any longer, given that the beautiful Nahi-Nava-Nahina, the beautiful Inès and the beautiful Amarou had put me off the species forever.

"'Bah!' said my correspondent. 'You haven't yet seen the Chinese women of Bidondo; when you've seen them, let me know what you think.

"The result of that was that, in spite of myself, I went to bed with matrimonial ideas in my head, and I dreamed that I married a Chinese widow who had feet so small, so very, very small, that I couldn't believe that she was a widow!"

XIX. The Hunt

"At five o'clock in the morning I was woken up by the barking of dogs and the sound of horns. I thought I was in The Hague again, on a day when King William was hunting in the park of Loo.

"Not at all; I was four thousand miles, more or less, from Holland, on the shore of Lake Laguna, and we were going hunting in the mountains of the Philippines.

"The game that we were going to pursue included the deer, the wild boar and the buffalo; the game that might possibly pursue us included the tiger, the crocodile and the ibitin.

"For the tiger, I was warned; if I saw a peacock take flight, or a flock of peacocks, it was necessary to beware of the tiger, which was never far away.

"For the crocodile, every time I drew close to the shore of the lake, it was a matter of paying attention to the tree-trunks lying on the bank. Those tree-trunks are almost always crocodiles, which sleep very lightly and grab you by the arm, a leg or a buttock as you pass close to them.

"As for the ibitin,[41] that's something else. It's a reptile about thirty feet long, a cousin of the boa constrictor,

---

[41] *Ibitin* is a Tagalog word meaning "hang" or "dangle." It was applied to the species now known as the reticulated python in accounts of travels dating from the seventeenth century, and reproduced, among other volumes, in the account of the Philippines given in André d'Orville's *Histoire des différents peuples du Monde* (1772). Such accounts inevitably exaggerated the size of the snakes.

which coils around trees like a stout liana, remains motionless, and then, at the moment when they least expect it, let itself fall on a deer, a wild pig or a buffalo, crushes it against a tree, flesh and bone, stretches out while crushing it, and finishes up by swallowing it whole. It goes without saying that it doesn't neglect humans and that, when the opportunity presents itself, it eats Tagalogs, Chinese and Europeans indifferently.

"For humans, the means of getting rid of it is quite simple, it's entirely a matter of knowing how to employ it. It's sufficient to carry in one's belt a razor-sharp hunting-knife; as the ibitin isn't venomous, and it's content to choke you, one passes the aforesaid hunting-knife between oneself and one of the coils it forms around the body and *snip!* one cuts it in two with a sideways thrust.

"As we were about to depart my host attached to my belt a magnificent hunting-knife with which he had already bisected two or three ibitins himself.

"As for venomous serpents, as there's no remedy for their wounds, it wasn't worth the trouble of looking for one.

"Two months earlier, Monsieur de La Géronnière had lost a charming Tagalog girl of sixteen or eighteen, whom he suspected of having been carried off by a tiger, devoured by a crocodile or strangled by a snake, given that poor Schimindra had gone out one evening and hadn't come back, and although several searches had been made since that time, no trace of her had been found.

"I confess that when my host enumerated all the dangers that we were running in our day's hunting expedition, I thought that hunting was a singular pleasure.

205

"We went on horseback as far as the place where the beating was to begin. There we dismounted and went into the forest.

"The first game that I saw flushed out was a magnificent flock of peacocks. I took careful note of the place from which they had risen, made a wide detour, and had the satisfaction of not disturbing the tiger that the departure of those magnificent birds announced to me.

"After ten minutes a rifle-shot was fired. Monsieur de La Géronnière had just killed a deer.

"In my turn, I heard a loud noise under my feet; I saw the undergrowth move ten paces away; I fired my shot at hazard; I won't say that my bullet encountered the wild boar, but the wild boar encountered my bullet. Everyone congratulated me; I'd just made a magnificent coup, with a single shot, killing a solitary—what's known as an old boar in your homeland?"

I nodded my head affirmatively.

"My boar was collected; it was put on the shoulders of four Tagalogs, and I was invited to continue my exploits, assured that at the first stroke I was a past master. Monsieur, there is nothing that dooms a man like flattery.

"It seemed to me, now that I had killed a wild boar, that I could kill a tiger, a rhinoceros or an elephant. I resumed walking through the forest, only asking to enter into hand-to-hand combat with all the monsters of the Philippines.

"So, in my ardor, I didn't notice that I was gradually drawing away from the hunt. I'd been told that we'd be climbing for about two hours and after barely three-quarters of an hour, I found myself on a downslope.

"Suddenly, thirty paces away from me, I heard a terrible bellowing. I turned in the direction from which the sound was coming, and I saw a buffalo.

"Ah! That was a fine coup. Except that, as my rifle was trembling in my hands slightly—I don't know why—I supported it on a tree branch, and pulled the trigger.

"Scarcely had I fired the shot when I saw two bloodshot eyes coming toward me, while the animal's muzzle labored the ground like a plowshare.

"I fired a second shot, but instead of slowing the animal down, that second shot seemed to augment its speed.

"I only just had time to drop my rifle, grab a branch of the tree under which I was standing, and lift myself up, by means of a gymnastic thrust, to the height of the branch, from which I was able to reach the higher branches. When I arrived there, however, I was far from having quit my buffalo. Not being able to follow me into the branches of the tree, it set about guarding the trunk.

"For the first ten minutes, I said to it: 'Turn away, turn away, fellow, I'm making a fool of you; go away.' But during ten more minutes, I began to perceive that the matter was more serious than I had thought at first.

"After an hour, I understood, by the tranquility with which it was making circuits of the tree, that it had decided to appoint itself my guardian until it could become my executioner.

"In fact, from time to time, it lifted its head toward me, looked at me with its bloodshot eyes, bellowed in a menacing fashion, and then started browsing the grass that was growing around my tree, and if to say to me: *I have everything I need, you see—grass to nourish me, morning and evening dew to slake my thirst—while you're a carnivorous animal, and you don't have the habit of nourishing yourself on leaves; eventually, you'll have to come down, and when you come down,* splat! splat! *with my feet,* zing! zing! *with my horns—and you'll spend a bad quarter of an hour!*

"Fortunately, Père Olifus is a man who doesn't sulk when it's a matter of forming a resolution. I said to myself: *Olifus, my friend, the longer you wait, the more your situation will deteriorate. You're going to give your buffalo an hour to go away, and if, in that hour, it doesn't go away...well, if it doesn't go away, we'll see!*

"I looked at my watch. It was eleven o'clock. I said: *All right, the two of us, until midday.*

"As I had suspected, the buffalo, instead of quitting the tree, continued its watch, raising its nose in the air from time to time and bellowing with all its might. For myself, every ten minutes, I looked at my watch, and I had a drink from my water-bottle. At the fiftieth minute I said to it: 'Pay attention, my friend, you only have another ten minutes; and if, in ten minutes, you haven't gone on your own, we'll go together.' At the fifty-ninth minute, however, instead of going away, it lay down, stretched out its head at the foot of the tree, opening its nostrils, and directing a rancorous eye in my direction from time to time, which seemed to be saying: *Oh, we have plenty of time, don't worry.*

"I had decided that things would happen otherwise. At the sixtieth minute I swallowed all the rum that remained in my water-bottle in one go. I took my knife between my teeth and *hup!* I jumped, calculating my distance in such a way as to fall two feet behind it and to grab hold of its tail with my left hand, as I had seen bullfighters do in Cadiz and Rio de Janeiro.

"Agile as the buffalo was, I was equally agile, and when it got up, I was clinging to its tail. It made two or three turns, which served to coil its tail more solidly around my arm. Then, seeing that while I remained solidly clamped to its rear, it could not reach me with its horns, I began to reassure myself a little, while the animal, on the contrary, began to bellow with all its might—only with anger, to be sure.

"'Wait, wait!' I said to it. 'Oh, you're bellowing with anger, my friend—well, I'm going to make you below with pain.' And, taking my knife, I plunged it into its belly.

"Ah! Right away I'd touched a sensitive spot, it appears, for it stood up like a horse rearing, and launched itself with such an unexpected shock that it nearly tore my arm off; but I held firm; I didn't allow myself to be carried away, and *bang! bang!* I riddled it with knife-thrusts.

"That's a race that I hope you never have to run. It lasted a quarter of an hour, you see, and in that quarter of an hour I covered more than two leagues through the undergrowth, marshes and streams; I might as well have been attached to the tail of a locomotive. And *bang! bang!* I was still striking, saying: 'Oh, wretch! oh, rogue! oh, rascal! you want to disembowel me; wait! wait!' So it was all the more furious; it was enraged, so enraged that when it arrived at the summit of a sheer rock, it made no bones about it; it leapt down—but I had seen it coming, and I let go. I stopped short at the top, while it rolled down *pit-a-pat! boom! boom!*

"I stretched out my head and looked over the rock; my animal was lying dead in the precipice. For myself, it's necessary to say, I wasn't much better; I was bruised, crushed, torn, covered in blood—but nothing was broken.

"I got up as best I could, cut a small tree to sustain me and made my way to a stream that I saw glittering, through the trees, a hundred paces away. Having arrived on the bank, I knelt down and had begun to wash my face, when I heard a voice shouting in French: 'Help me! Help!'

"I turned in the direction from which the cries were coming ad I saw a young woman, almost naked, coming toward me, her arms extended, giving signs of the most vivid terror. She was being pursued by a kind of negro who had a stick in his hand, and who was running with such agility that, even though he was a hundred paces behind her, he had soon caught her up, taken her in his arms and carried her off into the densest part of the forest.

"The sight of the young woman calling for help in French, the dolorous tone in which she had appealed to me and the brutality of the wretch who had loaded her on to his shoulder and carried her off into the dense wood concurred in rendering me strength. I forgot my fatigue and launched myself after him, shouting: 'Stop! Stop!'

"Sensing that he was being pursued in his turn, the abductor redoubled his effort. His pace scarcely seemed to slow down in spite of the burden he was carrying. I didn't understand how a man could be endowed with such strength, and I said to myself that when we came together, I might have cause to repent of playing the knight errant, as I was.

"Meanwhile, I was scarcely gaining on the negro, and I don't know whether, in spite of the kind of rage that I was putting into pursuing him, I would ever have reached him, if the unfortunate woman he was carrying off, while passing close to a tree-branch, hadn't clung on to it with such force that her abductor stopped dead, seizing her around the waist and making every effort to make her let go of the branch, while she continued to shout 'Help me! Help! In the name of Heaven, help me, don't abandon me!'

"I was no more than twenty-five or thirty paces away from her when the negro, seeing that he was about to be attacked, suddenly decided, apparently, to take the initiative. He let go of the woman and came toward me, club raised.

"In three bounds, he was in front of me. I uttered a cry of astonishment; what I had mistaken for a negro was an ape.

"Fortunately, I too had a staff, and as I wielded it rather adroitly, I assumed a defensive posture, for the aggressor had become the attacker.

"As for the woman, as soon as she was free, she had described a wide circle and had come to seek shelter behind me, while shouting: "Courage! Courage, Monsieur! Save me from that monster! Don't abandon me!'

"While playing the windmill in order to ward him off, and sending him jabs in the chest that made him go *phouac!* but didn't deter him, I examined my adversary. He was a great ruffian of an ape, very hairy, who was nearly six feet tall, with a gray beard, who toyed naturally with his stick with a skill and agility that nearly turned the contest his way. Fortunately for the honor of science, it wasn't to be. After ten minutes of struggle, his fingers crushed, his stomach staved in and his muzzle bloody, he began to beat a retreat—but that retreat had no other goal but to reach a tree, which he climbed rapidly, not in order to take refuge there but in order to launch himself from its height on top of me.

"Fortunately, I had seen the movement and had divined the ploy. I drew my knife and, at the full extent of my arm, extended it above my head. The two movements, of attack on the ape's part and defense on mine, were instantaneous. I felt a weight descend upon my head that I could not sustain; my adversary and I both rolled on the ground—but I got up alone. The knife had traversed his heart.

"The animal uttered a cry, bit the grass with his teeth, tore the earth with his fingernails, made two or three convulsive moments, and expired.

"'Oh, hunting's a fine thing!' I exclaimed. 'If anyone ever inveigles me into it again, may the Devil take me!'

"'Are you regretting having come here hunting, then?' asked a soft voice behind me.

'Oh, my God, no,' I said, turning round, 'since I've been able to be useful to you, my lovely child. But how the Devil do you come to be in the forest, what pleasure do you find in living with an ape, and how does it come about that you speak French?'

"'I'm in the forest because I was carried off here; I don't find any pleasure in living with an ape, since I called to you for help to deliver me, and I speak French because I was a chambermaid in Madame de La Géronnière's house.'

"'Then your name's Schimindra!' I exclaimed.

"'Yes.'

"'You're the young woman who disappeared two months ago.'

"'Yes, but in your turn, how do you know my name, and how do you know about my adventure?'

"'Because Monsieur de La Géronnière told me about your adventure and told me your name, of course.'

"'You know Monsieur de La Géronnière?'

"'I'm hunting with him. He's in the forest—but what part of the forest? I don't know, for, it's necessary to confess, I'm completely lost.'

"'Oh, don't worry about that—I know the way.'

"'Since you know the way, why didn't you come back to the habitation?'

"'Because that odious animal never let me out of his sight, day or night. I made twenty futile attempts to run away, and if Providence hadn't brought you to that stream, it's probable that I'd never have seen the houses of men again.'

"'Well,' I said, 'if you'll believe me, charming Schimindra, we should go back to the houses of men as quickly as possible, because, I confess, I'll think myself a lot safer there than here.'

"'So be it, and I'm ready to go with you; but first, let me tell you a secret in which you'll find the recompense for the good deed that you've just done.'

"'Bah!'

"'The frightful orangutan from which you've just delivered me belongs to the very race of apes of which you might have heard mention, from which the purest bezoar is obtained.'

"'Really?'

"'You can make sure of it, while I repair the disorder of my clothing with the aid of a few coconut-palm leaves.'

"I looked at the beautiful Schimindra, whose greatly disordered clothing was in need of repair; and, I confess, it needed nothing less than the idea that that disorder was owed to an ape for me to have no desire to augment it further.

"I therefore made a sign to the beautiful Schimindra that she could devote herself to the repairs she desired to make, and, full of curiosity, dread and hope, with the aid of the knife that had rendered me such great service during the day, I commenced the autopsy of my enemy.

"Schimindra had not deceived me. I found in the animal's entrails a beautiful blue stone, veined with gold, the size of a pigeon's egg. It was one of the most beautiful bezoars that one could see.

"'Now,' said Schimindra, 'if I might give you some advice, it's not to boast to anyone that you possess such a treasure, given that you wouldn't possess it for long, even if you had to be murdered to take it from you.'

"I thanked Schimindra for the advice, and as the coquette had made herself a charming loincloth out of coconut-palm leaves, and there was nothing to keep either of us in the forest, which, on the contrary, I experienced the keenest desire to quit, I invited Schimindra to serve as my guide and to take the shortest route to return to the habitation. Two hours later, we arrived at Hala-Hala, to the great astonishment, and above all to the great joy, of all the residents of the habitation, who had thought me lost, like Schimindra, but who saw me returning with her.

"I recounted my adventures and Schimindra recounted hers, but neither of us said a word about the bezoar."

XX. Vanly-Ching

"A week later I was installed at Bidondo, and as it was absolutely necessary for me to have a kind of housekeeper to place at the head of my household I had requested the beautiful Schimindra from Monsieur de La Géronnière, who was graciously accorded to me.

"My choice was made. The branch of commerce that I had decided to exploit was Manila cigars. In fact, the Manila cigar, even in Europe, offers serious competition to the Havana cigar, and throughout the Indian seas it is preferred.

"What had suggested that idea to me above all was that in Monsieur de La Géronnière's house, it was the beautiful Schimindra who was in charge of the cigar department. I therefore resolved, in order to realize greater profits, instead of purchasing the merchandise fully manufactured, to have it made up myself, and to put Schimindra at the head of the establishment.

"Nothing was easier. A kind of hangar was built in the garden; Schimindra hired ten young Tagalong women, some of whom came from the royal factory in Manila; the very next day I had the pleasure of seeing my enterprise in full activity.

"Thanks to Schimindra's active surveillance, and her knowledge of the business, I no longer had anything to do but stroll around; that was what doomed me.

"It's incredible how a remark casually dropped, even if it's not common sense, sometimes lodges in the mind and germinates in the brain. You'll recall the brief comment that was made at supper in Monsieur de La Géronnière's house by my correspondent about Chinese women and the fifth marriage projected by him. Well, there wasn't a single day, and especially not a single night, when I didn't think about it. Scarcely had I gone to bed, closed my eyes and fallen asleep than a veritable procession of Chinese women filed before my bed showing me their feet...feet to which Cinderella's slipper could have served as a clog. And, notice that, curiously enough, I had in close proximity Schimindra, who was what can be called a veritable beauty, and that I had in my cigar factory ten girls, among whom the ugliest, with her large dark eyes, with her velvet lashes, with...everything they had, in sum...who were made to turn a Parisian's head; and given all that, I dreamed of nothing but Chinese women.

"The result of it was that once I got up, I ran to the Chinese quarter, going into all the shops, bargaining for fans, porcelain and screens, learning a few words here, a few words of Cochinchinese there, jabbering all sorts of compliments to the tiny feet that remained hidden from me beneath the long robes, and coming back in the evening more determined than ever not to dispense with my Chinese fantasy.

"In the midst of all that, I had encountered a charming woman who owned one of the finest tea-shops in Bidondo, who had seduced me particularly with the fashion in which she ate rice, with the aid of those little knitting-needles that serve Chinese ladies as knives and forks; it was no longer skill but jugglery, and I believe in truth that it was by coquetry that the beautiful Vanly-Ching had a pilau brought for herself when there were foreigners there.

"You will remark in passing that the two words Vanly-Ching mean 'ten thousand lilies'; the parents of my Chinese woman had rendered justice to her and given her a name in harmony with her beauty.

"I sought information from my correspondent regarding the beautiful Chinese woman; at the first word I pronounced my correspondent raised his finger to the height of his eyes and exclaimed: 'Ah, rogue!'—which meant: *well, well, you don't have an unfortunate hand, to have put your finger on that one straight away.*

"I understood all that, and only insisted further; then I learned that the beautiful Vanly-Ching was an orphan who had been taken in by a famous physician, who had fallen in love with her when she was only twelve and had married her even though he was sixty-five himself. Providence had not wanted such a disproportionate marriage to have a long duration; after three months the physician had died of a malady whose cause he was unable to determine clearly, but he had died very happy, for no man could boast of having been cared for during his illness as he had been cared for by his young and worthy wife; so he had left her all he possessed, amounting to two or three thousand rupees. It was a paltry recompense for the devotion that the widow had shown during the illness, and the dolor she displayed after his death.

With the three thousand rupees she had inherited, however, the young window had founded a little establishment making fans in the least apparent quarter of the city, which, thanks to her economy and intelligence, began to prosper in a miraculous fashion.

"What was most remarkable of all about the premature widowhood of the beautiful Vanly-Ching, however, is that instead of listening to the proposals of all the elegant men of Bidondo, and instead of losing, by virtue of some imprudence, the reputation for wisdom she had acquired, she only ever wanted to accept the care of an old mandarin, a friend of her husband, who came every day to weep with her over the loss they had suffered. It resulted from those daily visits that the widow and the mandarin acquired the habit of weeping together, one for her spouse and the other for her friend—with the result that one morning, it was learned that in order to mourn the deceased more at their ease, the two inconsolable individuals were to marry.

"A year after the death of her first husband, the beautiful Vanly-Ching had, therefore, married the mandarin, but once they were united, and in one another's company from morning to evening, it appears that the newlyweds had wept so much that the mandarin, who was fifty years old, could not resist the deluge of tears, and had died after two months.

"The beautiful Vanly-Ching, who was only fifteen, was naturally better able to support dolor, with the result that, although she was weeping for both her first and second husband, she appeared more beautiful and more resplendent than ever through her tears.

"She had inherited five or six pagodas from her mandarin, with the result that with that small increase in her fortune she was able to launch herself in a more fashionable quarter and in a more extensive commerce. She therefore progressed from fans to porcelain, and the reputation of the beautiful merchant began to spread in Bidondo.

"That reputation spread to such an extent that the civil judge of Bidondo, who had known the beautiful Vanly-Ching's first and second husbands well and who, in consequence, was able to appreciate how happy the doctor had been during the three months, and the mandarin during the two months during which they had lived with her, offered his services in consoling her. Vanly-Ching declared that she had been afflicted so profoundly that she thought it impossible, but as the civil judge insisted, she ended up replying that she was willing to try.

"The marriage took place at the end of a year, for, although such a delay was not strictly required, Vanly-Ching was such a faithful observer of propriety that not for anything in the world would she have tried to console herself prematurely. But the civil judge did not have the satisfaction of arriving at a complete consolation, given that a month after his marriage, the day after he had inherited a rather considerable sum from a distant relative he had in Macao, and he had invited a few friends to dinner to celebrate that fortunate event, he died of an indigestion of bird's nests.

"Before dying, however, the declared that the month he had just spent had been the happiest month of his life. As he had just collected the sum, on learning that it had been bequeathed to him, the beautiful widow was able, thanks to that reinforcement, to extend her commerce and found in the main street of Bidondo the magnificent tea-shop in which I had seen her moving her head and eating rice.

"All this information, as you can understand, completed my change of mind. The beautiful Vanly-Ching had been widowed a great deal, but she had been so briefly married that she was necessarily the houri of whom I had dreamed so agreeably. I therefore confessed to my correspondent the keen desire I had to be her fourth husband, and to take her for my fifth wife.

"One never tells women anything when one tells them that one loves them, because they have always perceived our love before us. So the beautiful Vanly-Ching not only manifested no astonishment at my request but replied that she had expected it.

"The state of mind in which she found herself did not even permit her to make me wait for her decision. Her decision was favorable; I did not displease her; but as she had always had the self-respect to want to be loved or herself, she wanted me to make up a little account of my fortune. If my fortune equaled or surpassed hers she would believe in my love, but if my fortune was inferior, she would believe that it was base cupidity and not love that was prompting my action.

"That appeared to me to be powerfully reasoned. I had her asked whether she desired me to establish my calculation in francs, rupees or pagodas, and she replied that it was all the same to her, as she was familiar with the arithmetic of all lands.

"As I was not as good at calculation as she was, I preferred francs, and the following day I sent her the following calculation:

"Exact account of what Jérôme-François Olifus has earned in India and possesses:

"In Ceylon from pearl-fishing …….. 13,500 francs.

"In Goa from commerce in fruits ……… 7,400 f.

"In Calicut, in the cultivation of cardamom 12,500 f.

"In Bidondo, in the manufacture of cigars ……

"The last point was yet to be determined, the verification of the profit having not yet been made, but it was easy enough to evaluate. Total: 43,400 francs.

"You can see that it was a tidy sum, and that I had not wasted my time during the four years since I had left Monnikendam.

"For her part, she made her own liquidation and sent it to me. It was:

"Account of what Vanly-Ching, tea-seller of Bidondo, has earned in the various enterprises she has undertaken:

"In commerce in fans ....4,000 francs.
"In commerce in porcelain................17,000 f.
"In commerce in tea.....................22,037 f.
"Total ....43,037 f.

"One can see that, but for 363 francs, our fortunes were equal; I even had the advantage because I had nearly two hundred thousand cigars in my warehouse ready to be delivered. I confess, however, that instead of being proud of that advantage, I was glad to possess some pecuniary superiority over the beautiful Vanly-Ching, in order to compensate for all the physical superiorities that she had over me.

"That superiority established and the point firmly established that I was marrying Vanly-Ching for her beautiful eyes and not the beautiful eyes of her purse, the marriage was arranged for three months and seven days hence, which was, to the day, the expiration of Vanly-Ching's mourning for her third husband. She had had the delicacy, even though remaining faithful to the memory of the civil judge, not to make me wait a minute longer.

XXI. Cholera

The rumor of my future marriage with Vanly-Ching soon spread in Bidondo, and naturally acted in various fashions on the inhabitants of the city, habituated for two or three years to be preoccupied with the beautiful Chinese woman's every move. Some criticized her; others approved; finally, many shook their heads, saying that the first husband had died after three months, the second after two and the third after one, and that, in order not to belie the necrological calculation, I would probably die on my wedding night.

"The person whom the blow struck most violently, however, was poor Schimindra.. The generosity that I had shown to her had made her conceive the hope of becoming my wife some time ago. In a moment of despair she confessed to me what her ambition had been, but I quickly and easily made her understand the superiority that the beautiful Vanly-Ching, the widow of a doctor, a mandarin and a civil judge, had over her, who was only the widow of an ape.

"The result of that was that Schimindra, returned to her humility, admitted frankly that she should never have emerged from it, and, knowing that her rival had asked for an account of my fortune, limited herself to begging me not to include the bezoar in question in that account.

"Every evening, I was admitted to pay court to my future spouse, with the result that the time passed rapidly. As I spoke very little Chinese and she spoke very little Hindustani, and no Dutch and French at all, our conversations took place primarily in gestures, which sometimes gave me a boldness of expression that I would not have had in words; but I ought to say in honor of the beautiful Vanly-Ching that she conserved intact the reputation of virtue that she had made, and, while conceding me certain unimportant bagatelles, never allowed me to steal a serious march on the marriage.

"Finally, the day arrived.

"The day before I had experienced a great dread; several cases of cholera had been identified in Cavite and one or two in Bidondo, with the result that I trembled that the presence of the epidemic might determine Vanly-Ching to postpone our marriage; but the beautiful Chinese woman had a strong mind, and the event had no purchase on her.

"The great day was the twenty-seventh of October, which was a festival for the whole city of Bidondo. From the early morning there was a crowd at Vanly-Ching's door. It was the fourth time that that beautiful woman had been seen to traverse the city in bridal costume, and people had not tired of seeing it.

"The custom is that a Chinese bride is paraded through the city with a cortege of music and singing. It rather resembles, as a Dutch scholar living in Manila told me, ancient Greek orgies, except that at her first marriage, the bride wears a thick veil over her face as a sign or virginity. When she is conveyed the second, third and fourth times, a Chinese bride is paraded with her face uncovered.

"It was, therefore, with an uncovered face that my bride was paraded, and that to my great satisfaction, for I heard said all around me: 'Fortunate Olifus! That rogue Olifus! That rascal Olifus!'

"The rest of the ceremony strongly resembles that one practiced in Siam. When the couple are in accord, the relatives of the young man come to present the relatives of the young woman with seven jars of betel; a week later the fiancé comes himself and presents fourteen; then he lives in his father-in-law's house for a month, in order to see his future spouse and become accustomed to her; after which, on the day that the celebration is to be completed, the parents assemble with their oldest friends, and put into a purse, one bracelets, another a ring and another money; one holds a lighted candle, passes it around the presents seven times, during which all the others utter loud cries of joy while wishing long life and perfect health to the couple.

"After that comes a big feast, followed by a small intimate meal, itself followed by the consummation of the marriage.

"Vanly-Ching and I were dispensed of all that ceremony. She had shown me the purse in which her small fortune was contained; I had shown her the effects of my commerce certified by the correspondent of my Chinese captain, payable on sight and to the bearer; we each left forty thousand livres to the last survivor, that being well worth seven jars of betel, or even fourteen.

"As for relatives, neither of us had any. The ceremony of the purse and the bracelets, that of the lighted candle passed seven times around the presents, and that of the cries of joy wishing us a long life and perfect health, were therefore omitted; we restricted ourselves to the big sumptuous dinner and the little intimate meal.

"The sumptuous dinner was magnificent; Vanly had supervised it; it consisted of the most sought-after foodstuffs; there were mice in honey, shark in crustacean sauce; worms in rice oil; swallows' nests with crushed crab, and bamboo salads, all washed down with calamansi liqueur, which the domestics equipped with enormous silver coffee-pots poured continually; people drank to the emperor of China, the King of Holland, taking the cup in both hands and making *tschin tschin*—which is to say, moving the head from right to left and left to right like monkeys; then everyone showed the bottom of the cup to demonstrate that it was empty.

"In the course of the dinner the beautiful Vanly appeared to be looking at me anxiously and talked in a low voice to her neighbors. Two or three times she spoke to me in order to ask, in the softest voice in the world: 'How are you feeling, my love?'

"'Very well,' I replied. 'Very well.'

"In spite of that assurance, however, she shook her head and uttered such sighs that I began to get anxious myself, and when I left the table I looked at myself in a mirror. The examination reassured me; I was radiant with joy and health.

"It appeared, however, that I did not seem so well to the society, for two or three guests, before leaving, come to me to ask: 'Are you suffering?' and in spite of me negative response, drew away after shaking my hand sadly. I even thought I heard the word cholera pronounced in low voices, but when I asked whether someone of our acquaintance had been afflicted by cholera, the reply was negative, and I thought I had misheard.

"In the midst of all that, I sought out my beautiful bride, who came to me with anxiety in her eyes. I wanted to interrogate her as to the cause of that anxiety, but she contented herself with looking at me, turning away and wiping away a tear, and murmuring: 'Poor love!'

"I took my leave of the guests, whom I was in haste to see disappear, by rubbing my nose against theirs, as is customary. My correspondent was the last. I rubbed his nose with double ardor, given, as you will recall, that it was him who had served as intermediary in my marriage, and as I showed him with a sly smile the beautiful Vanly, who was heading very slowly toward the bedroom, to which I made her a sign that I was about to follow her, he said: 'You'd do better to call a doctor.' And, raising his eyes to the heavens, he left in his turn.

"I didn't understand at all. However, I didn't waste any time trying to figure out what all that meant. I closed the door and went swiftly to the bedroom. The beautiful Vanly was already at the table where a charming meal had been served, mingled with flowers and fruits, occupied in decanting a pink liqueur from one carafe to another. I had never seen anything as appetizing as that liqueur; one might have thought it distilled rubies.

"'Well, my darling,' I said to her as I went in, 'can you explain to me why, in my situation, which leaves absolutely nothing to be desired, seems to make everyone feel pity for me? People keep asking me how I am, if I don't feel well, and giving me the advice to send for a doctor—to the extent, word of honor, that I resemble the character that I once saw in a play in Amsterdam, whom everyone wanted to persuade that he had a fever, and repeated it so often and so firmly that he ended up believing it, and after wishing everyone good night he went to bed.'[42]

"'Oh,' murmured Vanly, 'if you only had a fever, it could be cured by quinine.'

"'What do you mean, if I only had a fever? I beg you to believe that I don't have a fever.'

"'My dear Olifus,' said Vanly, 'now that it's just the two of us, now that you have no more need to constrain yourself, tell me frankly how you feel.'

---

[42] The reference is to Beaumarchais' *Le Barbier de Seville*.

"'How do I feel? I feel the most ardent desire to tell you that I love you, and especially to....'"

"'And not the slightest stomach cramp?' asked Vanly.

"'Not the slightest.'

"'Not the slightest chill?'

"'On the contrary.'

"'Not the slightest colic?'

"'Get away! But if I had the cholera, my darling, you wouldn't ask me so many questions.'

"'Well, in fact, since it's you who have mentioned the word....'

"'What?'

"'People thought they noticed during supper...'

"'What?'

"'That you changed color, that you put your hand to your stomach several times, and that later...'

"'Oh. I can tell you, that was because to begin with, I couldn't stand the sight of the mice in honey; afterwards, you see, your crustacean sauce...we don't have the habit of those kinds of sauce in my homeland. Finally, your rice oil...but all that passed with a little air. Oh, what an idea, to think that I'd catch cholera on my wedding night! Ha ha ha!'

"'Well, my love, that thought was in everyone's mind, and I'm perfectly certain that, among the thirty friends who left us, twenty-nine were convinced that you'd be dead tomorrow morning.'

"'Dead of cholera?'

"'Of cholera,'

"'Oh, damn it!'

"'That's how it is.'

"'Come on, frankly, is it...?'

"'Ahem...'

"Oh, Monsieur, the imagination is a strange thing. After having laughed at Basile, who was persuaded that he had a fever, didn't I start feeling my stomach and my abdomen, and was near to believing that I already had cramps and was about to have colic. In any case, there was one incontestable fact, and that was that I was getting colder, and visibly.

"'Poor love,' said Vanly, looking at me compassionately. 'Fortunately, the malady hasn't yet made great progress, and my first husband bequeathed me an infallible remedy.'

"'Against cholera?'

"'Against cholera, yes.'

"'Oh, the worthy man. Well, dear Vanly, the opportunity has presented itself to make use of it, your remedy.'

"'Ah! You admit it, then?'

"'Yes, I'm beginning to believe it. Oh, what's that?'

"'Hurry up, my love, hurry up. Here comes the flatulence now.'

"'What! Flatulence?'

"It's necessary to tell you that the word is already barbaric in French, but in Chinese, it's even worse, which means that when she said to me 'Here comes the flatulence,' it was as if she'd said to me: 'Here come the Cossacks.'

"'Flatulence!' I repeated, letting myself fall into a chair. 'Well, dear Vanly, what needs to be done?'

"'It's necessary to drink, immediately, a glass of the red liqueur that I was preparing when you came in, in the anticipation, dear Olifus, that you were about to arrive.'

"'Quickly, then, the glass; quickly, the red liqueur. Oh, how the flatulence is coming! Quickly, quickly!'

"Vanly poured the red liqueur into a glass and presented it to me.

"I took the glass in a trembling hand and raised it to my lips, and I was about to swallow the red liqueur to the last drop when I saw Vanly go pale and fix her eyes on the bedroom door.

"At the same time I heard a familiar voice, which said to me: 'In the name of heaven, Olifus, don't drink!'

"'Schimindra!' I exclaimed. 'What the devil are you doing here?'

"'I've come to return the favor you did for me, to save your life,'

"'Oh, dear Schimindra, you too have a secret cure for cholera, then?'

"'I don't have a secret cure for cholera, and in any case that secret would be unnecessary.'

"'What! Unnecessary?'

"'Yes.'

"'I don't have cholera, then?'

"'No.'

"'If I don't have cholera, what's wrong with me, then?'

"Schimindra looked at Vanly, who was going increasingly pale. 'You've married a poisoner, that's all.'

"Vanly uttered a cry as if a snake had bitten her.

"'A poisoner?' I repeated.

"'Are you going to listen to this woman?' she demanded.

"'Schimindra, my good friend,' I said, shaking my head, 'it seems to me that you're going a bit far.'

"'A poisoner,' repeated Schimindra.

"Vanly was livid.

"'Let's count those you have poisoned, Madame,' said Schimindra, 'and let's see how you poisoned them.'

"'Oh, come away, come away Olifus!' cried Vanly.

"'No, stay and listen!' said Schimindra. Then she turned to Vanly: 'You poisoned your first husband, the doctor, with Saint Ignatius' bean, so common in Mindanao. You poisoned your second husband, the mandarin, with American ticuna. You poisoned your third husband, the civil judge, with Guyanan vooara. Finally, this evening, you were about to poison your fourth husband, Olifus, with Javanese upas.'[43]

"'You're lying! You're lying!' screamed Vanly.

"'I'm lying?' said Schimindra. 'Well, then, if I'm lying, drink this glass of pink liqueur that you've just poured for your husband under the pretext that he has cholera.' And she took the glass that I had put down on the table and presented it to Vanly.

"I expected that Vanly would snatch the glass from her hands and drink its contents—but not at all; she recoiled, reached the door while recoiling, opened it and ran away.

---

[43] Saint Ignatius' bean was described and named by the Jesuit Georg Kamel. It is now known as *Strychnos ignatii*, the generic term signifying that the beans are rich in strychnine. "Americam ticuna" was a term similarly found in the *Catholic Encyclopedia* to describe curare, so called because of its use by the Ticuna tribe to poison blow-gun darts. The poison rendered s "vooara" is probably that of the golden poison frog of Colombia, whose skin is coated in a powerful alkaloid toxin, also used on blowgun darts by native tribes. The term "upas tree" was and is widely used for a legendary tree that poisoned the ground around it, following a fanciful account given by Erasmus Darwin and further exaggerated by travelers' tales, but the actual Javanese upas, *Antiaris toxicaria*, is less dangerous, although it too was once a popular source of alkaloid toxins for coating arrows and darts

"I launched myself after her. 'Oh, my dear Vanly' I cried, 'have no fear, come back, I don't believe it, it's not possible.'

"'It's not possible!' cried Schimindra, in despair because I didn't believe her. 'It's not possible!'

"'No, unless I'm given proof…'

"'And if you were given proof?' cried Schimindra.

"'Well…'

"'You'd believe?'

"'It would be necessary.'

"'You'd believe that that woman is a poisoner, wouldn't you?'

"'Undoubtedly,'

"'And you'd no longer love her?'

"'What! I'd no longer love her? Not only would I no longer love her, but I'd denounce her, I'd pursue her, I'd have her guillotined, hanged or quartered.'

"'You swear it?'

"'I swear it.'

"'Well,' said Schimindra, 'that proof, here it is.'

"And she swallowed the pink liqueur in a single draught, in a single breath, before I had time to say: 'What are you doing?'

"I uttered a great cry in my turn, for after all, I had absolutely nothing against Schimindra except that unfortunate ape…but apart from that antecedent, I loved her with all my heart.

"'Now,' she said, falling into my arms, 'you'll understand why the rumor was put about among your guests that you were afflicted by cholera.'

"In fact, scarcely had Schimindra pronounced those words that I saw her go pale and, putting her hand to her breast, give the signs of the most intense agony."

XXII. Conclusion

"At that sight, I no longer conserved any doubt; Vanly was definitely culpable, and Schimindra really had been poisoned.

"I no longer had any but one desire—that of saving the poor woman who had just sacrificed herself for me.

"'Help! Help!' I cried. 'A doctor! A doctor!'

"Then, as no one replied, because Vanly had taken her precautions and the house was completely deserted, I opened the window. 'Help! Help!' I repeated. 'A doctor! A doctor!'

"Fortunately, a street-porter was passing along the quay at that moment. He heard my cries, recognized me and put himself at my disposal. 'A doctor!' I cried to him, throwing him a gold coin.

"He picked up the gold coin, nodded his head, and ran off at top speed. Five minutes later he came back with some kind of bonze who practiced medicine gratis for the people, and who had a great reputation for knowledge of holiness among the residents of the port.

"However, although scarcely ten minutes had gone by since Schimindra had swallowed the poison, the malady had already made terrible progress. Her respiration was noisy and interrupted by sobs, the muscles of the abdomen and thorax were beginning to contract, the moth was foaming, the head tilted backwards, and the vomiting commenced.

"I ran to the doctor and brought him to Schimindra.

"Uh oh!' he exclaimed. 'There's a woman who has cholera, or else...' He hesitated.

"'Or else?' I repeated.

"'Or else she's been poisoned.'

"'With what?'

"'With Javanese upas.'

"'That's it!' I cried. 'Yes, yes, she's been poisoned with Javanese upas. What remedy is there?'

"'There is no remedy, or, if there is one…'

"'What?'

"'It's so rare...'

"'But what is it, that remedy?'

"'It requires bezoar.'

"'Bezoar?'

"'Yes, but not cow bezoar and not goat bezoar...'

"'Ape bezoar.'

"'Yes, but where can it be obtained?'

"I uttered a cry of joy. 'Here,' I said, 'take it,' And I took my bezoar stone from its leather bag.

"Schimindra raised her head. 'Ah!' she said. 'He loves me a little, then!'

"'Oho!' said the bonze. 'Blue bezoar, veritable ape bezoar.

"'Yes, veritable, I guarantee it, given that I collected it myself. But don't waste time—look.' And I pointed at Schimindra, who was writhing in the convulsions of agony.

"'Oh, don't worry now,' he said. 'We have time.'

"'Bus she'll be dead in five minutes!' I cried.

"'Yes, if she isn't saved in three,'

"And, in fact, the bonze set about grating the bezoar into a glass of water with the same tranquility as he would have done with a sugar lump. The water immediately took of a beautiful azure tint, which gradually changed into opal, darting golden reflections.

"That was doubtless the point that the antidote had to arrive because, making signs to me to lift Schimindra

233

up, the bonze introduced the edge of the glass between her teeth, already clenched by the convulsions, where it nearly broke.

"At the first drops that moistened the palate of the dying woman, however, the muscles relaxed, the head swayed limply on the shoulders, the stiffened arms fell back by her sides, the gasping ceased, and a slight moisture beaded her arid brow.

"Schimindra drained the glass.

"Then, when the glass was empty, she said: 'Oh my God! It's life that you have made me drink.'

"Then darting a last glance at him, thanking me with one final smile, trying to touch me with one final gesture, she uttered a sigh, closed her eyes and fell into a lethargy that had nothing disquieting about it, for life could be sensed, muffled beneath that appearance of death.

"I couldn't leave her in Vanly-Ching's house, and I didn't want to stay there myself; my house was only fifty paces away from the one we were in. I took Schimindra in my arms. I went out with the bonze, locked the door, and gave the key to the bonze, asking him to take it immediately to the civil judge, the successor of Vanly-Ching's penultimate husband, and tell him everything that he had seen, while I carried my Schimindra home. According to the doctor, she no longer needed anything but tranquil sleep.

"Then, having deposited Schimindra in her bed, I went to bed in my turn.

"You can imagine what happened in my mind once the light was out and, vanquished by fatigue, I found myself in the state of reverie that is not yet sleep but is already not wakefulness, which would have been impossible.

"My four wives seemed to have gathered at the foot of my bed. There was Nahi-Nava-Nahina, Doña Inès, Amarou and Vanly-Ching; all of them were claiming me, pulling me, disputing me, more in the fashion of Furies than the manner of tender spouses, while poor Schimindra, to whom death had doubtless given wings, was floating above me, doing her best to defend me, shoving them aside and chasing them away. Thrown out of the door, however, that interminable series of spouses came back in through the windows, and threw themselves on my bed again, attacking me so forcefully that I sensed that I would be torn to pieces, and anticipated the moment when one of them would rip away an arm, another a leg, each taking a limb.

"Suddenly, the door opened, and I saw a kind of veiled phantom appear before which my four Indian wives fainted and who came to lie down tranquilly beside me, driving even Schimindra away with a single gesture.

"Oh, in truth, the last to arrive had rendered me such a great service that I took refuge in her arms, where, after an agitation that lasted a few moments more, I fell asleep.

"The next day, the first ray of daylight, striking me directly in the face, woke me up. I opened my eyes and uttered a cry of surprise. I was lying side by side with La Buchold—but next to a Buchold so pale, so changed, that I didn't have the courage to reproach her for her visit, so much did she give me the impression of not having long to live.

"Besides which, I recalled the service she had rendered me during the night. 'What! Is it you?' I said.

"'Yes, it's me, who, suffering as I am, have not hesitated to bring you some good news.'

"'Ah! Yes, you've given birth again?' I said.

"'To a daughter, a charming little girl; as I promised you, I've named her Marguerite.

"'And who's this one's godfather?'

"'Oh, you'd be proud of him, my love; he's one of the most illustrious professors of the University of Leyden, Dr. Van Holstentius.'

"'Yes, I know of him.'

"'Well, he's promised to love the dear child as if she were his own, but...'

"'But what?'

"'I'm very much afraid that, when I'm no longer there...'

"'What! When you're no longer there? Have you left Monnikendam never to return?'

"'Quite the contrary, my love, and I'm going to return there without delay; don't worry. But we're not immortal, and if, by chance, I died, our poor children...'

'Won't they each have a godfather, who loves them as if they were his own; won't they have Burgomaster Van Clief, the engineer Van Brock, the Reverend Van Cabel, Dr. Van Holstentius, etc. etc. etc.?"

"'Alas,' relied La Buchold, 'I know by virtue of what happened to me with you, what trust one can put in the promises of men. There were more vain promises than real ones in the engagements made by my illustrious protectors, with the result that today, my love, without your colleague Simon Van Groot, the harbormaster of Monnikendam, I don't know what would become of us—me, the children I have and those I might yet have.'

"'What do you mean, that you might yet have? What day of the month is it?'

"'The twenty-eighth of October.'

"'Yes, but what saint presides over that day?'

"'Two great saints, my love: Saint Simon and Saint Jude.'

"'Oh, that's too much!' I cried. 'This time I won't get away with anything less than twins!'

"'In any case,' said La Buchold, 'they'll be the last.'

"'Why is that?'

"'Yes, can't you see how changed I am?'

"In fact, as I've already said, that change had struck me at first glance. 'That's true,' I said to her. 'What's the matter with you?'

"She smiled sadly. 'Do you believe,' she said, that voyages like those I make aren't fatiguing? I've come to see you four times, without reproach; coming and returning is something like thirty-two thousand leagues every time—four times around the world. Could you find many women who'd do as much for...for a scoundrel of a man who thinks of nothing but deceiving her? Oh!'

"And La Buchold shed a few tears.

"What she said to me there was so true that I was touched by it. 'Well, why do you come?' I asked her.'

"'Because I love you, when all is said and done. Oh, if you'd stayed in Monnikendam, we could have been so happy!'

"'With your charming character? Get away!'

"'What do you expect? What spoiled my character is jealousy. And where did that jealousy come from? From the excess of my love. Let's see, now that five years have passed, will you say that your voyages to Amsterdam, Edam and Stavorin were innocent?'

"I scratched my ear. 'Well,' I said, 'in order not to lie...'

"'You can see clearly that you were in the wrong. With what do you have to reproach me of a similar kind?'

"'Nothing, I know, as long as I was there.'

"'But it seems to me that since...'

"'Since, that's a little confused. But in the end, there's still nothing to say, since, for me at least, appearances are there, and the dates match up, don't they/'

"'To the day.'

"I uttered a sigh. 'Oh, the fact is, I said, with a return of philosophy, that one goes a long way to find happiness...'

"'Yes, and one finds wives, doesn't one? Let's pass them in review, your wives.'

"'No, it's not worth the trouble, I know them—so I'm cured of marriage, or at least of marriages.'

"'Alas, my poor friend, there's nothing but the house, the hearth, children. Come back, come back, and you'll find all that—perhaps without me.'

"'Get away'

"'I know what I'm saying.' she said, shaking her head and uttering a sigh. But I'd die tranquil if I had the hope that, for want of a mother...my poor children..."

"'All right, all right...let's not go soft; we'll see about all that. Go home.'

"'It's necessary.'

"'And announce me,'

"'Oh! Really!'

"'Just a minute—I'm not promising. I'll do what I can, that's all.'

"'Adieu! I depart with that hope.'

"'Depart, my love. Who will live will see.'

"'Yes, who will live...Adieu.'

"And La Buchold kissed me one last time, uttered a sigh, and left.

"That apparition of La Buchold had left me with a very different impression than the preceding ones. Besides, as I'd said to her, the comparison between Dutch wives with Sinhalese, Spanish, Malabar and Chinese wives didn't work to the advantage of the latter; there was, therefore, only poor Schimindra who could counterbalance the European influence—but, you understand, she had the story of that wretched ape against her, to such an extent that, in sum, I was no longer able to think about anything else but putting my affairs in order and returning to Europe.

"Before leaving, though, my first concern was to ensure Schimindra's future. I left her my cigar exploitation, which was in full flow, and the rest of my bezoar, which was chipped, it's true, but which, even chipped, was still worth two or three thousand rupees—all the more incontestably now that it had been proven.

"As for Vanly-Ching, she had disappeared, taking her money with her, and during the five months that I remained in Bidondo, no one heard mention of her.

Finally, on the fifteenth of February 1829, about six years after my arrival in the Indies, I left Bidondo, after having realized a sum of forty-five thousand francs, which my Chinese correspondent banked, giving me excellent bonds in exchange, drawn on the finest companies in Amsterdam.

"The crossing took a long time because of the calms we experienced in the equatorial regions. Six months after my departure from Manila, Cap Finistère was sighted, and then we doubled Cherbourg and entered the Channel. Finally, on the eighteenth of August 1829, we dropped anchor in the port of Rotterdam.

"I had no reason to linger there, so I took the coach to Amsterdam the same day and then, having arrived in Amsterdam, a boat that would take me to Monnikendam. It was precisely that of my friend the fisherman who had taken me to board the *Jan de Witt*, whom I had not been able to pay for my passage, and who had promised nevertheless to drink to my health—a promise that he had kept religiously.

"This time, instead of a bag of pebbles, I had a wallet in my pocket containing a good forty-five thousand francs—with the result that, on disembarking in Monnikendam, as I not only owed him for the present passage but the previous one, with interest and the interest on the interest, for six years, I gave him twenty-five florins, which was a payment he had not touched for a long time.

Then I went to my house. At the door, I saw from a distance a nurse in mourning-dress, who was feeding two nurslings. I understood everything.

"I went into the ground-floor room, where my three sons and my daughter were. The three boys fled on seeing me. As for the daughter, as she was not yet able to walk on her own, she was obliged to remain.

"I understood that I was nothing to those poor innocents but a stranger; I picked up my little Marguerite, who uttered loud screams, and I went back to the door, in order that some neighbor might recognize me. Simon Van Groot, having just learned that a stranger had arrived and had headed for La Buchold's house, came running, suspecting the truth, and he arrived, having rallied the three children who had fled, and then the burse and the two nurslings.

"In a trice, everything was clarified.

"'And poor La Buchold?' I asked.

"'You've arrived two months too late, my dear Olifus," replied Simon Van Groot. "La Buchold died giving birth to your twins."

"'Yes, Simon and Jude.'"

"'That's right. In your absence I've taken care of the family. The creditors had sold the house but I bought it back; they'd sold the furniture but I bought it back. I knew full well that you'd return some day, and I wanted you to find everything in the state in which you left it, plus the children.'

"'That you, Van Groot.'

"'There's only our poor La Buchold...'

"'What do you expect, Simon; we're all mortal.'

"'You'll never find another like her, Olifus.'

"'That's probable.'

"Van Groot and I embraced, weeping, and then we settled our accounts. I reimbursed him for the house and the furniture, which I kept on Marguerite's behalf. Then I put six thousand francs on deposit for each boy, reserving the interest for myself until they came of age. Finally, I kept nine thousand francs for myself, in order not to be a burden on anyone and only to have to reach into my pocket to take out my bottle of tafia, rum and arrack."

"And you never saw La Buchold again?" I asked him.

"Yes, once. She came to tell me that I was rid of her forever, given that she had just married Simon Van Groot, who had been buried the day before and had asked, the old rogue, to be buried beside her. With the result," Père Olifus added, emptying his last bottle of arrack, that I'm rid of her in this world and the next. I hope so, at least."

On which note, Père Olifus burst into the laughter that was quite particular to him, and let himself slip under the table, from which, almost immediately, snoring emerged that left us in no doubt as to the serenity of the sleep to which that pure heart, devoid of remorse, had just surrendered.

At the same time, the door opened; I turned my head and a soft and harmonious voice made itself heard.

That voice was Marguerite's; she appeared on the threshold of the room, lamp in hand.

"It's time, Messieurs, that you went to bed," she said. "I'll take you to your room.[44] My poor father has been wearying you, hasn't he, with his stories? But it's necessary to have some indulgence for him. He spent six years in the insane asylum at Hoorn while our poor mother was alive. He didn't come out entirely cured. There are manias and fairy tales that plague his mind, especially when he abuses strong liquor, which happens often. As always, though, his reason returns when he wakes up, and he forgets his voyages to the East Indies, which only ever existed in his imagination."

We went to bed on that explanation, which appeared to us to be infinitely more probable than what Père Jérôme-François Olifus had told us.

The next day, we asked to see him to say our farewells, but we were told that he had left at daybreak to take a traveler to Stavorin, with the result that we left

---

[44] The author appears to have forgotten that the guests are already in their room, just as he had earlier forgotten that Olifus had claimed to have swallowed bezoar himself, whereas it transpired that he had actually given it to Schimindra. It seems likely that he had also forgotten at this point that Marguerite had only "spoken" in sign language previously, although he remembered that before reaching the end of the chapter, and deftly added the inconsistency to the final mystery.

Monnikendam without knowing which had lied to us, of the toothless old mouth of Père Olifus and the youthful and pretty mouth of Marguerite. However, one thing prejudiced us against the beautiful hostess of the Bonhomme Tropique, which was that the previous evening she had only talked to us by signs, but suddenly, the next day, she was able to speak perfect French in order to give us the explanation that we have just recorded above.

It is up to people who have been to India to judge whether Père Olifus had really seen the countries he described and that we have described in our turn in accordance with his account, or whether he had simply seem Madagascar, Ceylon, Negombo, Goa, Calicut, Manila and Bidondo in the lunatic asylum in Hoorn.

SF & FANTASY

Adolphe Alhaiza. *Cybele*

Alphonse Allais. *The Adventures of Captain Cap*

Henri Allorge. *The Great Cataclysm*

Guy d'Armen. *Doc Ardan: The City of Gold and Lepers; The Troglodytes of Mount Everest/The Giants of Black Lake; The Abominable Snowman*

G.-J. Arnaud. *The Ice Company*

André Arnyvelde. *The Ark; The Mutilated Bacchus*

Charles Asselineau. *The Double Life*

Henri Austruy. *The Eupantophone; The Olotelepan; The Petitpaon Era*

Barillet-Lagargousse. *The Final War*

Cyprien Bérard. *The Vampire Lord Ruthwen*

S. Henry Berthoud. *Martyrs of Science; The Angel Azrael*

Aloysius Bertrand. *Gaspard de la Nuit*

Richard Bessière. *The Gardens of the Apocalypse; The Masters of Silence*

Chevalier de Béthune. *The World of Mercury*

Albert Bleunard. *Ever Smaller*

Félix Bodin. *The Novel of the Future*

Pierre Boitard. *Journey to the Sun*

Louis Boussenard. *Monsieur Synthesis*

Alphonse Brown. *City of Glass; The Conquest of the Air*

Émile Calvet. *In a Thousand Years*

André Caroff. *The Terror of Madame Atomos; Miss Atomos; The Return of Madame Atomos; The Mistake of Madame Atomos; The Monsters of Madame Atomos; The Revenge of Madame Atomos; The Resurrection of Madame Atomos; The Mark of Madame Atomos; The Spheres of Madame Atomos; The Wrath of Madame Atomos* (w/M. & Sylvie Stéphan)

Félicien Champsaur. *Homo-Deus; The Human Arrow; Nora, The Ape-Woman; Ouha, King of the Apes; Pharaoh's Wife*

Didier de Chousy. *Ignis*

Jules Clarétie. *Obsession*

Jacques Collin de Plancy. *Voyage to the Center of the Earth*

Michel Corday. *The Eternal Flame; The Lynx* (w/André Couvreur)

André Couvreur. *Caresco, Superman; The Exploits of Professor Tornada* (3 vols.); *The Necessary Evil*

Gaston Danville. *The Perfume of Lust*
Camille Debans. *The Misfortunes of John Bull*
Captain Danrit. *Undersea Odyssey*
C. I. Defontenay. *Star (Psi Cassiopeia)*
Charles Derennes. *The People of the Pole*
Georges Dodds (anthologist). *The Missing Link*
Charles Dodeman. *The Silent Bomb*
Harry Dickson. *The Heir of Dracula; Harry Dickson vs. The Spider*
Jules Dornay. *Lord Ruthven Begins*
Alfred Driou. *The Adventures of a Parisian Aeronaut*
Odette Dulac. *The War of the Sexes*
Alexandre Dumas. *The Return of Lord Ruthven; The Man who Married a Mermaid* (w/P. Lacroix)
Renée Dunan. *Baal; The Ultimate Pleasure*
J.-C. Dunyach. *The Night Orchid; The Thieves of Silence*
Henri Duvernois. *The Man Who Found Himself*
Achille Eyraud. *Voyage to Venus*
Henri Falk. *The Age of Lead*
Paul Féval. *Anne of the Isles; Knightshade; Revenants; Vampire City; The Vampire Countess; The Wandering Jew's Daughter*
Paul Féval, *fils. Felifax, the Tiger-Man*
Charles de Fieux. *Lamékis*
Fernand Fleuret. *Jim Click*
Charles-Marie Flor O'Squarr. *Phantoms*
Louis Forest. *Someone is Stealing Children in Paris*
Arnould Galopin. *Doctor Omega; Doctor Omega and the Shadowmen* (anthology)
Judith Gautier. *Isoline and the Serpent-Flower*
H. Gayar. *The Marvelous Adventures of Serge Myrandhal on Mars*
Louis Geoffroy. *The Apocryphal Napoleon*
G.L. Gick. *Harry Dickson and the Werewolf of Rutherford Grange*
Raoul Gineste. *The Second Life of Doctor Albin*
Delphine de Girardin. *Balzac's Cane*
Léon Gozlan. *The Vampire of the Val-de-Grâce*
Jules Gros. *The Fossil Man*
Jimmy Guieu. *The Polarian-Denebian War* (2 vols.)
Edmond Haraucourt. *Daah, the First Human; Illusions of Immortality*
Nathalie Henneberg. *The Green Gods*
Eugène Hennebert. *The Enchanted City*
Jules Hoche. *The Maker of Men and His Formula*
V. Hugo, P. Foucher & P. Meurice. *The Hunchback of Notre-Dame*

Romain d'Huissier. *Hexagon: Dark Matter*

Jules Janin. *The Magnetized Corpse*

Michel Jeury. *Chronolysis*

Gustave Kahn. *The Tale of Gold and Silence*

Gérard Klein. *The Mote in Time's Eye*

Fernand Kolney. *Love in 5000 Years*

Paul Lacroix. *Danse Macabre; The Man who Married a Mermaid* (w/Alexandre Dumas)

Louis-Guillaume de La Follie. *The Unpretentious Philosopher*

Jean de La Hire. *The Fiery Wheel; Enter the Nyctalope; The Nyctalope on Mars; The Nyctalope vs. Lucifer; The Nyctalope Steps In; Night of the Nyctalope; Return of the Nyctalope*

Etienne-Léon de Lamothe-Langon. *The Virgin Vampire*

André Laurie. *Spiridon*

Gabriel de Lautrec. *The Vengeance of the Oval Portrait*

Alain le Drimeur. *The Future City*

Georges Le Faure & Henri de Graffigny. *The Extraordinary Adventures of a Russian Scientist Across the Solar System* (2 vols.)

Gustave Le Rouge. *The Dominion of the World* (w/Gustave Guitton) (4 vols.); *The Mysterious Doctor Cornelius* (3 vols.); *The Vampires of Mars*

Jules Lermina. *The Battle of Strasbourg; Mysteryville; Panic in Paris; The Secret of Zippelius; To-Ho and the Gold Destroyers*

Maurice Level. *The Gates of Hell*

André Lichtenberger. *The Centaurs; The Children of the Crab*

Maurice Limat. *Mephista*

Listonai. *The Philosophical Voyager*

Jean-Marc & Randy Lofficier. *Edgar Allan Poe on Mars; The Katrina Protocol; Pacifica 1, 2; Robonocchio; Return of the Nyctalope;* (anthologists) *Tales of the Shadowmen 1-13; The Vampire Almanac* (2 vols.)

Ch. Lomon & P.-B. Gheuzi. *The Last Days of Atlantis*

Camille Mauclair. *The Virgin Orient*

Xavier Mauméjean. *The League of Heroes*

Joseph Méry. *The Tower of Destiny*

Hippolyte Mettais. *Paris Before the Deluge; The Year 5865*

Louise Michel. *The Human Microbes; The New World*

Tony Moilin. *Paris in the Year 2000*

Michael Moorcock's *Legends of the Multiverse*

José Moselli. *Illa's End*

John-Antoine Nau. *Enemy Force*

Marie Nizet. *Captain Vampire*

Charles Nodier. *Trilby and The Crumb Fairy*

C. Nodier, A. Beraud & Toussaint-Merle. *Frankenstein*

Henri de Parville. *An Inhabitant of the Planet Mars*

Gaston de Pawlowski. *Journey to the Land of the 4th Dimension*

Georges Pellerin. *The World in 2000 Years*

Ernest Pérochon. *The Frenetic People*

Pierre Pelot. *The Child Who Walked on the Sky*

Jean Petithuguenin. *An International Mission to the Moon*

J. Polidori, C. Nodier, E. Scribe. *Lord Ruthven the Vampire*

P.-A. Ponson du Terrail. *The Immortal Woman; The Vampire and the Devil's Son; The Police Agent*

Georges Price. *The Missing Men of the* Sirius

René Pujol. *The Chimerical Quest*

Edgar Quinet. *Ahasuerus; The Enchanter Merlin*

Henri de Régnier. *A Surfeit of Mirrors*

Maurice Renard. *The Blue Peril; Doctor Lerne; The Doctored Man; A Man Among the Microbes; The Master of Light*

Restif de la Bretonne. *The Discovery of the Austral Continent by a Flying Man; Posthumous Correspondence* (3 vols.); *The Fay Ouroucoucou* (2 vols.)

Jean Richepin. *The Crazy Corner; The Wing*

Albert Robida. *The Adventures of Saturnin Farandoul; Chalet in the Sky; The Clock of the Centuries; The Electric Life; The Engineer Von Satanas*

J.-H. Rosny Aîné. *Helgvor of the Blue River; The Givreuse Enigma; The Mysterious Force; The Navigators of Space; Vamireh; The World of the Variants; The Young Vampire*

Marcel Rouff. *Journey to the Inverted World*

Marie-Anne de Roumier-Robert. *The Voyage of Lord Seaton to the Seven Planets*

Léonie Rouzade. *The World Turned Upside Down*

Han Ryner. *The Human Ant; The Superhumans*

Louis-Claude de Saint-Martin. *The Crocodile*

Frank Schildiner. *The Quest of Frankenstein; The Triumph of Frankenstein*

Pierre de Selenes: *An Unknown World*

Norbert Sevestre. *Sâr Dubnotal: Vs. Jack the Ripper; The Astral Trail*

Angelo de Sorr. *The Vampires of London*

Brian Stableford. *The Empire of the Necromancers (1. The Shadow of Frankenstein; 2. Frankenstein and the Vampire Countess; 3. Frankenstein in London); The Wayward Muse; Eurydice's Lament; The Mirror of Dionysius; The New Faust at the Tragicomique; Sherlock Holmes and The Vampires of Eternity; The Stones of Camelot* (anthologist) *News from the Moon; The Germans on Venus; The Supreme Progress; The World Above the World; Nemoville; Investigations of the Future; The Conqueror of Death; The Revolt of the Machines; The Man With the Blue Face; The Aerial Valley; The New Moon; The Nickel Man; On the Brink of the World's End; The Mirror of Present Events; The Humanishere*

Jacques Spitz. *The Eye of Purgatory*

Kurt Steiner. *Ortog*

Eugène Thébault. *Radio-Terror*

C.-F. Tiphaigne de La Roche. *Amilec*

Simon Tyssot de Patot. *The Strange Voyages of Jacques Massé and Pierre de Mésange*

Louis Ulbach. *Prince Bonifacio*

Théo Varlet. *The Castaways of Eros; The Golden Rock.; The Martian Epic* (w/Octave Joncquel); *Timeslip Troopers* (w/André Blandin); *The Xenobiotic Invasion*

Pierre Véron. *The Merchants of Health*

Paul Vibert. *The Mysterious Fluid*

Villiers de l'Isle-Adam. *The Scaffold; The Vampire Soul*

Gaston de Wailly. *The Murderer of the World*

Philippe Ward. *Artahe; Manhattan Ghost* (w/Mickael Laguerre); *The Song of Montségur* (w/Sylvie Miller)

Victor Margueritte. *The Bacheloress; The Companion; The Couple*

MYSTERIES & THRILLERS

M. Allain & P. Souvestre. *The Daughter of Fantômas*

A. Anicet-Bourgeois & Lucien Dabril. *Rocambole* (stage plays)

Guy d'Armen. *Doc Ardan: The City of Gold and Lepers; The Troglodytes of Mount Everest/The Giants of Black Lake; Doc Ardan: The Abominable Snowman*

Cyprien Bérard. *The Vampire Lord Ruthwen*

A. Bernède. *Belphegor*; *Judex* (w/Louis Feuillade); *The Return of Judex* (w/Louis Feuillade); *The Shadow of Judex* (anthology)

A. Bisson & G. Livet. *Nick Carter vs. Fantômas* (stage play)

André Caroff. *The Terror of Madame Atomos; Miss Atomos; The Return of Madame Atomos; The Mistake of Madame Atomos; The Monsters of Madame Atomos; The Revenge of Madame Atomos; The Resurrection of Madame Atomos; The Mark of Madame Atomos; The Spheres of Madame Atomos; The Wrath of Madame Atomos* (w/M. & Sylvie Stéphan)

Félicien Champsaur. *Homo-Deus; Nora, The Ape-Woman; Ouha, King of the Apes*

Jules Clarétie. *Obsession*

V. Darlay & H. de Gorsse. *Arsène Lupin vs. Sherlock Holmes: The Stage Play* (stage play)

Harry Dickson. *Harry Dickson vs. The Heir of Dracula; Harry Dickson vs. The Spider*

Séamas Duffy. *Sherlock Holmes in Paris*

Alexandre Dumas. *The Return of Lord Ruthven* (stage play)

Paul Féval. *The Black Coats (The Parisian Jungle; Heart of Steel; The Sword-Swallower; 'Salem Street; The Invisible Weapon; The Companions of the Treasure; The Cadet Gang); Gentlemen of the Night; John Devil*

Paul Féval, *fils. Felifax, the Tiger-Man*

Louis Forest. *Someone is Stealing Children in Paris*

Émile Gaboriau. *Monsieur Lecoq; The Casebook of Monsieur Lecoq*

Arnould Galopin: *Harry Dickson: The Man in Grey; Harry Dickson: Tenebras*

Goron & Émile Gautier. *Spawn of the Penitentiary*

G.L. Gick. *Harry Dickson and The Werewolf of Rutherford Grange*

Léon Gozlan. *The Vampire of the Val-de-Grâce*

Georges Grison. *The Heads that fell in Paris*

Paul d'Ivoi. *Around the World on Five Sous* (w/Henri Chabrillat)

Paul Lacroix. *Danse Macabre*

Jean de La Hire. *Enter the Nyctalope; The Nyctalope on Mars; The Nyctalope vs. Lucifer; The Nyctalope Steps In; Night of the Nyctalope; Return of the Nyctalope*

Rick Lai. *Shadows of the Opera: Retribution in Blood; Sisters of the Shadows: The Curse of Cagliostro*

Etienne-Léon de Lamothe-Langon. *The Virgin Vampire*

Steve Leadley. *Sherlock Holmes and The Circle of Blood*

Maurice Leblanc. *Arsène Lupin vs. Countess Cagliostro; Arsène Lupin vs. Sherlock Holmes (1. The Blonde Phantom; 2. The Hollow Needle); The Island of the Thirty Coffin; 813; The Many Faces of Arsène Lupin* (anthology)

Gustave Lerouge: *The Mysterious Doctor Cornelius* (3 vols.)

Gaston Leroux. *Chéri-Bibi* (stage play)*; The Phantom of the Opera; Rouletabille & the Mystery of the Yellow Room; Rouletabille at Krupp's*

Maurice Limat. *Mephista*

Jean-Marc & Randy Lofficier. *The Katrina Protocol;* (anthologists) *Tales of the Shadowmen 1-13; The Vampire Almanac* (2 vols.)

Richard Marsh. *The Complete Adventures of Judith Lee*

William Patrick Maynard. *The Terror of Fu Manchu; The Destiny of Fu Manchu*

Frank J. Morlok. *Sherlock Holmes: The Grand Horizontals* (stage play)*; Sherlock Holmes vs Jack the Ripper* (stage pla*y); Sherlock Holmes, Fantômas, Lupin, Raffles and More: The Spanish Plays* (stage plays)

Jean Petithuguenin. *The Adventures of Ethel King, The Female Nick Carter*

P.-A. Ponson du Terrail. *The Immortal Woman; The Vampire and the Devil's Son; The Police Agent*

Georges Price. *The Missing Men of the* Sirius

Charles Rabou: *The Secret Bureau: 1. The Secret Bureau; 2: The Brothers of Death*

Antonin Reschal. *The Adventures of Miss Boston, The First Female Detective*

Norbert Sevestre. *Sâr Dubnotal vs. Jack the Ripper; The Astral Trail*

Eugène Thébault. *Radio-Terror*

P. de Wattyne & Y. Walter. *Sherlock Holmes vs. Fantômas* (stage play)

David White. *Fantômas in America*

Pierre Yrondy. *The Adventures of Thérèse Arnaud of the French Secret Service*

NON-FICTION

Stephen R. Bissette. *Blur 1-5. Green Mountain Cinema 1; Teen Angels*

Win Scott Eckert. *Crossovers* (2 vols.)

Georges Grison. *The Heads that Fell in Paris*

Jean-Marc & Randy Lofficier. *Shadowmen* (2 vols.)

Randy Lofficier. *Over Here*

Brian Stableford. *The Plurality of Imaginary Worlds*